I0762959

THE GULF OF LIONS

ALSO BY CAITLIN SHETTERLY

Fault Lines: Stories of Divorce (editor)
Made for You and Me
Modified
Pete and Alice in Maine

HarperCollins books may be purchased for educational, business, or sales promotional use. For information, please email the Special Markets Department at SPsales@harpercollins.com.

hc.com

FIRST EDITION

Design by Elina Cohen
Cicada art © Mary Erskine / Shutterstock

Library of Congress Cataloging-in-Publication Data has been applied for.

ISBN 978-0-06-342107-3

26 27 28 29 30 LBC 5 4 3 2 1

THE GULF OF LIONS

A Novel

CAITLIN SHETTERLY

HARPER

An Imprint of HarperCollins*Publishers*

This book is dedicated to what Michelle Obama would call my "kitchen table" of female friends. I am so lucky to have so many vibrant and intelligent women in my life for whom Alice became a real woman, which made her that much more real for me.

And:

For Dan and my two incandescent boys, always.

There is a time for many words, and there is also a time for sleep.

—Homer, *The Odyssey*

FRANCE

JULY 2022

PART 1

Les Alpes

1.
ALICE

It is mid-July and I am sitting on a plastic chair with my notebook, writing it all down. Just across the soft tops of some feathery evergreens is Mont Blanc, whitecapped, even now in high midsummer, even in a heat wave, even with the Pyrenees blazing on the other side of France. It's evening, and behind the mountain, the sky is persimmon-colored. Not far away someone is playing Johnny Hallyday singing Edith Piaf's song "*Non, je ne regrette rien . . .*" in his low, sad, repentant voice. Iris is in the shower in the *cabinet* just inside the door behind me, and I can hear the splashing gurgle of water and her voice incanting a poem of words with secret French meanings: "*Myrtilles. Mirabelle. Mûre. Miroir. Mousse. Moi. Château. Chat. Champignon. Chèvre.*" She gets to the end of the list and then starts over, throwing in a new word, "*Fromage.*" And again, and again. This order has meaning only to her, but it makes me feel like this trip was not a mistake. Not yet.

• • •

To get here we flew N95-masked because we, in particular, still have to be cautious. Mask mandates have only just been lifted. Iris and I have recently been vaccinated. Our flight was non-stop from JFK to Geneva, the closest airport to the French Alps. Even though it was morning when we landed and, conceivably, we could have begun our odyssey immediately, I knew my body couldn't handle that kind of exhaustion anymore. If Pete were with us, we would have tried. Pete has unending energy for . . . well, everything. When we first met, I saw it as exciting, his zest for life, so to speak. Later, it wore on me.

Without Pete, the girls and I took the airport bus to a hotel, lugged our carefully packed (but very heavy) bags full of a tent, a camping set that included a small one-pot cookstove and stainless-steel dishes, sleeping bags, my notebooks, toiletries, bathing suits, shorts, both Keen hiking sandals and Birkenstocks (only Iris was allowed a third pair of shoes: her brand-new, hot-pink Crocs), light dresses, and T-shirts into the elevator, and arrived in a room I'd booked ahead with windows looking out at the planes coming and going.

We took off our masks, our faces marked with red lines, showered, ate a LUNA bar each, and the girls went, immediately, to sleep. Iris and I shared a bed, and she put the flats of her two feet against the side of my calf, keeping contact, *always* keeping contact. In her arms was Big Bear; *on* her arms were five friendship bracelets she'd made on the plane for herself from a kit I gave her for Easter. ("Why not?" I said, "as you must always be your own best friend.")

Sophie lay across the other bed, her long, smooth legs (did I ever have legs like *that*?) poking out of the blankets, her arms above her head, the comforter pulled only across her middle, the cold air from the AC blasting us, the hot sun glinting off the tarmac just outside. Lying there, I texted Pete on WhatsApp:

We are here.

Hi! How are you?

Exhausted. Iris wouldn't sleep on the plane. Kept saying it was too loud, too hot, she missed Ingmar. Cried and cried about "something happening" to him. By the end of the night she was a total mess. So was I. Sophie also didn't sleep but in her case it wasn't as annoying.

Ok. Where r u now?

I'm afraid I've bitten off more than I can chew, with the girls, myself. I'm already worn out.

I hear u. It will be ok. Go slow. There's no real time frame. The story is the journey. Are you still at the airport?

We are at the hotel. Both girls asleep now. I am going to sleep, too. Must be early there.

6. I'm up.

Ok.

Glad you're there.

Ok.

. . .

I could see he was typing more. I saw the ". . ." and suddenly it wore me out. I turned off my phone. I didn't used to be this way. I used to draw him out, help him find the right thing to say that actually made me feel seen. I used to wait on every word tripping from his tongue. But that was before. Before I knew about his affair and all that happened after. Now I find myself turning away, gulping for air.

• • •

When the girls and I wake up, we're hungry. We wear masks into the elevator. In the lobby, we see some guests with masks, others without; others have them half on, half off, dangling from their ears. Everyone, everywhere, is dying to get rid of the masks. No one knows what to do. And the stakes are higher for me, of course.

We make our way to a white-tableclothed dining room and eat, in seconds, it seems, two orders of pan-fried perch from Lake Geneva, one tomato salad, a plate of "Swiss cheeses, the heritage of our mountains," and three orders of a "Symphony of Red Fruits," which turns out to be a melt-in-your-mouth meringue at the bottom of a bowl piled high with raspberries, blueberries (which aren't red, just saying), red currants, and whipped cream. Drizzled over all of *that* is a sour berry sauce.

I almost can't describe what that dessert was like. I will think of it for the rest of my life, however long that is. I feel I have to say that, the "I have no idea how long I will live" part. Pete tells me not to say it in front of the girls. (Obviously.) But I think we all think about it. Five years is where most of the projections end. Five years is considered success. Five years is five seconds, if you ask me. (No one asked me.)

I'm only one year and change into my five-year odyssey. Still in Polyphemus's cave, so to speak, if anyone remembers who that is: All you need to know is that the Cyclops is just behind me. I can still feel his rancid breath on the back of my neck.

Thanks to chemo, I have almost no taste anymore. Most things taste like dust or like cardboard. But those tender, tangy berries, the sour *coulis* sauce on my tongue, well, it all *sings*, just as the name suggests.

After eating, we pull on our bathing suits and swim in the turquoise-tiled hotel pool until eleven p.m. We order fries in the lobby and then go back to our room unsure if we are ready for bed or awake enough for another adventure, the time playing tricks with us.

The girls want to talk to Pete, so I turn the phone back on, despite the fact that keeping it off makes it easier for me to focus on them, not to feel sucked back into *the everything* of the last two tumultuous years, the two years I'm currently trying to run away from in France. A text from him, the one I didn't wait for earlier:

> I'm really excited for you guys to have this trip!!! Can you call me later on? Would love to say hi. Love you guys.

Then:

> PS: Tell Iris that Ingmar is just fine—purring like a bandit next to me!!

I type out:

> Hi. We are back in our room. Just ate. Girls want to FaceTime. You around?
>
> Yes!

His exuberance annoys me.

I give the phone to Sophie, who pushes the buttons, and then I can hear Pete's voice ricocheting around our hotel room in Geneva, my legs pulled by the undertow of his infectious charm. The girls laugh and smile with their father and hand the phone back and forth. I smile and wave when Iris turns the phone to me. I am a good wife. A good mother.

Iris tells Pete about the flight and the pink sun coming up over the wing of the airplane and how she made those friendship bracelets on the flight and how she ate three orders of fries in the lobby and how the pool has a mosaic of a sun on the bottom, made of hundreds, maybe thousands, of orange or yellow tiles, but that she could not get down there to touch them.

When we finally pull the covers up, our heads on the crisp white hotel pillows, relief floods through me. I think: We're here, we've made it, we're together. How many times in the last few years have I said just that? Maybe families always feel this—relieved that, despite the spin cycle of life, the ordinary and extraordinary crises that befall us all, on this day no one's broken an arm or a skull and, for the moment, everyone is still glued together.

The next morning, after breakfast, the concierge tells me he will reserve an Uber to take us to a car rental kiosk in a nearby parking garage. He asks me how long we need. I say an hour or two to eat, swim, and pack. He smiles and says, *"Pas de problème."* This translates to "There are no problems," which, in that moment, feels like the kindest, most thoughtful thing a person could say to me. If only.

Breakfast is a conundrum, one I've known was coming. Last night's meal was a splurge. But am I truly going to eat so lavishly every single day, all day long on this trip? During my recovery, I subsisted on bone broth and a macrobiotic diet of rice, adzuki beans, leafy greens. I drank the broth in the morning; I drank it before bed. I took fistfuls of Chinese herbs. God, the work of illness! The eating or not eating. The conflicting information about fasting or dairy or meat or sugar. The incredible pain of it all, and the pain in the ass of it all. The portal messages, the administrative workers who call, often not having read the entire chart (they are well-meaning but clueless and can make you alarmed that the information they have on you might be all wrong). Then there are the bills, the insurance statements, the hurdles you have to jump over to get a prescription approved and filled. There's this insidious feeling that no one has *got this, got you, got "your one wild and precious life."*

It's been exactly a year and a half since the initial surgery, the shock of waking up without a breast, the first question on my lips being "Did you get it all?" Since then, I have worried that even a sip of coffee, a beer on a Friday night, two cupcakes at a party, any of these relatively minor splurges could, or would, start the cancer again. Food has scared me. The fact of which scared me, because I love food. I love cooking it. I love tasting it.

My oncologist, a vest-wearing man with red hair and glasses, smiles kindly at me, fondly, like we are now friends, soldiers in arms who fought the Crispin's Day fight together. "Go to France. You are free," he said just before we left. "Drink coffee. Have a teaspoon of sugar. Eat some cheese. Live your life. You are a survivor now." A survivor. Like from an avalanche, a shipwreck, a plane crash, a war, a genocide. I don't know how to wear that word. How to incorporate it into my full being. Not yet, anyway.

• • •

Halfway around the world, I am stuck. My thinking last night that dinner was my exception, my big night out, seems flawed this morning as I look longingly at the coffee people are drinking. My girls, gobbling croissants as appetizers, eye me suspiciously as I down my usual fistful of Chinese herbs with a glass of room-temperature water. "Mom, eat something," Sophie pleads. Here is my tender girl, bolting like lettuce in July heat, elongating into a teenage body that stretches while she sleeps, her feet already twice the size of mine. The girl/daughter/peer/woman/friend/child hybrid she is becoming is both disarming and comforting to me. Because she's my firstborn, my eldest, I often follow what she says. She is my soothsayer.

"Madame." A waiter appears with coffee in a silver pot.

"*Oui.* All right, what the hell? *Merci.*" I smile at my daughters. And that is that. Amazing how quickly the guardrails you've built can come right back down. How surviving becomes, simply, *living* if you let it.

A cup of plain black coffee never tasted so good! I follow it with a *café au lait*, because why not? Dairy! I feel full, but I want to keep going: next, a vanilla chia pudding with strawberries. It's so sweet it makes my teeth hurt. I eat a plate of silken, Gouda-like cheese riddled with holes and then a perfectly orange apricot.

Sophie and Iris are thrilled. We are, all three, together on an eating adventure now! The girls each eat a chia pudding. Sophie follows that with two apricots and both girls open yogurts in small glass jars. Iris sniffs the yogurt and says, "Yuck. It smells funny."

"Oh my God, Booby! It's amazing. So creamy," says an enthusiastic and almost giddy Sophie.

"Smells like cows," says Iris, frowning and pressing her nose flat to her face with her index finger.

"Can I smell?" I ask, and Iris hands me her little glass of lemon-flavored yogurt. I sniff and say, "I detect cream and grassy fields . . . and maybe a bit o' cow." I do my worst English accent.

I look at the girls and laugh. I haven't felt this light in, maybe, years. Then I taste it and agree with Sophie. "Iris, it's actually the best yogurt I've ever had. But yes, you are not wrong, it *is* laced with a tiny bit of cow-y funk." I try to hand it back to her.

"No," says Iris definitively.

Then both girls go back to the pastry cart making its rounds in the dining room and choose chocolate éclairs, bringing me one, too. And I can taste that, too! Hallelujah! (I can hear Leonard Cohen in my head.) A veil has been lifted, just in time! The soft, velvety smoothness of the crème, the crisp, lacquered outside of the pastry. Bite, sip, bite, sip. I am alive again.

My phone pings in the middle of my last bite. April. My editor and the reason we're here.

> Hey, saw your email! Glad you're on the ground. Have a great trip. Let me know if you need any support. My assistant, Ashby, can help if you get stuck. As much help as a, whatever the thing after millennial is, knows how to help. I mean she'll use her Siri and text you one-word answers. LOL. 🤣

What time does this woman wake up? Or go to bed? I can't tell which is the pertinent question to ask right now, given the hour it must be in Denver. One a.m.? From the look of the photos I've seen of her, she's probably run the entire Rocky Mountain range by sunup. Her mother got her name right: April, the month of surging change and, for me, anyway, bad omens.

I text back, all smiles: 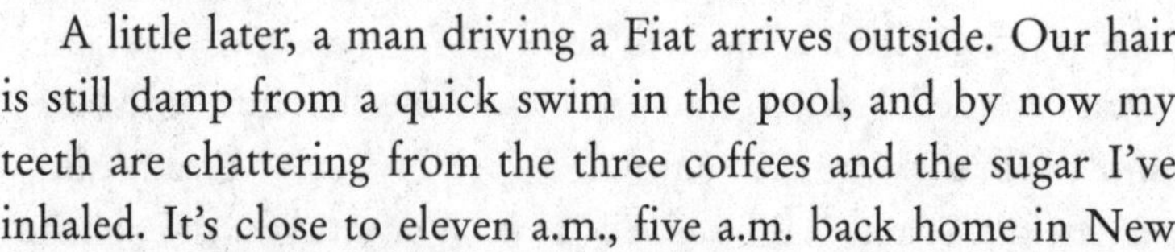

A little later, a man driving a Fiat arrives outside. Our hair is still damp from a quick swim in the pool, and by now my teeth are chattering from the three coffees and the sugar I've inhaled. It's close to eleven a.m., five a.m. back home in New York, three a.m. in the Rocky Mountains.

Our driver has a violet turban on his head and a Keith Richards T-shirt stretched across the hard hump of his belly. He wears a leather jacket, the kind with the little motorcycle neck straps swinging around his Adam's apple. Before he sees us, he's singing to the music on his radio. I immediately like him.

Inside his car it smells like coconut oil and mints. His smile is as big as the Cheshire cat's, and when he sees the girls, he booms, *"Salut les filles!"* and he reaches to turn down the Rolling Stones singing "Cherry Oh Baby." "I'm never gonna let you down / Never make you wear no frown!" In the back seat, I put my arm around Iris and smile. "It's okay," I say.

Ever since we left Maine in the middle of the Covid shutdown over a year and a half ago, to go home to New York City for my surgery and treatments, Iris has not been the same. New things rattle her. She wants to know where I will be at all times. "Where will you be when I am at school?" "Will you pick me up?" "Can you get there ten minutes early?" She wants physical contact, all the time. She wants to climb onto my lap, her gangly eight-year-old legs twisting around me and her knees jutting into my hips. Sometimes I think she wants to climb back inside the womb. Maybe, since she was early, since the NICU, she has forever wanted that. That is her journey: backward, a boat against the current.

But lately, there is something more jagged for me about Iris's behavior, something that makes me look back wistfully at our time in Maine, as challenging as it was, that weird year that divided our lives into the *beforetimes* and *aftertimes*. In Maine, Iris was blissfully free: her feet dirty, her busy hands making sod houses by the barn, talking to the birds, chasing the waves crashing interminably against the rocks. I would look out the picture windows to the field that slopes down to the stream that winds to the ocean and I'd see her traipsing down there, a bucket and a net in her hand, her Laura Ingalls braids hanging down her back. She thought I didn't know or didn't see that she was going to the water, because we had told her she must not, there were deep pockets, even in that stream. But she was too curious, too intent upon learning that landscape like one might learn a friend, that she couldn't heed our warnings and also hold on to her soul. So I watched her from the windows, my heart bursting with love and fear for this dear girl who was embracing Maine for everything it could give her. Sometimes parenting, I am slowly understanding, is about undoing everything you said before.

Our driver turns from the wheel to smile at me. "You 'ave beeooteeful girls," he says.

"Oh, thank you," I say.

He booms his big laugh and I feel Iris shudder again. Scared, even, of exuberant kindness, of love. He keeps talking, unaware that my daughter's anxiety is flooding the back seat. "There is an Arab saying, he says: 'For every mother, a scarab beetle is a gazelle.'"

"What's a sssssk-Arab beetle?" Iris pipes up. Her teeth sound like they might be chattering from anxiety as much as my own are rattling from the caffeine.

"It's scarab beetle, dummy. And stop worrying, it's annoying," says Sophie.

Our guide interrupts my children: "In ancient Egypt, the

scarab was the beetle that represented the eternal cycle of life. The sun died and was reborn each day as a beetle."

"Oh, weird," says Iris, her face opening a crack, her interest starting to overcome her anxiety. There you go, I think.

Sophie is googling "scarab beetle" surreptitiously on my phone, which she has slid out of my hand. "It's like a June bug or a Japanese beetle, Booby."

"Don't call me Booby. Mommy, Sophie keeps calling me that. I hate it."

"Sophie—we have discussed this. It's an unkind word."

"Elvis's mother called him that."

"Sophie Anne, you know exactly why you call your sister that word! I can't stand it."

"Really? Tell me? You think Iris is a booby, too?"

"Sophie, stop. For one, she's going to think you are calling her a breast. And that leads to body shaming. Stop it."

"Alice, it has nothing to do with boobies. It has to do with being special. Like Booby."

"My God, Sophie—"

"There are twelve million words in Arabic," our professor interrupts gaily, as if my daughters' fighting is a fun divertissement for all. "Twelve million! We have words for everything. English only has about two hundred thousand words and French even less! In Arabic we have twenty-three words for love! Just for love!" His tone is an infectious mixture of ecstatic and incredulous.

"Mommy, Sophie is rolling her eyes at me."

"Sophie, stop it. This is not good behavior. Come on. We have a long day ahead of us."

Our prof adds to the cacophony: "Something else we say in Arab culture. '*Celui qui n'a pas de fils ne connaît pas l'affection.*'"

"Yes, perfect for right now," I say, though I'm not sure I totally understand. I am trying to stay engaged with our chauffeur while dealing with the ping-pong balls getting lobbed at me by my girls.

"What did he say?" asks Sophie suspiciously. Even though I made the girls do some very basic French exercise books and watch French cartoons after school during all of May and into June, understanding actual French is going to be hard for them. Well, it's going to be hard for *me*: I am reaching back twenty years, more, to college and my one year abroad in France. All spring I used Fluenz and listened to French music and watched French rom-coms. But on the ground in real time? I'm not sure I'm going to be able to make this very seamless. It all sounds really, *really* fast.

"Girls, popcorn in a pan," I say. "I can't think."

"But . . . what did he say?" insists Sophie.

"I think it's this: If you haven't had children—well, sons, but you get the idea—you don't understand affection."

"Geez, too bad you didn't have boys," Sophie sneers.

"What, Mama?" It's Iris now.

"It's just a saying. It's a girls' world now. Don't worry. *You* are in charge, I promise."

"We are 'ere," our driver intones. Outside the car windows I see the cool darkness of the garage.

"Thank you so much, sir," I say, and hand him an extra ten euros.

"Why do you always do that? So embarrassing," Sophie grumbles at me while grabbing her backpack and getting out in a huff.

"What did I do?" I ask her after our driver disappears around the corner.

"Just. Everything." She sighs as though this fact makes her unbearably *fatiguée*.

The truth is that neither girl wanted to come with me. They wanted to go back to Maine for the summer. They wanted to see the grass turn from aspiring to lush as June rolled into July. They wanted the cold Atlantic Ocean.

When we left Maine, it was the dead of winter. We got home to New York City and were greeted by an ice storm and a full calendar for me of doctors' appointments, treatments, surgery, and then more treatments. Eventually, the girls went back to school in New York. But it was a long, dismal spring, and then a summer of confinement. The girls had hoped—well, we all hoped—we'd make it back to our house that summer, but it was too much. For me, for Pete to go without me. I felt that I was what kept us from Maine.

Instead of Maine, Pete and I let them watch pretty much anything and everything on screens. As if that were any comfort. They were caged, restless. It was an interminable year with me weakened and exhausted. And them masked, a lot of the time, even in my bedroom. How I longed to see their cheeks, their perfect lips! It was torture.

This summer Pete is working, and my daughters are a part of this story of mine, as kids often are, helplessly brought along on our currents. Luckily, this time it's a story I am writing, not more cancer. The story I was assigned. I feel so important when I say that: "I was assigned an article by *Get Out! Magazine*." And then, if someone asks, I say, "So glad you asked, actually. It's a piece about camping in France with girls—daughters. A woman/girl story. Best campgrounds in a few locales, part memoir/travel/

adventure. I haven't written something in so long. An assignment!" I am twittering. Spilling over.

This isn't exactly running away. Not in the way a man might run away when he has a midlife crisis. A man might buy a sports car, have an affair, start a Ponzi scheme, lie. This is an "Oh my God, I am still alive" running away. This is "I have a new shot at something, anything" running away. This is "I need some time with just my daughters" running away. And it is also a gift from the universe. When all you have is time, and the clock is ticking, you start to see things differently.

When the lump I felt that December day was revealed to be stage 2B breast cancer (yes, that B really belongs there; there's an A, a B, even a C; the numbers can go from 1 to 4; very rarely, and only with certain cancers, a 5 is used), I was rushed into a course of chemo, then a mastectomy, then some targeted radiation, then a short run of more (different) chemo, then hormone-suppressing drugs. That entire time is a dark hole, and I prefer not to think too much about it. The grief I feel about my breast. About losing it. When I found out that it was going to be too hard to get my largish tumor out and also keep my breast, I wept. Even though it's gone now, my mind still goes back, over and over that time, and I still wonder: Was there a way to save it? What if I'd seen someone else? Ack. "We just don't have enough room," the surgeon we had employed said, "to get the tumor and a handful of lymph nodes, and also keep your breast." This is what they tell me, what they told me.

My oncologist also told me that one in eight women gets cancer in the US. One in eight. And even that, he said, is old data. It's much higher now, he guesses, like one in four or five. "You're not alone," he told me. "You have so many people out there, all around you, who get what you are going through." I want that community of sisters and I don't. Will we scare each other once we find each other?

So, okay, a memory: Before I lost my breast, when I was still doing the first chemo, I was in that alternate universe of the cancer treatment, a universe I went to alone. Even if, like in the beginning, Pete was sitting right there with me, I felt so alone. It's almost unbearable to be that alone. It's different than being lonely. This is something I learned with cancer. When Pete was with me, I introduced him to the nurses and told him where to get a coffee out of a Keurig and asked him if he were comfortable, as I always, *always* have this problem of worrying about everyone else, all the time. And then, in the silence of the poison entering my veins, the freezing cold helmet on my head designed to save my hair, I would go to this other country, or planet, or universe. It felt that far away, and it scared me. While the nausea and exhaustion took over, I was yearning to reach out to Pete, and I wanted him to grab my hand and keep me in his world. Or, at least, I wanted my two worlds to come together, to make sense in the same room. But with the drugs mainlining, I was sliding, shifting into the other world, and I couldn't take him with me.

It's funny because sometimes I wonder now if I felt this responsibility for him, more than me even, to find a way to sew together the two places I was inhabiting in my mind, in my heart, in my body. When it was happening, I couldn't even describe it to Pete. So then I started going alone because it scared me less. I was more alone and also lonelier than ever, but at least I didn't feel his eyes on me while I slipped down an impossibly cold and fast river, too fast to reach back and grab for his hand.

Anyway, that's all "rly extra," as Sophie would write in a text. (I've had to look up what that "extra" means in this context; it means TMI, FYI.) And she is right. But to keep going with yet more extra, this is the other thing that started to happen once I was in the cancer-verse: When the drugs went into my veins and made me tired and the room was starting to spin and I knew I would soon vomit, I'd drift off and be back in the NICU with baby Iris. It was the beeps and scuff/squeak of nurses' shoes on the floor. Every time, I woke up, scared, looking for my baby.

But it wasn't the NICU, and I was the patient and I'm not a baby, though I felt sometimes like a small, frightened child. Here I could see only eyes above masks, and eyebrows and hats and scarves on bald heads and sometimes wigs or even bare, baby-chicken-feathered skulls. There were nurses whose job it was to be cheery and firm with their eyes and voices in the face of an interminable workday of abject losses of hope or faith or both.

One day, I was sitting there with my eyes closed and trying to breathe in a "4 square," trying to squelch that unbearable alone loneliness when I remembered France. This was a place I could go in my mind! It was an epiphany, a lifesaver. So I thought about Lyon, where I went for a year, and the two big French rivers that come rushing together like a miracle in that city, and the Musée des Beaux-Arts de Lyon with the Picassos and the room full of Louis Janmot paintings called *Poem of the Soul*, which tell a story about faith and love and death and an afterlife. I walked down streets in my mind and went food shopping at Les Halles. I thought of Paris, where I went on weekends from Lyon, and the countryside out the train windows, dotted with sheep and cows. I thought about everywhere in France I'd never been, like the cliffs of Étretat and Saint-Malo. I thought about wine and cheese and fruit and hot sun and fields of sunflowers. And I decided: If I get out of this alive, I will go to France.

On the way home that day, I listened to Beethoven: the

Moonlight Sonata. It was in my earphones and only I could hear it, but the entire city felt like it was moving to that beautiful, ethereal music. I walked as many blocks as my legs would carry me, until I was tired, my legs were too weak, and I got a cab. I was crying. Crying for Beethoven being deaf. Crying for my legs, my body, this fight. Crying because I was too tired, sometimes, for a fight. And, anyway, was this a fight? More like a submission. (Fighting, like a war, which always ends in certain death for someone, is the oddest metaphor to give a person who is terrified: You get so weak, it's not fighting, really; it's clinging to our most animal instinct to survive. Those sisters who did not make it still fought the good fight. Some tyrants can't be toppled in one lifetime. I know that now.) But even with that sadness and the music and how weak I was, I now had France and I held on to it in my mind. It was mine and I could go there anytime I wanted, no matter where I was. And, one day, I might actually go back in person, I told myself.

So that fall, after the worst was over, I'd lost a breast and four lymph nodes ("lost," as if I'd misplaced them, dropped the breast and nodes somewhere along the road or on my floor, like Toad losing a button in *Frog and Toad Are Friends*), I realized I was going to live. I had five years to be sure that I'd go another five years or another ten years or twenty. But inside I knew that, for now, I could, and had to, seize whatever living was left, and there *was* some left.

By then, I'd done radiation, which fried my skin and made it peel and blister and bleed under my arm. I'd done some more chemo, bought a wig, then traded it for a scarf because my hair never truly fell out, it just sort of thinned. I'd started Tamoxifen, which is like a Red Bull and a whiskey at once—jerks you up, sends you down. After all that, I'd been plunged into the hot flashes, the skin-crawling feeling of "formication" (which sounds like "fornication" but is nothing so pleasant; this means, literally, "skin crawling with ants" and is an apt description if you imagine that the little feet of the ants feel like razors rasping your skin), and the mood swings of chemically hastened perimenopause, along with the insult of chin hairs—which, all of a sudden, just as the hair on my head was thinning, had decided to poke out with uncanny regularity, spiny.

But as I said, despite all that misery, when that horrible and bloody part of my "fight" was over, I realized, like cold water being splashed on my face, that I was done hovering in the no-man's-land of "fight." It almost hurt to feel it. My doctors and Pete and the girls were so joyful we'd won. We'd done battle together and the foe had been vanquished! I saw them all feel this victory, like it was something we'd all done together (we had, we had!). Of course, for me, there was the regret—mine, not theirs—that my breast couldn't be saved, but these were just details—to them, not to me. And there was my fear, which would become my constant companion, even when I allowed myself to feel a tiny bit of hope again.

When that hope came back, as it miraculously did, even despite the ants and the fear and the bleeding skin, it was rosy-fingered and cool to the touch. So, I started a newsletter. So many people had been posting notes on my Facebook and Instagram pages in response to little things I put up. Like: An image of a nurse with her mask down and a smile, under which I wrote, "Doing this alone and never seeing a smile. Until today." Or a hand-painted aphorism on a piece of driftwood hanging in a bathroom of the treatment center: "Cancer is an opportunity for gratitude." These photos weren't very profound; in many ways, I found any false cheeriness infuriating. Like when a nurse handed me a cloth bag of cancer swag at some point in the early weeks: a little pillow, a binder, ice packs. I didn't want her little bag. I didn't want the support group's handout, much less the actual group. Sometimes I was sharing images for my friends with few or no words under them, and definitely with a dose of irony, even fury. I let everyone else decide how they felt. The responses, which were prolific, surprised me. People's words and support made me want to share more of my journey. This surprised me. I'd no idea I'd want to do that. Slowly, oh so slowly, I started writing sentences for the newsletter. I named it "After Cancer: France." I didn't ever think I'd *really* go to France. What I was writing about was the dream of it, the halcyon fields of somewhere else. France seemed better than, say, Iceland, where it might be cold, and I'd have to hike.

This was when April Betancourt, a friend of a friend from college who was apparently (thrillingly) reading my newsletter, wrote to me and said,

> Hey, I'm the editor of *Get Out! Magazine*. And I like what you're writing. I'm wondering if you'd like an assignment to actually *go* to France with your daughters and travel to campgrounds—maybe 5—and write about them for me? We've got a sponsorship package in the works for a whole initiative on women and girls adventuring into the great outdoors. I mean, *Get Out!*, let's face it, has been pretty male. But we want more women readers. We'd need you to take photos, too. I can pay for the plane tickets and the campgrounds and a food stipend. Then, assuming the piece goes to publication, I can pay an even $5,000. This would be a big cover feature for us. I'd want some of the frank openness about your health and life in there, the stuff you put in your newsletter about what you endured: the bone broth, staring out the window—that stuff.

> Surviving! But also good assessments of France, the land, the food, what camping is like—we'd need you to go east to west, north to south. Your girls and you doing it alone without your husband. 😀 What do you think?

The first thing I did was this: I sat down and went online to find all the photos I could of April Betancourt. I learned her father was French and her mother English. And that she'd gotten a graduate degree in wildlife conservation from the University of Arizona, Tucson. In all the pictures, she was wearing tank tops made of the silky nylon material that athletes wear. Her arms were muscular and she had a year-round tan, posing for pictures camping, skiing in Aspen, her dark hair pulled back in a ponytail. She wore red lipstick, even on the slopes. To me, at that low point in my own life, she looked like the picture of health and strength. If I could have just crawled into her sleeping bag and reemerged, like a butterfly coming out of its chrysalis, as *her*, I would have been eternally happy. So I said yes. Yes! I had no idea what I was saying yes to, really—it was almost a year away. And I was still so weak!

The morning I told Pete, he looked at me like I was absolutely fucking nuts. "You know," I said, "a lot of decisions have been made for me, or not by me, I should say: Your affair. Covid. Cancer. This is a decision I can make. And I've made it. Please don't make this about you."

"Okay," he said as I was adding a quick little chaser: "For once."

He paused. Took a "patient" breath, then said, "It's a ways away, anyway. Do you need anything before I leave for work?"

"Ice water. And send in the girls. I want to say goodbye." I cracked him a smile to soften my bossy tone.

"Okay." He paused. "I love you?" He gave me one of those tender looks where he's soft and lovely and relieved that I have smiled but he's also unsure of where we are in the morass of our marriage. I could see above his smile his dark circles from a year of worry, and that some of his stubble was coming in silver. Even now, his handsomeness killed me. Even when I was walled off, it got inside, clamped onto my heart valves like some kind of jumper cable, and gave them a jolt.

"Thank you. I really need this."

"I know you do." And if love could be described as being as expansive as the Atlantic Ocean, stretching all the way from Manhattan to the cliffs of Étretat, then that was what we had pounding between us like waves.

2.

ALICE

At the car rental, after we've said goodbye to our driver and heaved all our gear onto the concrete floor of the parking garage, we are given a hybrid/plug-in Peugeot the color of the shiny green tiger beetles we have back in Minnesota and about as big as a beetle, too. As we start to pile our bags into the trunk, a man in a dark coat with a name tag that reads "Amir" helps, saying *"Allons-y"* to me, which, if my college French holds, means "Let's go!" And then he says *"Hop"* each time he lifts a bag into the car. The girls clamber in, their carry-ons too disorganized now to zip closed. Sophie is in front with me; Iris and the contents of her bag are already spilled all over the shiny black pleather seats in the back. I can see Iris sorting her items thoughtfully and mashing with her foot both Sophie's bag and my purse into the small space behind Sophie's seat.

"Sophie, I think you should sit in the back."

"Alice, I'm not sitting in the back with Iris."

I glance behind me. Iris has Big Bear buckled into the seat next to her; her coloring books, bracelet-making kit, sketch pads, and a pencil bag are now arranged on the center console. Behind Sophie's seat, Iris has smoothed out the chaos of Sophie's and my bags with a sweatshirt draped on top, and on top of that she's made a little table with a Garfield book. There, she has placed an unopened LEGO set Pete gave her for the trip. Iris looks content, her jean shorts exposing her tender knees; her green T-shirt, with the words "Maine, Vacationland" scrawled across it in vinyl ink as blue as the Atlantic Ocean. Her hair is snarled but still soft.

"I'm not sure of myself here. Of driving. It would be safer, Sophs." I look at her pleadingly, thinking, Please don't fight with me. But part of me, if I am honest, needs her eyes and body next to me, and I am fairly sure she can see that, too. I am still so fragile. Amir taps the back of the car, as if it were a horse, and says, "*Ça va?* Ees you o-kay?" I nod. But after a beat, when I don't seem to move the car while I look for my glasses, I hear him say, more loudly, "*Mah . . . Vas-y.*" The car is on, an enormous screen lighted up in front of me in the dark garage.

"Oh my God, okay—which one is drive?" I push some buttons, and the wipers and headlights go on, as well as the car, which lurches forward like a frog. I slam on the brakes. The car shrieks at me in French—a woman's computer voice saying something alarmist. The dashboard is flashing red at me.

"Oh my God, Alice. You. Are. The. Worst. Driver." Sophie looks away like, if she could, she would certainly transport herself "rn" to Greenland.

I put the window down and say, feebly, "Pardon." To which Amir smiles and says a jumble of words in French that are likely car parts. I look at him blankly. And then he says, "SOS?" but in an American accent. Is he teasing me?

"Sophie, is he offering to help?"

"No. I don't know. Just drive, Alice."

"Sophs, I have no idea how to drive this car. Everything is in the wrong place, and there are lots of buttons I don't understand." I try to inch forward, and the car woman yells at me again: "*Attention!*" Red lights are flashing on the dash.

"Mom! At least turn the wipers off. My God, this so embarrassing."

More harshly than I should, I say, "You could help me, you know."

Gamely, Sophie starts pushing buttons on the screen. Suddenly the heat is pounding at us full blast and French rap is blaring into our ears. Our buddy Amir comes next to the car again. He taps on the window. He has the look of someone watching an *SNL* sketch in a language he does not understand; he can tell it is amusing, but he just isn't sure he totally gets it.

"*Ça va?*"

"*Oui. Ça va. Fatiguée,*" I shout over the music. Yes. I am tired and fine.

"*Ouais.*" Something about the way that *oui* drawls out to "yeah" makes it seem like he's in a Western, maybe *Shane*. It does not make me think he believes I am okay.

"Sophie, turn that off. The music. It's too loud. It's embarrassing. And I can't fucking breathe, it's so hot in here." Sweat is running down my forehead, pooling in my bra. A hot flash. Perfect.

"I am trying. Could you just drive the car?" Sophie's sneer is as thick and sour as that berry symphony of fucking coulis.

From the back seat, Iris starts to complain, her timing always impeccable. "It's too hot in here. I need the windows open. Take off the child safety lock! I need to unlock the windows." She is kicking the back of my seat, like she is back in the womb and she needs to tell me something important.

"Iris. Stop. Kicking. Me." I am thinking that this idea of

France and me alone with these two is just about the worst nightmare of my life. Cancer can't hold a candle to this, I think angrily. My rage is molten all of a sudden. Iris stops kicking and is silent.

Lurching forward, I get the car from one end of the garage to the other, our breath fogging all the windows. Someone in a car behind us beeps; they know how to drive and want to get out of here. I pull into a handicapped spot by the entrance, bright summer sun pours into the front seat. In the light, I'm able to figure out how to put the windows down, and we all breathe a fetid combination of car exhaust and stifling concrete-garage-in-summer smell. The man who beeped roars by, swiveling his neck to glare at me. I want to give him the finger. Instead I just wave.

But I am not calm. I turn back to my children. "Guys, I need my fucking glasses. And I need to get the map part of the screen up." I am crying now. Everything is out of control. Ever since my avalanche of perimenopausal symptoms, my eyes don't work anymore, my body is on fire, I pee my pants regularly, and sometimes I have tantrums. Like actual door-slamming tantrums. My one remaining nipple hurts as badly as it did when Iris chewed on it as a baby. But because of the cancer, my doctor has told me I will have to white-knuckle through the ups and downs of hormone insanity. Use alternative therapies, like acupressure, which, I'm sorry, does not fucking work. The bottom line is: No hormones for you, lady. No help. Try meditation. Fuck you.

At home in New York, my bedside table is now covered with turmeric and lemon balm capsules, reishi mushroom powder, Chinese herbs from my acupuncturist, CBD gummies that leave an acrid taste in my mouth, CBD cream for my sore nipple, arnica for my joints, and Tamoxifen, Advil, Tylenol, Lexapro, and Klonopin. Also: tweezers and a small mirror for those long black spiky hairs that keep appearing on my chin. (Truth: I love to pull them out, that valedictory deep-down tug giving me such satisfaction.)

The mean joke of defeating cancer only to be hurled into peri-or-full-on-who-really-knows-which-is-which menopause while my daughter blossoms into puberty is not lost on me. As she goes up and down emotionally, I do the same, but we're never in sync. How has evolution not fixed this problem? I mean, how is this even okay to do to us? Can't someone fix this? No. There's no one to fix anything anymore in our broken world.

Sophie pushes a bunch of buttons, and a map miraculously comes up on the enormous screen. I pull my email up on my phone. "Okay." I am trying *so* hard not to sound screechy. I am trying to sound like the mother. But instead I've got John-Cleese-in-*Fawlty-Towers*-clenched teeth. I say to Sophie slowly, I'm sure condescendingly, "What you need to put in is this . . ." I point to the words "*Camping le Grand Champ.*" Sophie pushes some buttons. Then the female voice starts to tell us again what to do in French—but she is calmer now and sounds more like she is a traffic cop in Paris, suffering an American fool. Of course, none of us understands. "Sophie, goddammit! Is there English?"

Sophie grimaces and growls like a young female lion. "I thought you learned French in college, Alice."

"Yeah, I can't remember shit. Don't tell the lady who assigned me this piece, though."

"Wow, somebody is swearing a lot," pipes up Iris acidly from the back seat. She hands me my glasses. Finally.

"Thank you, Iris. For the glasses." I slide them onto my sticky face.

Sophie pushes more buttons. A French singer is singing in English a song I've heard emanating from her Snapchat on my iPad: "Ooh-ee. Makeba. Makes my body dance for you."

Iris starts singing along and bouncing in the back, making the whole car jive. She thinks this is fun. My God, it's not! We haven't even left the garage.

"Iris, stop it. Sophie. Anne. Use the fucking phone and get this in English. Plug it in or whatever."

"Jesus, ADHD much? You never said that, Alice."

"Well, I did. Say that. I said, 'Use the phone.'"

"Not out loud. I hate you, Alice."

"Can you please just put it on the phone. And we need to find a cord somewhere—Iris, can you find a cord in Mommy's bag?"

Iris isn't moving.

"Iris! What are you doing?"

When I turn back, Iris is crying. "Are we ever going to see Daddy again?"

"Oh my God, Iris. Not right now," I say.

"I'm worried about Daddy," screeches Iris. "And Ingmar."

"Your worry is annoying, Iris. Shut. Up." This was Sophie, not me. But did I agree? Yes. But I am busy trying to retrieve any wits I can possibly find. Someone here has to be the adult, and I guess today it's me, which feels so grossly unfair.

I sigh a huge sigh. Then I say, "Sophie. Not helpful. Iris, honey—we can't do this right now. We can FaceTime with Daddy when we get to France and the campsite. Right now we are in Switzerland, and I don't know what the hell I'm doing."

"I want Daddy!" Iris starts a full-on wail.

Under the wailing, I can hear Siri on the phone. Blessedly, Siri is speaking in beautiful, comprehensible American English.

Sophie has found a cord. She has pushed the right buttons. It is working! Siri is telling me to exit the garage and then turn left. These suddenly feel like instructions for my entire life: Exit and turn left. Exit, turn left. Turn left! Turn left! Over and over.

"Sophie, you did it!" I yell. I am laughing now, joy has come back to me. I hit the gas and move the car, the glorious summer sunlight streaming through all the windows as we come out of the garage. Iris is crying in the back seat and saying something about how "nobody cares that I'm upset." To which Sophie says, "That's right, so shut up."

And then there are mountains right in front of us, enormous, towering, whitecapped mountains unlike anything I've ever seen before—huge and majestic and beautiful.

"Look, Iris, look! Those mountains. We are driving to those. To sleep right under them in our tent!!"

"Wow," says Sophie, craning her neck next to me. "Those are big." The silence of awe settles into the car. This is one of those moments when, as a parent, you can't believe you are being graced with a second to think your own thoughts and yet all you want to think about is how tender and amazing your children are. Love bubbles up inside me, cooling my hot, sweaty cheeks. I think anything, everything, is possible now.

3.

PETE

What Pete would remember most about Alice's sickness was the terrible, hovering stillness. Like the entire city, even the birds in the magnolia tree outside the windows had been silenced, gagged, snuffed out. Behind a closed door, he could hear the tinny laughter of a cartoon that Iris was watching on Netflix. Maybe the rustle of Sophie in her room. But other than the movements of these mice, it was silent, still. Some evenings Pete would try to find reasons to stay out longer, linger at the grocery store, at CVS picking up prescriptions for Alice. Any reason not to go back to their home. On replay in his mind, day after day, he heard an old recording his father used to play on LP of W. H. Auden reciting his famous poem: "Stop all the clocks, cut off the telephone . . ."

He'd remember this feeling: No matter what he did, no matter which of the very best doctors he got, he couldn't change the fact of what was happening. Cancer had happened. It had happened to them. Well, to her. Also, yes, to all of them. His wife had lost her breast. Across her chest, she had a scar as big as his foot. Cancer could come back. And he couldn't, no matter what he did, outsmart or outplay it. He had realized this fact with a crushing futility that threatened to drown him.

Some days, he couldn't shake the feeling that he had traveled back to Maine, to his family, just before Christmas in 2020, not because his wife wanted him, really. And not because she wanted the marriage. But because, just like when Covid descended, something pulled them back together and into a family again, something outside their control. Life, circumstance, inertia. Cancer.

The guilt he felt, pulling his girls away from Maine when he took Alice back to the city. He had to adhere to his deep belief that whatever this cancer thing was going to be, it had to be dealt with in New York, where it was familiar, where he knew people, where his father's roommate from college was the head of NewYork-Presbyterian and had connections to, literally, everyone. Handling it in Maine, where everything seemed slightly foreign, too far away from research—he couldn't do it. So they went back, and he set up the Meal Train with friends from the kids' school, taking the dinners at the door of the apartment or when he picked up the girls. He spent his waking hours trying to protect Alice's fragile rest. The importance of it all, the mundanity of it, the question marks that hovered over his head, these things behaved in his mind and his body like the weight of a thousand-year-old turtle shell: hard, calcified, worn, and also cracked in places.

A moment he'd never forget: Coming home with Alice, his girls, and Ingmar to their apartment. Walking in with their eyes in his mind, their female and feline abilities to pick up on clues that he never noticed. He was worried about the remnants of that bleak period in late November when he'd strayed again, and before he'd begged Alice to let him come back to them in Maine, after she had told him she had a lump. The dust everywhere that Ingmar walked through, leaving paw marks, the takeout containers piled high, the stifling airlessness. He was afraid Alice might see what he went through: the days he had lain in bed after he betrayed her again, staring at the ceiling, the sheets around his chin. He'd taken some time off from his job—not much, paid sick leave—while he lost his fucking marbles for a second, for a month, who knew. Enough time to make him remember lying in the fetal position and feeling scared.

Finally, able to climb out of bed to get help, first at the ER one night when he thought he might be going crazy, then in the appointments that followed, he realized that his life had gone off course. Pete needed help.

He had, he consoled himself, started to tell Alice that night on the phone; started to tell her everything he had done, started to confess and tell her how bad it all was for him, started to . . . what was he doing? Was he asking for a divorce? It sure sounded like it. What the fuck? But like some kind of divine intervention, an angel or a demon, whichever, the conversation had changed, moved, slid away, hit the bump of her tumor, the fear. And he'd felt too scared to put it back on track; *his* track. Scared she'd hang up. So he never confessed.

When he arrived in Maine, ready to help, thrown back into the girls' and Alice's lives, he was rosy-cheeked from the cold, city-dude-parka'ed, leather-gloved, and he had a new haircut and breath mints. He'd driven all night to get there, the knight. No matter the squishy doubts he'd had lately about not just his own life but, more importantly, his "character," a word his father might have used, he was willing to shove those all down and use action to climb back.

In the back of the car were a dozen Absolute bagels and garlic-chive cream cheese. He laughed at himself in the car, this image he'd conjured of a white stallion charging up I-95, seeing the New Hampshire liquor store and popping in for a bottle of Aperol, a bottle of prosecco, and a large plastic bottle of grapefruit soda to make grapefruit spritzes for Alice on New Year's, her favorite drink.

Those first few days at home with Alice and the girls were bliss. Like life had started over. They had the fire roaring by night. By day, he cooked, finding recipes on the *New York Times* app. He sat with Alice by the fire and rubbed her feet. The girls didn't know about the tumor, so he spent a good part of each day upstairs doing surreptitious research, calling doctors, making notes. An appointment was set for January in Bangor, a city in the middle of the state, one he'd only driven through on his way home to New York via the Bangor International Airport. "I'll take care of everything," he told Alice.

And he did. He did!

He also said, "We need to enjoy the now." And Alice nodded, docile, thank God. Every evening he made her a cocktail and they sat by the fire. She asked him no questions. They were suspended in a time free from recriminations, old wars, and new wounds. The emptiness of what the unsung future might hold was so large that it was best to cleave together, not talk, hang tight.

For Christmas, Pete made a prime rib and a new recipe, mashed potatoes *à la Pépin*, a French chef he found on YouTube. The secret appeared to be garlic and lots of butter; they were so smooth that everyone oohed and ahhed.

Pete started feeling his old self come back to him. He worked remotely, he did well at his job, he felt vigorous again. How had he lost track of how good this all was? he wondered. At night he and Alice made love and looked out the windows at the moon and the ocean. They talked, remembering how they had shown up at this house that March of 2020, when the entire world was frozen in time. He remembered how they had hung together and how that had mattered.

As Christmas passed and their January appointment loomed, Pete cleaned the house. After the biopsy and results, he made more phone calls and asked for favors from people he knew and got Alice in with a well-regarded surgeon back home in New York. He packed them up and moved them all back to the city for her treatment. He told her it would be fine. He held her hand.

In New York, he tried to manage everything the same as he had in Maine. But almost a week to the day from when they got back, just as the medical mayhem of the entire thing took over, this new darkness that belonged to him, or was in him, or had attacked him (which was it?), came back, seeping like an ink stain on soft rag paper. He held it off as best he could. Looking blearily at his girls, he could see they were caught in their own storms. But what could he do? He felt helpless. These were beasts rising out of a dark sea which no man could control.

As winter turned to spring, Alice was deep into post-op and then radiation. He went through the motions: took his pills, stashed behind the Celestial Seasonings lemon zinger in the cupboard above the toaster, doled out lasagna from aluminum tins. He ordered Chinese on the nights when no one left them anything or he, Sophie, and Iris couldn't bear another bowl of chili, or someone's creative attempt at "gourmet pasta," as if pasta could ever be gourmet. He and the girls ate quietly as Alice slept in their bedroom with a white noise machine. He'd never been truly afraid before in his life, not really. He'd gone along for so many years with fear not on the menu of options, even notions. He'd had that brief period alone in New York, but that was internal to him. This was outside him, there was actually nothing he could do to influence what was happening. He was feeling scooped out like an avocado, the crinkly peel turning gray/brown on the counter. That empty space.

His therapist, Dr. Bruno, whom Pete met on FaceTime from his desk at work, the door shut, would say, "One foot in front of the other. Baby steps, Peter. This is no small thing, all this—all of it. You will find a way back to your wife if you can take stock, repair. It's slow work. And right now, the world is upside down. So many people are in crisis. Your wife is in a very serious crisis. And so are your girls because their mother is. It's a hard time to start a process of repair in some ways."

"But I have never really had a crisis before."

"Tell me more about that?"

"I just—I don't know. I haven't felt like this before. I can't pinpoint any other time when I felt like everything was a true crisis, not like lately. There's always been so much in my life to make it better."

"What things?"

"Money. My parents. Alice. A vacation. A nice meal."

"Things sometimes catch up with people. And then there are the aftereffects of this really crazy time . . . I mean, just look at the stress, on top of the stress you already had in your marriage, the stress you caused."

When, in the fall, after that interminable summer of surgery and poison and then recovery, Alice suggested taking the girls and going to France the following summer, part of Pete felt relieved. As bad as being alone had been that fall and winter of

2020, while the entire world waited for a vaccine, and before he went back to Alice and the girls in Maine, there'd been something private about it all that Pete missed. The prospect of some future time alone—this time with meds, thank heavens—to adjust to the person he was trying to become, or becoming, seemed okay, even better than okay. Didn't it? To recover a bit himself, too? Maybe when she came back, tan and strong from a trip, her health restored, maybe then Pete could start to do the repair he kept promising himself and Alice that he would do. Maybe then the time would be right. He knew repair and change—her words, not his (of course)—were waiting for him. It was understanding how to do it. The how, what, and when were still confusing to him in the blur of illness and his daughters. Even so, it was all he thought about: how, what, and when. It was a math equation. All he needed was to find the right symbols to connect the variables. Maybe now he'd finally have the time.

4.
SOPHIE

At home in New York, Sophie could see her friends that spring. She spent time outside on the city streets and in parks, hanging with a group of kids on scooters and skateboards. Somehow, in the intervening time of their "Covid Banishment to Maine," as she liked to call it, and then coming back to New York so that her mother could have surgery and chemo, Sophie had gotten older. Or anyway, her parents acted like she had. They let her go walk around Riverside Park at dusk with a gaggle of other thirteen-year-olds. They let her go get ice cream drumsticks by herself around the corner at the bodega and come home and flop down in front of a movie. Her dad let her leave the table before dinner was over to go Snapchat in her room. There was this silence, this distractedness, this tired and heavy feeling like the dust was settling everywhere in their house. No cleaning people came anymore, her dad did what he could, but sporadically and badly, Sophie thought. She and Iris did small chores when he remembered to ask them to.

Her mother barely ate, and what she did eat seemed to consist of, from what Sophie could tell, raw turmeric root, brown rice, some sort of turnip, dandelion greens, dark meaty-smelling broths, and sometimes salmon. The rest of them ate whatever neighbors left, or they had takeout. Gone were her mother's pancakes, eggs, hot buttered toast, bacon, smoothies, stir-fries, garlic mac and cheese, lasagna, honey mustard chicken, salads. The salads! One night she asked her father to make a salad. He tried. But he bought the wrong lettuce—stiff, overly tough romaine—and tomatoes with little white dots inside them, store-bought dressing. And though technically, her father could have made a delicious salad, he seemed unable now. Sophie averted her eyes when she looked at him. She knew too much, and her love for him pierced.

In the evenings, she and Iris would put masks on and get into bed with their mother and watch the *Bake Off*. Even if she hated to admit it, the coziness felt good, like she was young again. It was annoying when her mother fell asleep only to wake up and ask, "Who won?" But the breads and cookies, the colors and shapes, the creamy puddings and frostings, they lulled her into a place where their lives seemed normal, okay. Sophie fell asleep in her own bed dreaming of matcha-colored cakes and sticky toffee-apple puddings, only to wake up to the rude reality of frozen waffles.

• • •

When Sophie saw the mountains beyond Geneva for the first time, the snow on them in the middle of summer, she felt small and powerful at once. The world was so big! After all the confines of the last two years, freedom felt delicious and terrifying, like that time she went on the Cyclone with her dad and screamed and laughed and cried all at once.

5.
IRIS

The French word for rock is *une roche*. In the Alps, everyone talks about *les rochers*. And *les sommets*—the peaks of the mountains. *La neige*. The snow. "Mama, you can see how we get from *roche* to 'rock' in English," Iris explains to her mother after inspecting the French word on a flyer she's found at the campground. "Iris, you're brilliant," answers her mother.

After getting groceries at the Monoprix grocery store, after the drive, after setting up the tent and then eating a baguette with butter for dinner at a picnic table, it's now nighttime and Iris is lying on top of her sleeping bag braiding orange and red and yellow into a new bracelet and she's singing the words she's learned on their first day, "*Roche, neige, sommets,*" in a kind of incantation.

At the Monoprix, as she peered above her pink KN95, Iris realized that American supermarkets were full of plastic junk. At their local Gristedes and even the Whole Foods where she went with her mother, there were toys at the register, and rows and rows of snacks in plastic bags in a dizzying array of colors. She would never admit it was junk when she was back home—she was always bugging her mom for a new magazine or toy or candy as they waited in line—but in France, she could plainly see that they had books and wooden toys in the regular supermarket here. Clothes, too. Cool ones. And smaller portions of everything—not the enormous vats. Instead, an amount that made you excited to try whatever it was, roll it around on your tongue without committing to eating it all week. The vegetables and fruits were not on Styrofoam or covered in plastic. Instead, they were laid out in piles that looked like they had just been picked: long dark grapes, tiny green plums, enormous bumpy tomatoes, zucchini. Shiny glass jars of every yellow of mustard you could imagine, from brown to electric, lined the shelves.

There was an entire aisle just for yogurt. "Wow, these people love yogurt," said her sister. Her mother told them that yogurt was called something like "*yah-ooh-tuh*" in French, which made both girls giggle. The butter selections were dizzying. Iris watched hungrily as her mother piled small bags of chips (large bags didn't exist), cheeses, crackers, yogurts, fruit, sliced ham, and a jar of mustard into her arms. Although they had all looked for a shopping cart, no one could find one, and it seemed too complicated to ask for help. Sophie held two jars of jam, red raspberry and apricot, and Iris held two baguettes and a package of Président butter. While the check-out began, Alice ran back to the housewares section and found a small steel skillet, a sharp knife, six cloth napkins, five forks, five knives, and five spoons. And a package of paper towels, which, she informed the girls, was hard to find, "*tant pis.*"

"What does that mean, Mommy?"

"Isn't that funny? It means 'too bad'!"

Iris giggled in glee and said, too loudly, "*Tant pis,*" pronouncing the "sss." The woman behind the register seemed to glare at Alice and then said the price so quickly that Alice had no idea what it was so she just proffered her card.

"*Voilà!*" the woman said, and then, unexpectedly, reached behind her register and handed each girl a Chupa Chups lollipop.

Back in the car, Sophie broke off hunks of bread and slathered them with butter and jam before handing them around. Iris noticed that her mother was happier and so was her sister. If her mother and sister weren't fighting, then Iris could calm the little bird that flap-flap-flapped in her chest all the time, no matter what she did to try to still it, quiet it, make it go to sleep. With the French radio on low in the background and the mountains following them, the sky looked so blue, like one of her crayon drawings. They drove in chewing silence the rest of the way. Soon they got to the gates of *Le Camping.*

The turnoff was soft grass, giving way to a patchy dirt road that meandered through poplars flashing their leaves—silver, green, silver, green—and wild mountain roses. Just looking out the window, Iris could almost feel that grass under her feet, and she immediately started pulling off her plastic Birkenstocks in the back seat. Just above the tops of the trees loomed a huge mountain, so close it seemed you could touch it, even the snow.

"Oh my good God," said her mother. "Look at *that*! It's Mont Blanc. So close."

"Wow," said Sophie. Iris noticed that her sister's face was soft, full of wonder, like she was younger than Iris thinks of her.

Iris watched her mother go into the office, her pink linen blouse puffing in the wind over her cutoff jeans. She was focused on her mother's hair, which had grown in frizzier, grayer, wispy around her face. It wasn't as long anymore, or as soft and golden as it used to be. Her mother often kept it pulled into a knot at her neck.

Iris missed that soft, long hair that used to fly around, bouncing between her mother's shoulder blades. Iris used to love to braid and play with it when they snuggled. Before the trip, her mother finally had enough hair to go get a cut, to tame the odd assortment of lengths. "Every follicle has its own idea of how to grow back," she told her girls the hairdresser had informed her. "Even so," Iris heard Sophie say, "it's loads better, Mama. You look ten years younger."

"Thank you so much, Sophie," her mother exclaimed, bursting with gratitude. Iris could hear that, the bursting. But Iris was looking carefully now and noticing how thin her mother still was, so full of bony contours rather than soft places to cuddle, and also the weird bounceless quality of the fake boob in her bra next to the real boob in her bra.

When her mother had been sick, Iris had practiced the words "My mother is dying. My mother is dead. My mother died yesterday." She said these terrible sentences like a mantra, hoping that if she tempted fate, playacted what her dad called the "worst-case scenario," then of course it would never ever happen. But as with a ghost story conjured in the dark, she scared herself with her own words and thoughts. If she had been older, she might have understood that what she was searching for was a period at the end of an excruciatingly painful sentence. The haze around the ending was the problem. It reminded her of when they were in Maine and the fog would roll in, blanketing the fields and house, and you couldn't see out the windows, couldn't see the stream or islands or waves. For a brief moment, you could feel scared that the world had vanished.

After a few moments of waiting for their mother who had disappeared into *Le Camping* office, Iris wanted her sister's attention. "Sophie, I'm thirsty."

"Drink some water, Booby."

"I don't want water. I want a cold drink."

"Do you have any idea how spoiled you are? Drink the water. Where are we getting a cold drink right now?"

"See? The sign there? Right there? Oh my God, Sophie—over there. You are looking in the wrong direction. See! There's a picture of a soda."

"That just means they sell cold drinks in the office."

"That's what I'm saying."

"Booby, we are just waiting for Mama. I'm not going in there. She'll just get mad at us for not waiting."

"I don't care. I'm getting out. I'm going to tell Mama we need a coh-old drink!"

"Yeah, you do that, Booby."

But Iris didn't get out. She knew her sister was right. So she waited, squirming, sighing, making whiny noises about how hot and thirsty she was. Sophie had stopped responding. She was on her mother's phone, scrolling her friends' Instagram pages, even though Sophie, herself, is not allowed to be on the grid.

When her mother finally reappeared after what seemed like forever, she was carrying, as if she could read Iris's thoughts, three orange-colored teardrop-shaped bottles of soda.

"See, Booby? Aren't you glad you didn't go annoy her?"

"Mama! Mama, what are those?" Iris started climbing out of the car and reaching all at once.

"Let me get in the car, honey. I got us each an Orangina—look, these are little French orange sodas! Look how pretty the glass bottles are! Let's go set up our tent."

They drove a little farther down the grassy road and turned into a square of birch trees; Iris recognized them from their papery bark. All around the trees were tall pink lilies that were spotted with purple dots and smelled like what Iris imagined fairies might smell like. The ground was covered with a thick shag of creeping thyme. Iris got out of the car in a shot, her bare feet on that thyme, yelling, "It feels like moss or a carpet! Sophie, take your shoes off!"

Iris is always thrilled to share with Sophie, to forge connections—she does it reflexively, without thinking, her big sister is her mirror. She often feels poised to be let down; she knows how much power Sophie has to reject her, slap her back. But oh, when Sophie reciprocates! To Iris's delight, her sister was smiling and pulling off her leather thong Birkenstocks to sink her own big feet into the woolly thyme, and she was also bending to smell the sweet, heady perfume of the lilies.

As the girls investigated the campsite, Iris saw her mother pulling out the bags of food from the grocery store and placing them on the picnic table. Iris wanted to see all the lovely and unusual things again, so she came to sit at the table to watch. Her mother pulled her two insulated food bags out of the suitcase and moved the cheeses and yogurts into those, sliding in the two cold packs she had picked up. Then her mother went to the car and retrieved the big duffel with their tent, stakes, sleeping bags, and camping pillows inside. While her mother and sister puzzled the tent together, Iris began to wander the perimeter of the site alone, peering into the hot-pink blossoms of the lilies to find bumblebees with furry white butts, buzzing from flower to flower. Iris could hear the flap-flap of the tent and the rain tarp and her mother and sister arguing over what went where, banging stakes into the hard mountain soil with a rock. And then the zippers and her mother calling, "Sophie, can you hand me the mats," and then Sophie trudging back and forth from the car with their suitcases and backpacks.

Her mother had thought to bring a cotton April Cornell tablecloth covered with tiny pink roses. When the bedding was all inside the tent, they sat down on thick, rough wooden chairs at the square wooden table covered with the pretty cloth; the chairs scratched at the backs of Iris's thighs. They ate the tiny green plums with golden centers that her mother said were called *mirabelles*, and more bread and butter, and her mother and sister ate a stinky *Camembert*. Then they took a walk around the campground, scoping out other people's homey tents and campers. All the while, Sophie and her mother were discussing the various merits and demerits of each camping spot. Iris found a periwinkle blue and very furry butterfly, and she chased it down the grassy road.

By the time the clouds rolled in, threatening rain, they were back at the campsite eating crackers and more *mirabelles* for dinner. Darkness descended. It was so dark here, no lights anywhere, just the sky a dark blue-black.

In the tent, with Big Bear beside her, Iris takes a break from bracelet making and FaceTimes with her dad. Iris tells her father in immense detail about the grassy path and the blue butterfly with the white outline on its wings and the Oranginas and the high, high mountains. She shows him the bracelet she is making. She teaches him some French words and explains what they mean and laughs when he tries to pronounce them. He does a funny French accent for her, even goes off to find her costume box and comes back wearing a beret, glasses, and a mustache, and that makes Iris laugh. Sophie and her mother are laughing, too, and that makes Iris oh so happy.

By the time the rain starts, Iris is falling asleep. In the vague background, she can hear her sister talking to her father, and then she hears her mother say goodbye. But Iris is so cozy in between her sister and mother, she can't hold on anymore.

Iris feels her mother kiss her cheek and hears Sophie say good night to her mother, she hears breathing and, later, snoring, and no bad dreams come that night. Iris couldn't know that her mother is wide awake, lying on her own mat and holding her breath against the fear that presses in most nights. She couldn't know that each night her mother contemplates how to get through four more years. How to accept that she'll be looking over her shoulder, peering into darkness for a monster, half expecting it to arrive, day after day after day. A never-ending story. Iris couldn't know that her mother is wondering how in the world she got to France and how and why this gulf between her and Iris's dad is so jagged, so unrelentingly treacherous to sail across. She could not know that her mother is also thinking about what they would eat in the morning, because they have already eaten almost everything in their grocery bags save for the mustard and the yogurt. Iris is not old enough yet to understand how many layers a mother holds in her mind. Iris only sleeps, as that is all she has to do, and for once, it feels okay to let go.

6.

ALICE

This all appeals to me. The slow pace, the way the light hits the mountains and flowers; the lush woods. It's the way the buildings look in the little towns, the way the bakeries smell when we go for bread and croissants every morning. The cobblestones and old doors with the iron knockers; the way the exterior details were created, I think, by people who seemed to understand that pleasure, beauty, will change a moment, a life, make it all that much more precious. I love the tile floors and the balconies and the old ladies with their carts of groceries talking on the corners, their voices like tinkling glass. And the girls. *My* girls. They are radiant here in France. Since that first morning after the long drive and after setting up the tent and then the wind that made the tent huff and puff like a dragon, when the sun came up and hit those mountains the next morning, I knew this was right: France, I am here. I am here.

We have left our masks in the car. No one here wears them. Back home, everyone is still so cautious. And our family has had to be extra cautious. But now we feel so free. I am letting myself feel free. I don't know the last time I felt this way. It's been years, at least.

My last chemo infusion, I got a new nurse. Before that, I'd gotten to know the faces of the regular nurses and their rhythms, and I almost didn't want that part of it—the club—to end. When I went there, it felt like that *Cheers* song. At least everyone knew my name. I would miss it. I loved how we'd talk about things like Meghan and Harry or Beyoncé, stupid stuff about the world, and somehow, just in doing that, it always made me feel more a part of things than when I went in. That is the incredible gift of nurses. I think they do that for most everyone, nurses do.

My favorite nurse was a guy named Steve. He was from Wisconsin and tall and muscly. He had tattoos all over his arms and thick black hair and a beard. I imagined putting my hands in that thick hair. Would they get stuck? He had a slow handsome smile, and he told me he'd been in Iraq and Afghanistan, ten years all told. One day he told me how the US government had told the Iraqi translators and others who had helped the US in Iraq that they would be given visas to get out, a reward for their services, he said. These people who had served this country, they arrived at the airport, their bags all packed, their kids with them, and then the US said, "Sorry, no." Steve got choked up. Then he told me about the sun coming up over the hills in Afghanistan and how for a moment it was the most beautiful, peaceful place in the world, an image he will never ever forget. "But just as the sun would touch your face, suddenly, there were bullets flying. They knew where we were. They always knew," he said. He said the military told you to never trust any Afghani—or Iraqi—no matter how much they meant to you. "But those guys—we had fun times. They couldn't shoot worth a shit, the ones who were our guides, our translators. I got to know them like they were my own soldiers. But we could never trust. That's the thing, your heart wants to trust. It just . . ." Again, Steve was at a loss for words. I looked forward to Steve. And every time I lay back in my chemo lounge chair and felt warm in the blankets he gave me, they were so heavy on my chest, and it all felt so familiar, I was willing to lean in, to succumb, to the medical industrial complex. It was going to save my life, they said. No question, don't worry. One year from now you will forget all this. A bump. A blip.

But that last time at the center, I didn't see Steve. Instead, I had a nurse with purple hair. I asked for a blanket, which arrived warm, as usual. I had put my feet up, lounging. But the nurse wanted me to put them down because, she said, she was tall, and it was awkward for her to lean over to put in my IV. Wait a minute, I thought, aren't I the one with a deadly disease? Can't I keep my feet up? Reluctantly, I lowered my feet from that enormous chair. Then she sat down, so I put my feet back up.

She looked at me, annoyed. "Why did you do that?"

I looked back at her, confused. "Because I thought you needed them down while you were standing?"

"Well, I have back problems. Been in and out of the hospital." And then she shoved the needle into my arm, hard.

"May I have another blanket, please? I'm cold. The IV makes me cold." She brought another blanket and plunked it on my lap. I had to reach, one-handed, to try to undo it, without dislodging the needle in my arm, to spread it over my body.

"I will never come back here," I said to myself. Like I was deciding never to go back to a diner that had overcooked my eggs. Across the room, a man, maybe my age, with a trucker hat and nice jeans sat in his chair with his laptop perched on his lap. He was very thin. All the patients sat in their own little Jetsons pods, with their reclining chairs and IV drips and snacks and drinks. A little universe.

It comes over me sometimes: My body will always be inscribed with the map of what has happened. My breast is gone, there are scars. By some incredible grace from God my hair is growing back. When it was over, though, it was over. Instead of "I have cancer," my childhood friend Betsy told me I could now say "I had cancer." Then, a cliff drop. My God, if someone had only told me that the afterward bit would be the worst. In that purgatory, I tried not to obsess on the five years. I tried to think of my cancer as a groove in a river rock. A rock has so many stories to tell. So much water from so many places will ripple over that groove, smoothing, always smoothing, until the end of time.

And so I went to France. With the girls. And here we are.

• • •

Sophie is back in the tent, reading, while Iris showers and someone plays Johnny Hallyday. Sophs has been reading *Are You There God? It's Me, Margaret.*, despite my raised eyebrows; although to be frank, I was also her age, maybe younger, when I learned about Two Minutes in the Closet from Judy Blume.

Last night, when the girls called Pete, I took the phone, too. I feel tenderly toward him. I can see he's been shaken by my cancer. Sometimes, back home, when he says goodbye in the mornings, before leaving for work, he hovers in the doorway. Like he wants to talk. But I want him to go, I want the house to be quiet, only Ingmar as my companion. I want to collect my thoughts and turn to the quiet place I have found when writing my newsletter. I have a ritual now: I make myself some green tea mixed with mint. I put a little honey and oat milk in it. I go to my computer and look out across the Hudson and watch the light spill across the buildings as morning comes and turns the corner heading for noon. And then I start to write.

There is a sadness that overtakes me sometimes in the afternoons, when the sun starts to slide toward evening and I know everyone is coming home and there's going to be this need or want for me. More than I can give yet. Or want to give. It's this, I think: Knowing it all could go, that they could lose me entirely, that sometimes makes me distant. I feel shitty saying it.

I, weirdly, also have gratitude for the cancer: For the first time in years, the cancer has opened this door, this quiet, this space—I get to think, I get to write. Gone is the expectation that I will micromanage the backpacks or laundry or schedules. Instead, I am left alone. That's a gift, one I didn't expect, one that only cancer gave me. My mother used to say as I was growing up, "Gifts come in packages you often don't expect."

Soon enough, though, after the worst was over, my girls needed me back on my feet, running the ship, carrying the mental load. But I kept thinking, Just a little longer, a little more time to fall into my thoughts and words every morning, to exist as my own person and reach into my chest to pull out a voice. I don't know this new person yet, this new voice.

Somehow, as cancer receded into the rearview mirror, I held on to that voice. I kept going.

You wouldn't believe it, but I have four hundred followers. Mostly mothers I know and people I grew up with. Nonetheless, there are followers out there. Of me. Who read my writing. About my cancer. And my survival and losing my breast and being a mom. Of course, I can't say everything. I can't. Well, isn't that what we all do nowadays? Expect lives to look like

Instagram posts, the light falling just so, a flower arranged to dip at a certain elegant slant. Everyone is their own author of their own curated memoir, doled out in images and pithy posts that scream, "I was here, I existed, I did some things right."

Coming to France, though, I am back in the saddle of mothering. I feel a little out of step. I have to go at this carefully. My girls are watching.

• • •

The lovely, sleepy jet lag in the warm sun since we got here has been honey-sweet. Every morning we awake early, and the girls and I stretch and get in the car, still bleary, and drive to Chamonix to pick up bread, and I get coffee, which is sour and terrible but gets the job done. I wear this bra now that has a floppy fake breast sewn into the left side; I even wear it to bed so I don't have to deal with it in the morning. I also have a few crocheted cotton "breasts" which I can slip into a normal bra. The first morning here, when I woke up and started to pull off my nightgown, I saw Sophie eyeing the breast/scar/bra situation as I fumbled to find a bra and slip in one of those soft cotton breasts. I quickly pulled on a tank top and my jean shorts and decided that, for the rest of the trip, I'd just keep things as covered as I could. So many pieces I keep holding for everyone, for myself.

I wear the same shorts every day here—they pull up above my belly button, flare out around my thighs. I love how the denim gets softer each wear, no matter that they aren't clean. I feel like it molds around my body, hugs me, and makes me feel like I am centered, alive. I haven't felt this in so long. So odd, now, come to think of it, when I have only one breast, I am camping, I am alone with the girls: I suddenly feel almost beautiful.

Each morning Clotilde, at the bakery, sings out *"Bonjour!"* I've taught my girls how to say *bonjour* and *merci* and *s'il vous plaît*. I stand there, tiger-momming, and make them say it. I make them sort out ordering their *éclairs* and *brioche* in as much French as possible. We leave, a bag overflowing with hot *chouquettes*—which are these puff pastries that are round and studded with big sugar crystals—and three baguettes and a few more sweets we couldn't resist. Then we make our way down the road to the open-air market, where we buy dew-covered rust-red lettuces, bright orange carrots, olives as big as silver dollars, yellow tomatoes, green olive oil, a roast chicken, butter, and the local Tomme, which is a hard cheese like cheddar but much milder. I swallow another espresso from the local café, letting it burn my throat with its fiery acidity, while the girls drink *une limonade*, and then we pile back into the car, back to our camp table, where we eat and eat and eat. Oh, these olives are not like the olives of yore, which came from Amazon during Covid in glass jars and were wrapped in Bubble Wrap. These are green and fruity and mellow and spicy all at the same time, their flesh smooth as an unripe pear, no mush. The girls inhale these olives. In fact, Iris will eat only these olives and the one Tomme we've found called Le Chat (the cat), which is particular to this town and creamier than the others. Everything else, she says, is gross. The yogurt, "disgusting." The smelly cheese, "disgusting." The chicken, "too rich." Oh, she'll munch on a lettuce leaf on a baguette with salt and olive oil. And we all eat *les mirabelles* by the pound. (Makes me think of those William Carlos Williams lines "I have eaten / the plums / that were in / the icebox . . .")

In the afternoons, when we lie down in the tent, there is such peace, despite our bags exploded all around us, Iris making more bracelets and singing more new words. Sophie has her Judy Blume and I've got an advance copy of the new Barbara Kingsolver novel a friend at *Time* sent me. *Demon Copperhead*. Quite a book, if you ask me—I can't put it down. I keep emailing my friend new revelations; she's read the book twice, she said.

Oh. That's another funny thing about getting cancer, about writing this newsletter. People send me presents! Magazine subscriptions, advance copies of books, codes to watch screeners of movies or series not yet released—friends from college or high school who have gone on to work in publishing or movies. One friend sent me a small, intricate painting of a bluebird, which I hung on the wall next to my bed.

Another friend sent me a manuscript about a mother who decided to have an open marriage after she found out her husband had been cheating. (She couldn't have known about Pete's affair—or did she? New York is a small town in so many ways, it can make you paranoid.) I tried to read it. I did. I hated it.

The door of our tent opens to trees. They are poplars, lindens, and ash, or at least this is what Charlotte, who runs the campsite with her tall Swedish husband named Nils, tells us about them. She tells us that down the mountain road, "dat way," she motions with her long-fingered hand, "there ees a festival of the leen-den tree, we call that tee-you'll. The 'oney from the bees in the flowers, *c'est magnifique*!" She kisses the tips of her fingers.

When we nap in the afternoons, if we crane our necks just right, we can see the peak of Mount Blanc from where we are lying, far above us, way above the leaves of the trees, reaching to the heavens above. Sophie always says she doesn't need a nap, that she will read. But after a while I open my own eyes with that funny startle I have had for years now, ever since I first learned that Pete was cheating on me and I kicked him out. It's a terrible feeling, never being able to sleep deeply. Some women say it's hormones. Others it's chemo. Others it's fear. No matter what it is, it makes me feel broken inside, like I am never totally mending.

When I open my eyes, I see Sophie asleep. Her sweet face that has gotten longer, her nose thinner, like a figure in a Modigliani painting. My firstborn, who teaches me day after day how to become.

On those afternoons, I wake up and remember when I first was diagnosed with cancer in Maine, before we came back to New York. Pete was back in Maine then, and he drove me at dawn to Bangor, through the freezing January tundra of Maine, only the crows awake and scavenging from the snowbanks on the side of the road. Down a long green hallway, we saw a doctor with cold, probing hands. I was shuffled along to a mammogram, then an ultrasound, then a biopsy. And then we came back home, the weight of answers unbearable. I remember that, for a solid week, I lay in our bed upstairs, watching the light and how it traveled across the room, carving shapes into the white-painted walls, setting in pinks and purples over the water. I would miss this light, I remember thinking. I would miss light.

In a day, the girls and I will leave this magical place in the Alps and move on to the next camp, even though we've made this our home for three days. From here we will go south, to the fields of lavender. Our next campsite is on a farm, by the looks of it, where we will camp for free. Sophie is already missing the mountains, already attached to this piece of earth. But Iris is excited to be in motion, to see more. As long as we are together, as long as she can see us, touch us, Iris has decided in France that she likes to move. She is my little adventurer now. France did that. Funny how your kids will surprise you, change roles, rearrange internally, break out of what you expect, say something that stops you.

7.

IRIS

When they got back to New York and her mom was sick, Iris and her sister had to go back to school. Everyone was still wearing masks. No one had a vaccine yet.

But none of those kids were just starting in the middle of the year. They had their routines and friends; they had an easy-peasy attitude with their parents at drop-off. They knew what was in their backpacks. By then their grown-ups had sorted out that Maisie definitely hated dried mangoes, and Claire would never eat any kind of pasta in her lunch, and Addyson would tolerate only the thinnest schmear of SunButter on her SB&J, which had to be three quarters grape jelly, and the bread couldn't be toasted, only soft, and def no crusts.

Iris was thrown in midstream with her father making lunches and her mother in bed. She got halves of take-out burritos from the night before; bagels with olive cream cheese, which she decided she hated more than anything but forgot to say so; an overly handled apple; a Nature Valley granola bar in the familiar green and mustard-yellow wrapper, so dry it tasted like sand; two slippery cheese sticks; pretzels. All these things were pressed into her insulated lunch bag, which took on the smell of soft apples and granola bars crumbled past wanting.

To make matters worse, Iris was signed up for soccer three days a week and, on the other two, aftercare. Basketball season had come and gone without ever happening, and dance was on indefinite hold. Zoom classes had been a failure for kids, teachers, and parents alike. But spring outdoor soccer was on, at least for Iris, who had never played soccer before. Her father had to work, her mother had to recover, she needed to be taken care of. "I want to be home," she said. "And we have to wear masks on the bus, and the bus ride to the fields is long, and all the other kids actually know how to play soccer." Her mother put an arm around her and Iris could feel her mom shuddering like she was crying, but she didn't want to look. Her mom said, "I know. This is just a little period. Everything will be okay. You will remember doing this tough thing. You will come out the other side. You might even start to love soccer."

"Pickle, it will be okay." Her father rubbed the top of her head.

Her older sister said, "God, you're such a baby about everything, Booby. Aren't you glad to be back in the city? I am."

Iris wailed, "No, I hate New York, and I hate you guys." She could feel this hot, wet, molten lava in her eyes, like they were full of fire, and her mouth felt stretched taut in her face. Her sister laughed at her and called her "Booby" and "crybaby." They were all ganging up on her!

Iris charged at her sister and tried to punch her, and her sister shoved her, walked away, and slammed her door.

"Sophie Anne, you are very rude," her dad yelled. Iris turned to her mother. "Mama, I miss Maine." Her chest heaved and she cried and her mom held her against her less comfy chest and she knew her mother knew and she also knew it hurt her mother to know what she knew.

• • •

To get to soccer, Iris needed to get on a yellow school bus and watch the city fall away until they got to Riverdale, where they had their practice fields. She knew the girls on her team, many of them. She'd known them in preschool, but no one remembered *her* very well. Iris wore her mask and a sweatshirt, her brown hair braided in two straight lines down her back. There was a girl named Sylvie with whom Iris made friends. Sylvie wore pink soccer socks and a pink mask. Sylvie had ten or twelve or twenty—Iris could not count because Sylvie was always moving around, and it seemed rude to be obvious about it—little braids all over her head with different-colored beads at the end of each one. She told Iris, when Iris asked how long they took to braid in the morning, that they stayed braided for days and days and she slept with them braided and she used a powder shampoo instead of the wet, gloppy stuff Iris always got in her eyes. Iris went home and asked her mother for braids like Sylvie's, and her mother said, "Iris, you'll need to be content with two braids, my love." That was the kind of answer her mother gave now that left everything murky. Why couldn't she have twelve or twenty braids? Why no beads? Iris had no idea. She knew she couldn't keep bothering her mother the way she used to. She had to push it down inside, bite her knuckles if necessary.

Most of the soccer games that spring were at four in the afternoon. And her father could not come, and most weeks her mother was either at the "hostible," as Iris called it, getting her infusions, or too weak to go downstairs to take a taxi and come because she'd had her infusions earlier that day. So Iris went on the bus and played her game, then got back on the bus and took it back to school, and then her father picked her up from aftercare. Sometimes she was one of only three or four girls on the bus going back to school; all the other girls had gone home with their parents. Iris barely saw her sister anymore; she was in the middle school wing now, and sometimes Sophie went home earlier than Iris to do her homework.

Iris had a lump in her throat all the time. She asked her mother if that was like the kind of lump she had had in her breast. Her mom said no, she guessed Iris's kind of lump was from being sad. "Is that right, honey?" Iris nodded, and tears seeped down the sides of her face onto her pillow. "Your lump will get smaller with time, lovey," her mother reassured her.

Iris missed Maine so much she could barely think about anything else sometimes; it would take her breath away. She missed everything, even the time when they were stuck in that cold house quarantining after Covid began and all they ate was olives and cereal and saw no one. She missed her dirty knees and the crash of the ocean and she missed her friends the bluebirds and the fields and the snow and the smell of clean air. And she missed the house with its creaking floorboards and her mother cooking and their garden. She missed being free. And more than being free, she missed knowing where everyone was. Now she had no idea where anyone was. "I keep losing track of everybody," she told her mother one night.

"We're right here, we're not lost," her mother said.

"You don't understand what I mean," Iris said, even though, actually, she thought her mother probably did understand. But when she looked up, hoping her mother might ask what she needed to understand, Iris saw her mother had fallen into another one of those feathery, soft sleeps, here one second, blown away another.

If her mother had asked, Iris would have told her: "It's like you guys are those gray, puffy dandelion flowers, like in our field up in Maine, and when the wind comes up, the seeds go everywhere, and you're all too small for me to run after and catch and put you back into that perfect lollipop shape." Someday she would explain this. But for now she just had to be vigilant and keep her eyes on everyone. Keep track.

8.

ALICE

The morning before we leave the Alps to drive south, we go for a hike to an old crumbling manor at the top of a steep path. By then, our jet lag has passed, though my lower back aches from sleeping on that thin compressible mat. Like every morning, the first thing that went through my mind this morning after I awoke was wondering if the cancer had come back. What's crazy is I'm starting to feel better than I have in a long time. And yet, somehow, instead of that making me joyful, I have these moments of scanning for dangers lest I get too comfortable. I don't want to be surprised, made a fool of. Today, I shook it off before the girls woke up. I told myself, Don't do this to yourself.

Honestly, it's easy here to change the channel to optimistic: The air is dazzling, the food is amazing, the sunlight is luxurious. As we hike, I'm humming "*The Sound of Music*," much to Sophie's irritation. The more irritated she becomes, the more I want to hum and throw in the odd dissonant word I remember.

"Alice, you're so immature," Sophie says. But she is smiling because she can see I am happy, strong enough to hike and sing, I am laughing.

I have chosen our next campground because I've never been to Provence. I found it on Hipcamp, which, in my cursory online education, is like Airbnb but for camping. Many years ago, when I was in college and went to France for a semester, I went to Normandy for the summer after and was an au pair. I haven't been back in years and years, other than a very short trip Pete and I took to Paris when we were just married. This idea of France has been like a candle I've kept burning inside me, through starting my career in New York City, the marriage and kids, then 2020 and cancer. Then comes April Betancourt, with her tan, muscular shoulders, and Patagonia outfits, offering me a ticket.

What I want this summer is the Peter Mayle Provence of old houses and daffy carpenters and lavender fields. When I tried to find a true campground, nothing was even moderately redolent of what I had been imagining. The place I finally found on Hipcamp has a field for a tent overlooking a body of water called the Gulf of Lions, to the west of Marseille. There's a small, dusty town nearby. Okay, I thought, this is perfect. This is the kind of rugged individualism *Get Out!* wants.

After our hike, we eat more olives and bread and cheese, fill our water bottles, and then get back into the car. The drive is going to be long and winding. One route I looked at had us drive briefly into Switzerland and then all the way to Turin, Italy, all on highways, only to come back to France along the coast. The one I chose, eventually, would have us drive up and down through three national parks. I need to show my girls the French countryside, I told myself. My goal for this trip is to have them go home having experienced the heart of France, not a world city like Paris, and certainly not a bunch of highways.

Charlotte comes out with a basket of raspberries she's picked this morning, still warm from the sun, all perfectly fresh little thimbles. *"Faites attention dans les montagnes,"* she says. Be careful in the mountains.

This morning I texted Pete: Leaving for the ocean. Well, I guess it's actually a sea. Weird. Never used that word for real! I'm in a Jane Austen novel when I say sea! 😆 We'll go through the mountains now. Will text when we arrive. No idea about service on the way. In the back of my mind, of course, I worried about fires in any mountains, even these seemingly lush ones.

The heat seems to radiate off the tar of the roads and fields on the sides, baking the world dry. Back home, on the NPR site, we did read about the fires in France on the Spanish border, and of the record heat waves everywhere. So here we are, in the pan but not the fire. An email from my mother, "Are you ok there? Are you near the fires?" "No, Mom, on the other side of the country." Even Pete, who knows we are going to be miles and miles away from the fires, warned me as we got on the plane, "Watch out for fires, okay?"

Google Maps is telling me now that it will take seven hours to get to the Gulf of Lions. This seems insane: How could one route that would take us through two other countries be four hours and the straight shot through the mountains be seven? I head into the mountains. Google gets things wrong all the time, I tell myself.

9.
SOPHIE

It's a hot afternoon when Sophie gets into the car. Her mother hands her the container of raspberries, and Sophie arranges the water bottles in the various cupholders. Iris clambers in, clutching a wax-wrapped Le Chat cheese. Sophie's mom has made sure to pack a knife and has bought a little wooden cutting board that Sophie can use as a table as they drive.

Sophie's mother doesn't argue anymore about her sitting in the front seat, which Sophie feels is a victory every time she gets in. Sophie makes jam and butter sandwiches as her mother starts driving. Sophie is thinking to herself, as she spreads the butter and then the jam, that it's possible that everyone in the entire town of Chamonix was telling them it was *not* a good idea to take that long drive through the mountains.

She sifts back through the evidence: There'd been the reluctant enthusiasm of the woman at the bakery and also with the man at the café. Charlotte had said something about wild berries along the way, *myrtilles* and *cerises* (blueberries and cherries, her mother had translated) and *incroyable* vistas. Another person had talked about having a *frère* (a brother) in Sestriere, on the Italian border, in case they needed to spend the night.

Sophie heard her mother say, too loudly, "I want my girls to see *the real* France." Sophie has no idea what that meant. All of France is real, isn't it? This isn't Disney, for God's sake. Iris has no idea what is happening at all, of course. Iris! Making bracelets in the back seat, picking her nose. Iris being so clueless and babyish makes Sophie feel very alone. I am the only logical person here, she mutters to herself.

"What, Sophie?" Iris pipes up.

"Never mind," Sophie grumbles. Oh, they are both so annoying! Sophie thinks.

Earlier, Sophie watched her sister sitting on the dusty floor of the bakery, petting a black cat missing an eye, cooing over it and saying, "Mommy, look, this cat looks just like Ingmar." Ingmar. Booby.

When they left for France, Booby cried and clutched Ingmar like she'd never see him again. Sophie couldn't stand it. On the plane, Iris kept saying over and over that she was worried something would happen to Ingmar. Sophie said, "My God, Booby, nothing will happen to Ingmar. He's there, with Daddy."

"Mama, what if Daddy lets Ingmar out or forgets to feed him?"

"Pickle, I understand." Her mother was always indulging these absurd ideas of her younger sister's. "I promise, Daddy will take good care," her mother placated. The night before they flew to Europe, Iris had taken Ingmar into her bed, matting her face into the poor cat's struggling body, holding him hostage under the covers. Sophie said, "Oh God, Booby. Seriously. You're hurting him."

In the bakery, after three days in a tent, Sophie had had it with

Iris and her behavior of crouching on the floors everywhere, her legs spread and the crotch of her underwear showing from underneath her dress, her dirty sneakers, multiplying friendship bracelets, long braids, and tendency to act two, not eight. "Get up, Booby," she told Iris in the bakery. "Booby, get up. That cat doesn't like that." She wanted to kick Iris.

Her mother's voice from left field: "Did you hear girls, the cat's name is *Fraise*, for the eye that's lost? Strawberry. Sweet thing. I think she's saying it lost the eye in an accident, maybe a fight. I am not totally clear on that part."

Sophie looked down at the cat and saw that, indeed, its eye was all scarred and pulverized, like a red berry. Gross. Sophie got her mother's perfectly healthy eye and made the "Get us out of here" face.

Setting out on the *chemin*—"That's the French word for road," her mother told her, "kinda sounds like 'sha-men' but they say it fast and more elegant and the mouth is more open . . . like this," and her mother demonstrated—even Sophie can admit that it is stunning: deep gorges and peaks above, flowers and trees everywhere, streams and deep blue ponds and lakes.

But from practically the moment they start, Iris is piping up from the back seat, asking how much longer the trip will be, then complaining that she needs to pee every five seconds.

When her mother finally pulls over, not even forty-five minutes into the drive, they bushwhack together through tall grass and weeds to a stream that's burbling and cool. Just as they get there, Iris starts screaming and sits down, writhing on the ground. She is screeching, "Bees!" Sophie can feel her own legs stinging, too, and she looks down and sees welts all over her legs. Suddenly fearful, Sophie hears her voice come out younger than she wants, needier, "What is it, Mama?"

"Sophie, hold on." Her mother is running past her to Iris, whose mouth is open like a big O. Sophie can see that her mother, too, has red welts all over her own bare legs. "Guys, we must have run through a hive. Sophie, come here, let me look." Sophie is fighting back tears. It's so hard to be the older sister. Iris always gets her mother first. Sophie always has to be strong, grown-up, she always has to wait. It feels awful sometimes, the pressure. Her legs burn and so do her eyes. Sophie goes and hovers next to her mother. Iris is saying she won't pee now, she doesn't need to anymore. Typical, thinks Sophie. You probably never even needed to and now look at the situation you've caused! "Try, honey," her mother tells Iris. Obeying the instructions for her younger sister, Sophie goes behind a tree and pees. "Let's run back," her mother says, and Sophie nods bravely.

"Maybe they won't get us on the way back?" Sophie offers. But they are stung anew. In the car, all of them breathing heavily and Iris still screaming, Sophie says, "There weren't any bees this time! What is this? What is it, Mama?" Sophie's growing fear feels drowned out by her sister's meltdown.

"I don't know," shouts her mother. "I just don't know. Sophie, here's a napkin—hand me the water." Her mother pours water on napkins and hands them around, and everyone puts the cool water on the welts, and that feels a bit better.

"Sophie, look on the phone. Is there a town nearby? We might need a hospital. I have no idea what this is."

Suddenly, Sophie feels angry. Everything is going to be bad now, she can just tell. "Alice, stop it, you're screeching. So is Iris."

"My God, of course I'm screeching. Of course Iris is! So are you!"

Sophie worries that this is one of those moments. Like when they first got to Maine during Covid and someone cut their trees down. These things, in Sophie's experience, don't reverse course and get better. The trip might be ruined now.

Fighting through pain, Sophie picks up her mother's phone, teasing her fingers across the screen to reveal the next town on the map. "There is a town about ten miles away," she says through clenched teeth.

"Okay. We will go there. Find out."

"Find out what?"

"What I said, Sophie! Is there a hospital?"

"How would I know?" Sophie asks.

In a little while, the stinging subsides and the welts go down a little bit and Iris eventually stops screaming. They all drink some water and Sophie hands around some chocolate. She puts on the radio.

When they get to the town, they find a small store on the bank of a rushing stream. It has a big wheel for milling flour that sits just above the stream. The wheel goes in huge circles, dumping pailfuls of water back into the stream. Inside, it's quiet and cool. There are small bags of chips, chocolate bars that fit in your palm, books for kids, and boxes of colored pencils. Small sodas—none of those liters—and large waters in green glass bottles are in a fridge.

"*Buongiorno,*" says the woman behind the counter.

"Ah, Italian," answers her mother.

"*Sei Francese?*" asks the woman.

"*No, Americana*. Do you speak English? I need help. My girls and I got these stings, do you see?" Her mother is pointing to her own legs, then to Sophie's, showing the woman. "Stings," she says loudly. Sophie wants to crawl under the shelves. Mama is so embarrassing, she thinks.

"Non parlo inglese." The woman has dark hair pulled back from her long, lined face and glittering green eyes; she is wearing a black dress. For a moment, Sophie considers whispering to Iris that maybe this woman is a witch, hoping to scare her, but when she turns, she can tell by the way Iris's eyebrows are drawn tightly, like a cat putting back its ears, that this thought is already crossing Iris's mind. For a second, some of the hardness inside Sophie melts for her sister. "My God, how little of this she understands," Sophie hears herself say out loud.

"What?" asks her mother.

"Nothing."

"She's Italian, Sophie. Why in the world would you assume she speaks English?"

"I wasn't talking about *her.*" She can tell from the dark look on her mother's face, her brows frowning like a manga, that she doesn't believe her. "Never mind," mumbles Sophie, and looks away.

The woman turns and shouts, "Roberto!" And then *"Dai,* Roberto! *Mamma mia. Rispondi!"* She mutters something about *"È un vecchio sordo . . ."* and shakes her fist in the air while hobbling to the back of the little store, her cane scraping the floor. She raps on a wooden door and yells loudly, "Ro. Ber. Toh!"

A coughing voice emanates from behind the door. *"Sì,* Angelica, *cosa vuoi?"*

"Roberto, *c'è una donna Americana con due ragazze. Parlano inglese e ci chiedono aiuto per delle punture d'ortiche."*

"Ortiche? Lei e le ragazze? Tutti ce l'hanno le punture?"

"Sì, Roberto."

"*Balle.*"

"*Ma, sì.*"

"*Va bene, Madonna.*"

An old man dressed in dungarees and a dusty black collared shirt comes shuffling out of the room then. He looks as though he has been milling flour for the last hundred years; even the tips of his hair have flour in them, it is under his fingernails and on the pointed end of his nose.

"*Buongiorno.*" He smiles shyly at the girls, and Sophie sees that he is missing a tooth on the bottom.

"I am so sorry. To disturb you." Her mother is still yelling like he is deaf, which maybe he is, he is very old. "But my girls and I got these horrible stings." She gesticulates a little dramatically, Sophie thinks, to Iris's legs. "And I wonder if you have any *crema* or if you know what it's from?"

"*Eh, sì sì,*" says the man called Roberto, pulling a pair of dusty black-framed glasses off of the top of his head. "*Fammi vedere.*" He bends down and peers at a spot that her mother is pointing to on her own calf, awkwardly hoisting her leg up to the counter. Sophie is dying. The man scuffs over and looks at the tingly marks on Iris's arm and then peers at Sophie's legs, too.

He straightens his dusty frame and puts his glasses back on their perch. "*Sono ortiche urticanti. In inglese . . . è . . . aspetta un attimo.*" He puts his hand up as if directing traffic and shuffles to the register to pull out a small, rotten-looking Italian-to-English dictionary. "*Sono needles. Needles.*"

"Needles?" echoes her mother, looking in a panicked way at Iris's legs. "I don't think it's needles."

"*Sì. Sì.* Needles. In the mown-tans." Roberto stares at her mother for a second, silent.

Sophie is remembering when they were in Maine and went to

a farmers' market how there was a farmer selling "nettles." She is willing her mother to just please understand. Nettles, Mama! she thinks. After a long moment, Sophie opens her mouth to speak. "Mom." She nudges her mother.

"Not now, Sophie, I'm trying to understand. I can't handle any more."

"Mom, I think—"

"Sophie. Hang on—"

"Alice, Jesus. He means nettles. I think."

"Oh my gosh, Sophie. You are so right." And her mother brightens that radiant way she always used to, like a flower standing up in the sun, her whole face beaming. And Sophie feels like she has done a good thing, the right thing. "I am so sorry, *Signore*. Nettles, we say in English," explains her mother.

"Neh-tyles," the man tries. His mouth looks like it is sucking on a booger.

"Yes, yes." Her mother smiles again, huge, warm; people everywhere love that smile.

"*Ecco, metti un po' di crema.*" The witch-woman is also smiling now and nodding and handing her mother a white tube of something. Outside the little store Sophie can see that the sun is going down. She has this sinking feeling that they are nowhere near the Mediterranean, that the drive might be long, that her mother has terribly miscalculated.

She hears her mother ask Roberto how much longer it might be to Nice. And she hears him respond, "Ah, long time. Long time." He throws his hands in the air like only God could supply more information about the incredible length of time he is talking about.

Sophie's mother pays for the cream and buys three glass bottles of Orangina. The witch woman presses a sugar-coated cookie shaped like a heart into each girl's hand. Sophie looks at the sky pinkening to gold and blue and wonders what her mother will do. Drive all night on those windy roads? Will they eat dinner?

"Girls, the cream" is all her mother says. She hands Sophie the tube, starts the car, and swipes to the map on her phone.

10.

IRIS

It is dark now. Iris is looking out at the shadows along the side of the road, and it all looks unfamiliar, scary. Her anxiety is back. The car seems to be careening on narrow roads that drop down hairpin turns with mountains on all sides and her mother is gripping the steering wheel and swearing and Iris keeps yelping, "Mama!" and Sophie keeps telling her to shut up.

The moon is coming up white gold to hang in the sky over the dark trees. Iris is hungry and they haven't had dinner. Luckily, there are olives and cheese and more bread, which Sophie doles out each moment they catch their breath. Iris is remembering how, when she was little and scared, her mother would read her this silly book that she now knows by heart: *Hand, Hand, Fingers, Thumb*. "One thumb / One thumb / Drumming on a drum . . ." The rhythm of it always calmed Iris down and, even now, in a time of stress, she finds herself whispering in the back seat, "'Hands play fiddles / Zum zum zum.'"

In a little while, as they come to a flat stretch of road with fields on both sides, her sister spies on the side of the road a blue-and-white-lettered sign that reads *"CHALET MILLE HUIT CENT."* On the picture is a drawing of a wooden-looking building and there is a light on the post above the sign and then a long driveway with lanterns hanging from the trees.

"Mom—that?" Iris hears her sister say. And Iris cranes her neck to see what her sister is saying.

"What, Mama?"

"Hang on, Iris."

"No, tell me! I don't like it when you don't tell me!"

"Let's drive up," her mother says to her sister, a conversation that is private, just the two of them, not including her. The car turns, and her mother's window goes down, and Iris's nose is filled with the green smell of trees mixed with the musky smell of the earth cooling down. This is a smell Iris remembers from Maine. Leaves rustle in a breeze, and the lanterns along the drive make them look golden.

At the end of the long drive, Iris can see a large wooden building made from planks, with porches on every side and so many windows shaped like the kind in gingerbread houses. The car crunches on gravel, and in the beams of the headlights, Iris can see massive red clay plant pots next to the driveway, filled with enormous red tomatoes. There are plants growing up the sides of the building that have dark midnight-purply flowers, and Iris can smell roses and lake water. Above a thick wooden door is a sign that reads "Welcome" in English.

"What is this place, Mama?"

"I don't know, Pickle. I think it's a lodge of some kind. It's called a chalet. So, maybe for skiers. *Chalet Mille Huit Cent*, that must mean Lodge 1800. It's late, and I want to get off that crazy road. I was thinking I would ask if we could put up our tent to sleep here. What do you girls think?"

"I think this looks amazing," says Sophie.

"It's creepy," says Iris.

"Let me go in and check. Girls, do you want to come?"

"I'll stay here," says Sophie, who generally hates to be the first one to approach anything, Iris knows.

"I wanna go," says Iris.

"Okay, Pickle. Come with me. Sophie, are you okay here alone?"

"Yes."

"I'll lock you in."

"Alice. Overkill."

"Anyway, that is what I am doing."

Holding her mother's hand, Iris walks gingerly in her bare feet over the gravel to the smooth plank steps and takes in the cozy-looking couches and tables strewn around the porch. She can hear people laughing and dishes clinking somewhere deep inside and the music of someone playing piano. She can smell onions and beef, maybe a stew, and fresh bread. Together they walk to the door, and her mother reaches up and takes an old, rusty owl-shaped knocker in her hand. She taps once, twice, again. Iris hears a dog bark and then someone is coming, footsteps along a corridor, muffled over rugs, perhaps, and she can hear a man singing to himself. As the door unlatches and opens, Iris hides behind her mother, barely peering out.

11.

ALICE

The man who opens the door with a "Wheeee" has a dish towel in his hands and a yellow-and-red-striped apron tied loosely around a pair of jeans turned up at the ankles. I notice that his feet are bare and long and that he is tall and his hair is blond mixed with a few grays. His smile precedes him, as if he just always opens the door expecting good things. "*Ah, bonsoir,*" he says, alpine-river eyes sparkling, dancing.

"Hello, monsieur," I say. A white and tan dog with fluffy hair and enormous ears darts between the man's legs, almost taking him off his feet, dark eyes and black nose peeking out at me.

"*Ouah,* Salsa*! Va-t-en, la chienne. Allez! Au lit!*" He points behind him, and Salsa slinks back down the hall toward the tinkling dishes and light.

This man's arms are muscular, with flecks of milky-colored blue paint in the hairs, as if he has spent the day painting shutters or doors. His teeth are slightly crooked with a gap between the front two, just a tiny one, that makes his smile more charming. Under his apron, he wears a V-neck white T-shirt and a silver chain. Something, some sort of pendant, is on that chain, and I find my eyes traveling down his neck to where the chain disappears and searching to know what is under there. My stomach does a flop. Forgetting about Iris for a second, I open my mouth to say something more, my eyes traveling back to his square jaw and sideburns, then back to those gleeful blue eyes. His skin is the color of toasted marshmallows, like he's been outside hiking, gardening, swimming nude all summer. Why does my mind go there?

"*Oui?*" His eyes laugh.

"Hello. I mean: *Je m'appelle* Alice. *Je. Cherche. Une chambre.*" What? Am I suddenly living in *The Canterbury Tales*?

A smile breaks out across his tanned face. "I speak English." His accent is like cool water smoothing rocks.

"Oh, phew. I'm exhausted." He radiates back a calm I didn't know I needed. With children, even though you love them to pieces, you can sometimes feel like your shoulders are up in a "me against them" attitude just to survive the next minute, the next hour, the next week. "You don't by any chance have a room tonight? My girls and I are on our way to the sea, in Provence. And it's longer this way than I thought. They need dinner and baths. Honestly, I need a glass of wine!"

Instead of answering, he wipes his hands one more time on his dish towel, sticks out his right one to shake, and says, "Didier. *Enchanté*, Alice." Ah-leese.

"*Enchanté. Oui.*" Our eyes are locked and my whole body is tingling. But Iris, Iris is right here. I feel about fourteen all of a sudden. A crush, a ridiculous crush. Immediate and absurd. "You have one boob, Alice": I can hear Sophie in my head. I push it away and forge ahead.

"This is my younger daughter, Iris. My older girl, Sophie—

she's in the car." I'm stuttering. My breath sticks in my throat. My heart is beating like mad. Like mad. That line. Where did it come from? Oh, yes, *Ulysses*. I only read the sexy parts, skipped the rest. "We were supposed to be camping," I say.

"Camping? Wow." His eyes are still locked in. I am starting to experience my own personal heat wave. He continues, "I have a room—luckily, someone got sick and couldn't come—*c'est dommage* for them. So, I have a nice room, chalet-style, with three beds, actually. Two little beds for the little girls. And one big bed for you—they have a little door in between, and a bathroom and a desk to write or draw—people like to come here and look out at the mountains. Create masterpieces!"

"Masterpieces! Well, I won't do that. Just one night. Not enough time! Then we will take off. We are on our way to Provence."

"Oh, Ah-leese, you never know. We had a famous American novelist here three weeks ago. And Spike Lee, he came 'ere once. Depardieu comes often. Years ago, Fellini would come—before my time—and eat and write. When Agnès Troublé needs to get away, she comes here to sketch her fashions, you know, for agnès b. This is now a long story . . ." He booms a laugh. "But. You know, during the war, my grandparents invited their friend Henri Matisse 'ere. Sometimes he brought Jewish artists. Chagall was one. Get this: Matisse put him in the root cellar whenever Nazis came to inspect the place!" He gestures behind him toward the sounds of dishes and the amazing smell of stew and bread and maybe some kind of fruit pie, toward the lights at the end of the hall. "They never *ack-two-alley* found 'im, but they did take all the wine!"

I clear my throat. The dog, Salsa, has reappeared, peering around her owner. My God, she's as big as a pony, I think.

"Okay." He smiles and rubs his hands together. Then, "Shall I show you to your room? You must be very 'ungry."

"Let me get my daughter. My other daughter."

"*Bien sûr*. And let me get you a glass of wine. Salsa, *tu viens?*"

"Okay, I'll be right back." I smile again and am embarrassed and surprised that I still feel warm in my stomach and into my shorts. "Iris, let's go get Sophie. I am so hungry, aren't you?" Alice, get ahold of yourself.

"Yes, Mama. Did you know who those people were he was talking about? And what was the war? Is that now?"

"No, no. A long time ago. We'll learn about Matisse when we get to the south, where he lived."

Salsa decides to follow us out, nudging her wet black nose into my hand and hovering close. When we come back, each carrying a bag, we enter the hall through the door Didier has left open, Salsa leading the way. We soon enter a brightly lighted dining room, where long wooden tables are graced with glinting china and silver. Over the mantel is an enormous Matisse collage of palm fronds with a naked woman and a pitcher and stars. "Ah, girls, waiting for that lesson on Matisse isn't going to be necessary—there's a piece of his right there."

The girls stand blinking in the light, as if they have just walked through Narnia's wardrobe into another land entirely, taking in the elegant people speaking quietly at tables and drinking wine, the man in the corner wearing a sky-blue suit with a lavender tie and playing the piano, the candles and silver.

12.
SOPHIE

Sophie is watching her mother from the car. The way Iris has her hands knitted into the back pockets of her mother's jeans, the way the door opens. The dashing handsomeness of the blond man. Even Sophie can see that. He looks like a movie star, Brad Pitt before the airplane episode, before the divorce. And, on top of all that, French. And then Sophie feels it in her stomach, the physical switch that is turned on in her mother. She can't name what it is, though. She feels it like it is happening to her. The line between them so porous, one feels what the other feels. It has always been this way.

It occurs to Sophie that this fact of blurred lines might be why parents like to say, "Kids are resilient." Sophie heard other mothers whisper that to her mother when they came back to New York, when her mother was getting treatments, when everything seemed pretty bleak. And Sophie wanted to yell, "Do we have a choice? Anything, be it plant or animal, that wants to survive is, in fact, *resilient*. What are the other options?" More ideas come to her, examples for her thesis: a squirrel with one leg hobbling its way from peanut to peanut in the park; the child of a drug-addicted mother. Kids who have to tell their parents they were born with the wrong gender parts, then suffer the outside world's judgment. People who survive car crashes, deformities, terrifying illnesses. "This resilience business doesn't mean we don't carry it in our bodies forever, whatever happened and didn't happen," she wants to say. Maybe parents just need kids to be resilient, to endure, she thinks, because they are so connected, it's a matter of their own survival, too.

Sophie is unable to keep thinking this thought through because her mother is getting her out of the car, and there is this big fluffy white dog with the strange name of Salsa, and they are walking into that amazing-smelling hallway that opens into a room unlike anything Sophie has ever seen in her life: the fire, the handful of well-dressed guests—jeans and nice linen shirts, sandals. The French—Sophie has noticed this—will wear the exact same materials—jeans, linen, leather—and make it look amazing, elegant and perfect, while the Americans' jeans are somehow always just slightly wrong for the figure, the linen shirt a bit too boxy, the sandals not quite strappy enough. How does this happen?

There are candles in lines all the way down the long tables—Sophie counts three rectangular tables in total—and paintings cover the walls. Over the fireplace hangs that massive Matisse. Near it hangs a smaller painting of women who are brightly colored and lounging by a river, naked. The women are made with little flicks of a brush in every color you could possibly imagine. Sophie notices that that painting is unfinished; one corner of the canvas devolves into nothingness, where the artist has taken some black paint and scribbled a futile little "harrumph."

The man who answered the door, Didier, is telling her mom that "it was a study" for the "*famoose* painting," and then he says some words including "calm," and her mother is oohing and ahhing in a way that drives Sophie absolutely batshit.

Didier leads them to yet another painting of a young girl, maybe Sophie's age, sitting in a blue chair, wearing a gray dress, and she has a black collar or ribbon around her neck. He says, "This is Marguerite. Matisse's daughter. She was about this one's age." Didier turns to Sophie, and Sophie feels her cheeks get hot. Like the other painting, this one also feels unfinished, like the artist was hurrying or maybe lost interest. Sophie is looking at the strange collar on the girl and she's thinking about her art class last year when they got to experiment with oil paints on small canvases that the art teacher, Mrs. Robinson, showed them how to stretch and gesso themselves. Each student had to bring in their own objects for a still life. Sophie painted an orange next to a deep blue vase of her mother's that had purple hydrangeas in it, which Sophie immediately regretted having chosen, as there were so many separate flowers. In the end, she'd made the flowers blurry but gotten the color just about right. She had decided to focus her attention on the orange and the shadow the vase threw, both of which Mrs. Robinson had praised. Sophie loved the smell of the oil paints and the fact that they had to use turpentine to clean their brushes.

Next to her, Iris is stroking Salsa's fur with such intensity! Sophie feels so strange here, her mother enraptured by this French guy, and Iris obsessed with the dog. This leaves Sophie where, exactly? Their threesome is being splintered, she thinks. So soon—this trip has only just begun.

Her mother calls to her, "Sophs, let's go see the room. Can you grab the bags?" And her mother is following Didier—empty-handed, typical—and Iris is also empty-handed, and they are going out a glass door into a little courtyard. Sophie sighs, grabs two of the bags, and follows her family.

13.
ALICE

I remember some things. Like when I realized I thought my friend Maeve was crazy. I know you aren't supposed to use that word anymore (are you?).

It was when everyone was getting vaccinated for Covid. We were back in New York, and I was halfway through the first chemo regime and was puking my guts out as they tried various fixes and medications to make my stomach comply. That day I had rallied on my way home from a treatment and gone to the grocery store to pick up ingredients for this recipe I'd seen in the waiting room on my *New York Times* cooking app earlier that morning. I always tried to do my treatments in the morning because it seemed better to get them over with. Otherwise I would wait all day, and the waiting to know how terrible I would feel was disastrous for my mind. Anyway, it was this tater-tot casserole. At that time, I was thinking that it would be fun for the girls. I hadn't made them anything in so long. This must have been April, May. I remember it was warm outside, and there were flowers coming up in those little gated places around trees where dogs shit.

I, myself, couldn't bear to eat anything that was greasy or buttery—that feeling on my lips made me want to heave.

This recipe, though, had tater tots on top of ground beef and this kind of milky mixture with carrots and celery and onion, and then on top of all that there was grated cheese—I guess it's kind of like shepherd's pie. I have no idea why I wanted to make this in particular. I mean, given the grease, I was unlikely to eat it. And just thinking about it now, I realize it sounds terrible. But there I was at Whole Foods on my way home, pushing a cart slowly down the aisle and getting everything for this casserole. I missed my girls. That's the thing. Illness takes you out; it takes you away; it throws you into this lonely orbit, and that makes your kids lonely, too, because they feel so much, they are so mixed up in it all, being so resilient.

So, Maeve, she'd decided that everything to do with the medical world was wrong and dangerous. In her defense, she had a baby who was stillborn two weeks before the due date. That kind of thing can change a person. She told me to eat macrobiotic and drink chaga tea, or some such thing. Chemo was poison. I didn't listen, my God, how could I? I was being told I had one way out of hell, and it was called chemo. So I took it. No looking back.

Everyone around me was getting vaccinated, but I couldn't yet, seeing as I was in treatment and wasn't strong enough. So I needed everyone around me to get their shots. But there were all these moms at the girls' school and on Facebook and everywhere talking about how *no one's really studied these things*, and I'm thinking: I get that, I do. But look: *We have a getaway car right here. Are you actually complaining about its wheels?*

So, Maeve told me she wouldn't get vaccinated, and it had created this huge fight with her husband, who did get poked. She wanted me to take her side, understand. But I didn't understand. And that was disturbing to her. She wouldn't listen to her husband, and she told her elderly mother and her teenage son that it was a bad idea, dangerous, to get these vaccines. She created this fault line in their family where her husband couldn't reason with her.

(I did notice how, suddenly, everywhere, everyone was talking about their immune systems, like we were all natural-born immunologists. Did you notice that? I did. Even the dads at pickup were clearing their throats, no masks, and talking about their immune responses and how they were building up their immunity with zinc and vitamin C.) Anyway, Maeve said she actually wanted to get Covid. She said "to build up" her immunity, get stronger.

"But what if you don't? Get stronger?" I asked.

"Oh, Alice, stop it. I'll be fine. It's like a bad cold."

"That seems crazy," I said. (Right, I know. That word.) "And even if you aren't worried about you, there are people like me. Who need you to do it. You know?"

"Alice, you'll be fine." She sounded tired. And irritable.

"I might not be fine, Maeve."

"I can't discuss this with you, Alice. You're not reasonable lately." Did she actually yawn after she said that?

And then we said some things about the kids and hung up. And that was that. Later she sent me some texts with data from God knows where—maybe the bad Kennedy—about the vaccine. And I just hit delete, delete, delete. No time, though all I had was time. Maeve had been my best friend in New York, I'd thought.

I remember another thing often. It's the man who gave me the anesthesia when I lost my breast. He had an Egyptian name, I do remember that. I said, "Beautiful name," and he told me he was from Cairo and had gone to medical school at Columbia. His family was still in Cairo, he said. He had these amazing green eyes, I think about them. He looked right into my eyes as they were prepping me to remove my breast. God, I felt so small in that bed, waiting while they did their jobs around me, for me. He stayed right there, titrating to the right dose whatever they were giving me. And there was this funny moment when I said to him, "Hey, I can feel it, the tug." They hadn't started anything yet, God help us. They put you under to saw off a breast, thank goodness. But they must have been adjusting something around my breast, or putting some painkiller into the nerves, I don't know. I never found out. But I saw the doctor—she was this spitfire of a surgeon to the New York stars—and she just put her thumb up and gave him the signal to pump it up. And he did and I was out. But I went out gazing into those green eyes with long lashes, the kind of looks my grandmother would have said were "wasted on a boy." Once, later, I passed him walking down a hall. He was with a tall woman, also in scrubs. They were talking. I was too shy to say anything. He wouldn't remember me, why would he?

Another inchoate thought about that whole time, smashed into my head all higgledy-piggledy like bubble and squeak, a headline in the paper: "America's Mothers Are in Crisis. Is Anyone Listening to Them?" I already had cancer by then, we were on our way back to New York, it had been decided. The appointments were made. And I remember thinking, Ah, yes, we sure are in a crisis. It's the mental load and the feeling like we can't breathe all the time, the feeling that we're stuck with the kids at home during Covid with the failure of online school and the exhaustion of the whole thing. It's the years and years piled up on our shoulders of being COO of the dinner plan, the lunch plan, the breakfast plan, the birthday plan, the piano lesson schedule, the ferrying to the dance studio, the soccer moms' bake sale plan, the teeth cleaning schedule, the teacher appreciation gifts, the basketball coaches' gifts, the Meal Train for the family who lost their house in a fire, Spindrifts and chips for the school dance, the interfacing with other moms (my *God*, the other moms are *the worst*), the gerbil's annual checkup plan, the aging parents' plans, and then our jobs. *Of course we're losing our fucking minds.*

And then I left the mental load and went into this very odd time warp where I had cancer. I read poetry by Jane Kenyon and cried and did absolutely fucking nothing. I was indoors, caged. I was watching plastic bags and leaves drift through the sky and into the Hudson River. This was a benefit and a curse from my privilege, privilege I married into and did not earn. I could have been spending most of my days calling my insurance company and writing applications to the United Way to help pay for my mortgage and electricity bills given the incredible, punishing, unethical cost of cancer. I was lucky. I am lucky.

In my case, I just had the mental load of worrying about the mental load, which is its own mental load. Like, worrying that Pete was feeding the girls nothing but takeout. Worries about Pete being in charge at the grocery store. I have no idea why I hated that, since I hated grocery shopping. But then, God, I wanted the grocery store to be mine again. "It's not forever," Pete would say. And "You're in recovery." Over and over I was "in recovery" from chemo, surgery, radiation, then chemo 2.0. (I'm not actually sure when recovery truly begins and cancer ends, that part is still lost to me.)

In that blurry and ineffective period in my life when I couldn't find my purpose, sometimes I threw things. Like books or my bottle of Tamoxifen. Never at someone. Usually when I was alone. Being taken out of the action, or having no purposeful action, I thought, may be as bad—or worse—than the mental load. All I had to do was survive. Such a mundane task, it turns out.

14.

ALICE

The suite Didier shows us into is fashioned all in weathered wood, with an enormous plush bed, a woven white cotton coverlet, and a gray woolen blanket folded at the end. The pillows are square and miles thick, and there is an enormous fireplace, cold now, it being summer. Another room with two white-covered beds, also with thick pillows and gray blankets smoothed at the end. On the walls is more art—smaller paintings that will need later inspection—and black-and-white photographs. The windows are cut out in diamond shapes, with louvered cranks that open, without screens, to rose-scented night air. A glass bowl of fresh rose petals in clean water sits on each bedside table, and there are tall iron candlesticks with years and years of drips down the sides and fresh white candles ready to light. Each bed has a tarnished silver water pitcher and a glass next to it. A chair next to the fire is covered with the furry pelt of some poor animal long gone, and there are fire tongs and leather gloves sitting atop a basket of wood. A bottle of red wine and a corkscrew are waiting on a table to the side of the fireplace, and next to them is a small glass orb under which sit two cheeses with gray-ish rinds. A blue bowl of orange apricots sits next to the cheese. An old-fashioned radio glows yellow at the dial, a Chopin nocturne playing ever so softly.

With a small bow, Didier says, "I will leave you. Dinner in thirty minutes, *mesdames*?"

"That sounds amazing," I say.

Sophie says, "There's one more bag, Mama."

And Didier says, "Not to worry—I'll send a boy."

"He's so nice," I say to the girls, smiling. I catch Sophie's eye.

"I don't like him," she says.

"Stop that, Sophie," I scold, harsher than I mean to. She looks at me, wounded. "I'm sorry. You're allowed not to like someone. Thank you, by the way, for your help with the nettles. And the car. And navigating." My daughter looks away. I can see her skin looks greasy; there are blackheads on her nose and on her brow. Her chin is misshapen with the promise of a cystic pimple. This is one of those small moments I'll regret later: Softness and empathy were necessary, but instead, I've done the opposite. And I am not sure I can undo it.

She turns to me, a slight smile, and at first my heart almost breaks with the thought that she will have mercy. But no. "Yeah, you know, you did that thing you always do with the nettles, where you tell me to shut up—you do it to Iris, too—and you're not listening. I hate you when you do that."

I want to react. I want to tell her how irritating she is sometimes, how irritating Iris is, how neither one of them can ever let me finish a conversation, a thought, a sandwich, a pee without forcing their way into my tiny little moment and that I've just had it lately. But I smile and say, "You are right. I can do better."

Immediately, her shoulders go down. I am hauling her back

to me, thank heavens. "Okay," she says. Vulnerable. My girl. Then a boy does arrive, maybe around Sophie's age, tall, with dark hair and dark eyes; he drops the bag in the room with an efficient nod and leaves.

When it's just the three of us again, there is silence, finally, and we all take it in. I see Iris eyeing the dead animal pelt on the chair and Sophie looking out the windows into the garden and at lanterns hanging from trees and little twinkle lights along a wrought iron fence, illuminating white chairs and lush, droopy roses, making it look like a place in a fairy tale.

Sophie turns to me, her face full of innocent awe. "What is this place, Mama?"

"It's like we turned off the road into some other world, some fairyland, isn't it," I say.

"Who would Didier be?" Iris asks. "A fawn? Mr. Tumnus? Or the wolf, grrrrr . . ." Iris is playing along.

I run to her and scoop her up and we fall onto the big bed with her laughing as I tickle her. "Now we just need to find the wicked witch," I say, nuzzling into Iris's neck. Sophie had looked amused until I said that. Now, suddenly, she scowls again and mumbles as she goes into the bathroom, "Yeah, Alice, I think that might be you. And, Iris, you're as annoying as Edmund."

"Touché!" I call after her. "Do they use that word in French, you think? Like we do?" Iris takes this opportunity to jump on me and start growling and tickling, saying, "Where is the Turkish delight? Where is the Turkish delight?"

"Sophie," I call, "Sophie! Come save me!"

She doesn't respond. I've lost her again.

When she finally comes out of the bathroom, she has slicked her hair back into a neat ponytail and added some mascara and blue eye shadow to her eyes. She's tucked in her T-shirt, like French girls do, and her cutoff jean shorts are pulled up a bit higher. Something about these slight changes time-travel her from fourteen to more like seventeen, and it takes my breath away, scares me. She looks lean and tall; her legs look ten miles long. "I'm hungry, can we go eat?" she says. She looks away from my face, down at the floor.

"Surely. Give me a second." Iris and I take turns using the bathroom, and I pull on jeans and a loose cotton blouse I got years ago on a trip to Mexico, the kind with embroidered flowers across the top, a box-cut with a wide neck; it shows a tiny bit of my bra strap. I reach into my shirt and try to adjust my prosthetic breast, moving it around to look a bit more natural (it doesn't). I add some lip gloss and redo my mascara. I don't want to look like I have tried hard, just natural enough that I can look effortlessly attractive. Am I actually thinking this way? Yes, I confess, I am.

Suddenly, in rebuke, my grandmother's voice comes into my head: "God in heaven, she looked like lipstick on a corpse." I catch my eye in the mirror. And then look away, shake my head, trying to get the word "corpse" out of my mind.

• • •

The dining room is almost empty of people, save for two couples. One couple, at the corner of a long wooden reddish-hued table, is youngish, thirties. The man has dark curly hair and a navy collared shirt. The woman wears a white dress and sandals, her hair cascading down her shiny shoulders. I feel suddenly ridiculous in my Mexican peasant shirt, my jeans; my poochy mom stomach that, no matter how much weight I've lost thanks to my cancer diet, never really went away; the breast that isn't a breast. At the other table is an older couple, white-haireds. The woman has a Queen Elizabeth stature—a middle area that is thick, legs that get wider where they should get thinner, as if some body parts have slipped down. She is wearing a light blue dress and he a white shirt, all very pristine. When we pass them, I can hear her saying to him, "Daah-ling, I called Callie and told her we'd meet her at the Picasso Museum in Paris in three days."

"Yes, yes," he puffs, eyes protruding from under bushy white eyebrows.

"Mommy." Iris pulls my hand and gestures for me to come down to her level. She whispers into my ear, her breath hot and sticky: "Oh, I wish no one ever got old. I wish they would get to twenty and just stay like that. Don't you, Mama?" She looks intensely into my eyes, and I know what she is thinking: Don't get any closer to dying on me. I hug her closer and I can hear her stomach growling.

Didier comes over to us, his apron dusty. He is wiping his hands on a clean white kitchen towel and brandishing a bottle of red wine by its thin neck. "Welcome, welcome, *les filles*," he says, and beckons us to the third long table, where three places have been set near a painted door that stands open and looks out into the fairy forest. On the table is a glass bottle filled, a little white label tells me, with cold mountain water, ready for us to pour. Didier opens the bottle of wine and pours me a glass, taking the bottle to his aquiline nose for a sniff. The wine, he explains, came from just on the other side of "dose mow-n-tains," gesturing out into the darkness. "My friend Alexandre, he, eh, he grows this variety of grape that likes the mountain air and cold spring waters. He only makes a small amount each year, makes his own labels."

I take the glass to my nose and sniff. "I know nothing about wine," I confess.

"What do you smell?" he asks. "Try again—we can all become wine experts."

"I smell, I don't know, something like fall leaves. And brown sugar. Maybe peaches? Vanilla?"

"*Exactement!*" Didier exclaims excitedly, his eyes shining. "Take a taste."

I do, and the wine is indeed rich and luxurious, smoky like a campfire. "It's amazing," I say. I can't think of anything else to say, even though "amazing" seems like the kind of description Sophie would call "basic." I look up to his face, and my eyes stay with his for a second too long. I duck my head back to the girls in embarrassment. I see Sophie taking me in. "What?" I mouth. She rolls her eyes. Didier has vanished, and when he comes back, he is carrying three little glasses of something liquid in his hands; two of them are held in the large palm of his right hand and the other in his left.

"*Des petits amuse-bouches,*" he says. "To tickle the taste buds!" This makes Iris laugh. He puts each glass in front of us, and we all pick them up while he waits expectantly. "You sip it!" He beams. It's like essence of gazpacho. I can't even really explain it except to say that it's like tasting only the essential flavors of the freshest, most perfectly salted vegetables; I could drink just that for dinner and be very happy.

"Is good, *non*?"

Then comes a warm, crusty bread, just fished from an oven, and a small dish of whipped butter with herbs. "Our farm, for the *chalet*, is just down dat rise," Didier says. He says "chalet" as if it were a Frisbee he's tossing off a mountain, that "lay" sound at the end disappearing with a puff into the clouds. "And our milk and cream come from our cow, Bernadette." He turns to Iris. "Tomorrow, maybe, you can meet Bernadette. She loves *les petites filles.*" Didier reaches over my shoulder and pours me more wine from the bottle, and as his hand retracts, I feel his wrist touch my shoulder, and my body burns all over.

Next is a *viande*—steak—perfectly charred, served as one large piece, which he cuts for us at the table and serves on small plates along with a crisp onion salad flecked with teeny-tiny shavings of lemon rind and herbs. I try not to let my mind wander to the idea that it might have been Bernadette's brother or father we are eating. Whoever the cow is, they are delicious, with a creamy green peppercorn sauce and the tangy onions.

After that, we are served an endive and Roquefort salad. Next, we have slices of bright orange persimmon. And then cheeses, which come with another warm bread and are laid out on a board. There is a small goat cheese, a Crottin, Didier tour-guides, and a local Tomme, and then something soft, nutty, unctuous, the name of which I never caught. All modest amounts, but nonetheless, Sophie groans when she sees the cheeses and says, "I'm not sure I can eat any more." And Iris says, "Eeeww, they smell."

Didier fills my glass again as I slather the cheese on the bread and eat as much as I politely can.

Just as we are hoping for bed, we hear Didier coming to the table once again. "*Hop! Et voilà, un pot de crème.*" Each of us is handed an old-fashioned teacup covered with flowers outlined in gold filigree—my flowers are pink, Sophie's are green, and Iris's are yellow—and inside each one is a thick chocolate pudding. He hands me a tiny, tinkly glass and pours something grassy green into it and says, "Chartreuse. From the monks—just above, there," and points somewhere I take to be north, over his shoulder. “One hundred and thirty herbs in this stuff,” he tells us. “In France we believe that Chartreuse will cure any ailment!”

“One hundred and thirty,” I echo.

After he has poured the Chartreuse, I feel his arm touch my shoulder again. Despite being almost inert from the jet lag, the food and wine, the driving, I feel that old electricity, that pulse, travel through my body to thrill and terrify me. How long have I been dead to that?

I hear my phone buzz. A text from Pete:

> Hey. Looking at Life360. You guys don’t seem to have made it to Nice. Everyone ok?

15.
ALICE

When I was recovering from the surgery, the poisons, the entire ordeal, Pete took me to a town in Massachusetts, not far from the city, where there's a famous art museum and a hotel with a year-round outdoor pool and a sauna. It's the kind of town where capsule-wardrobe-wearing Gen Xers and Millennials go with their families for a weekend of culture. The town itself is a little gray and run-down. Well used, I'd say. My friend Solange stayed with the girls; Pete called her and asked.

This was the kind of hotel where you went when you were trying to spend time together, be intimate. I remember thinking it was not the kind of place you went when you were (maybe) still dying. Or when you felt like you were dying. Or just looked like you were dying. I remember seeing my hip bones when I looked down at myself in the bathing suit I had brought along, a navy blue Speedo Pete had bought me online, exactly the same as the one I always got, only two sizes smaller than the year before.

The sauna was warm. The pool was cool. We went out to dinner. We looked at bad modern art, save some incredible concrete tubes outside, made by Taryn Simon, that looked like enormous pinhole cameras or, I thought, crematoriums. The rain that day came through the tops of the tubes, and we couldn't sit down on the little benches inside. But we waded in through the puddles and could hear our voices echo; "Hey-oh, hey-oh," we called over and over. We looked up at the sky through the open tops and the rain splattered our faces and we were grateful we had seen those concrete objects, they saved the day. They also made me think of silos. And how alone I felt. How alone I had been. Still was. How alone I would always be with my fear.

Memories kept surfacing that weekend, unwanted and unbidden. One: In that weird in-between pause after Christmas and before January, when most people feel the darkness rush into the house in the late afternoon like a monster who intends to crush them, I was vacuuming the downstairs bathroom in our house in Maine. I had the lump but no diagnosis. Pete was back. Nothing was real yet.

And there was a cellar spider, dangling—long-limbed, wispy, more delicate than a daddy longlegs, its body a mere fluff of dust—from a wooden drying rack. At first I poked it, thinking it was dead. It jumped down and I tried to grab it so it wouldn't get swallowed by the vacuum. Spiders kill mosquitoes and no-see-ums and houseflies; we need them. But it was terrified, circling, panicked, trying to get away. Finally, I got it by one tiny leg and moved it to a counter, but it fell down into the clothes hamper and then to the floor.

"Stop it," I shouted, louder than I meant to. But the creature was hell-bent on getting away from me, its body full of fear. And as though I were watching from above, I realized I hadn't turned off the vacuum, and the spider, now on the floor as I scrambled after it, was sucked up. After all that! After the effort it was making, *I* was making. I turned off the vacuum and tried to open the bag and find it. Nothing. It was gone. Vaporized. For days after that, I replayed how lumbering and slow I had been, how stupid leaving the vacuum on. How, compared to the panicked spider, I was practically stuck in aspic, in a dream. How, if I'd just left well enough alone, it would have stayed on the drying rack. How much it wanted to survive, to live, to stay here on this mortal coil; and don't we all?

Anyway, on this weekend with Pete, we went to another museum and saw Rembrandts there and silver polished to the hilt, and we splurged for the first time from my restrictive diet and ordered huge, juicy hamburgers at a place in town. I could barely eat mine; it was too much, too overwhelming, still too soon to let it all hang loose. Pete ate my burger when I gave it to him, even though he was full. That was a kindness he did for me. When we got back to the hotel, I lay down while he was in the bathroom showering. I was still in my coat, as I was always, *always* freezing at that point in my recovery, and I fell asleep. The next time I woke up, it was dark and Pete was under the covers next to me and I still had the lined raincoat on. Pete had carefully taken my shoes off and put them neatly by the door.

On Sunday morning, when Pete went down to get me green tea and himself coffee, I somehow felt invigorated enough to grab a notebook from my bag. I had awoken thinking about an old John Cheever story I loved, "The Swimmer." So, I started a play about a couple going to that hotel after the woman had chemotherapy. (Ha, right, I wonder where I got that idea.) As with everything, I thought that maybe there was a germ there, in my real life. In the play, the woman got up in the middle of the night and swam alone in the pool in the dark. And while she was swimming, animals—a fox, a raccoon, a rabbit, a deer, a frog, a salamander—came to the edge of the pool, and she talked to them. I imagined these animals as larger than real animals. In my mind, I could see humans dressed in elaborate animal costumes, with Julie Taymor–type masks. In the nightly conversations the woman was having, she and the animals were discussing the world—wars, climate change, the dangers of highway crossing, human detritus. In the morning, she told her husband about her swim, about the animals, about the conversations. He thought she was losing her mind, maybe she had cancer in her brain. He scoffed and looked panicked as she spoke. Anyway, they stayed in that hotel for seven nights. And even though, each night, her husband begged her to wake him and take her with him to swim, as he wanted to verify it all, wanted to show her she was dreaming, he fell asleep every night after they made love. And she went down alone: This was hers and hers only. That was as far as I got. A sketch of the idea, really, no more.

When Pete came back up, I stopped writing and we were quiet and then we went down to breakfast. There was granola which we ate with almond milk. And then we went back to the city.

I didn't know what Pete wanted from that weekend, but here's what I got: In the hollowed-out quiet left by the grenade of cancer, I found words in a notebook. I was a writer again. Cancer was this horrible aloneness and loneliness, which are two different things, I know now. I was constantly realizing, the entire time I was sick, that this was happening only to me. That weekend, when I started writing again, I found comfort. That was a gift. A gift Pete gave me, actually. He just let it be.

In a month, I had started my newsletter; soon I'd even finished that play and called it *Woman Swimming*. Before we came here, to France, I got word that a small theater, over in the Meat-packing District, would do a short run in a year. I found a new agent. It's this thing back home, waiting for me; something I have just begun that does gleam a bit.

• • •

After that weekend, I was thinking about Pete and the ache of whatever it was that hovered between us. I was thinking about how quiet we were that entire weekend. How he let me sleep. How I'd been sleeping for months by then. How everything felt like one long wait for me to get back to myself, though I think we both knew I'd never be the same. One morning, when he was dressing for work, I sat up and asked, "Pete. What was it you wanted when we went to Massachusetts. When we drove up there."

"Nothing, really." He sat down. His shirt was crisp, and he smelled of sandalwood and juniper.

"Nothing?"

"I mean, not nothing. I just wanted to get us outside of this." He waved his arms wide and looked around at our room. "And this." He gestured now at the space on the bed between us.

"Ah," I said. "Well, thank you. I started writing something there. Maybe a play. In my notebook."

"Is it good?"

"How could I ever know," I said, looking away.

"I bet it will be good. Keep going."

I looked back at him and thought I saw, I might have been wrong, his eyes fill with tears. "What is it you want now?" I whispered.

"I don't know." His voice was ragged. "Things to rewind. Another chance. You to be okay."

"All things that may not be possible." I felt my chin set, defensive, almost. I could tell he hoped for something else from me.

He kissed me on the shoulder and left, taking the girls with him after the noise of breakfast and lunches and shoes and bags and door slamming, the unbearable noise of family life.

No. The affirming and delicious sounds of life.

Later that day, I got a text from my friend Skylar, who lives in one of those ridiculous Connecticut communities with houses like castles where the women have all had cosmetic surgeries, plural.

How are you doing?

The same.

Meaning?

Waiting for the days to pass. For this to be over.

Meaning?

Jesus? To die or live.

I thought they are pretty sure you are going to live? Didn't they say?

Yes. But. I can't explain. Sometimes I hate my husband.

We all hate our husbands.

You, too?

Is there anything likable about the white male? Our children excepted. 40 + up.

I am angry a lot.

Mansplaining, manspreading, clutching power. Gross.

Is Gary working a ton?

Working, gone. Who knows what he does. I don't even care anymore.

I wish I could not care.

I'm dead inside. You don't want this.

I'm trying hard not to die on the outside.

Switch it up. Die only on the inside.

I can't seem to turn off my feelings. They are huge, more huge now than ever. I am stuck. In my head, in my tiredness. In my love and then anger . . .

. . .

Oh shit gotta go—work.

Yes.

Yes.

Bye.

Ciao.

And then I was alone again in the house, breathing, exhaling, trying to get up the gumption to put words on a page, another solitary action that screams with each letter: I. Was. Here.

16.

ALICE

Didier has caught the eye of another patron and gone off with the bottle of Chartreuse dangling by his side, like a swan, or a goose, or an albatross. I watch him and then feel the phone vibrate again, insistent that I click and answer. I see it is Pete.

I feel myself blush all of a sudden. I have been caught. This flash: A friend of a friend who worked at a bookstore and "had a torrid affair" with the bookstore owner. Whispered by another friend. "Torrid." That word.

I quickly text Pete: We are ok. We had to get off the road, dark, winding roads, taking a long time. We have found a charming chalet to stop at. Girls and I are ok. OK?

In the background, I can hear a Sam Cooke song start singing: "Another Saturday night and I ain't got nobody . . ." Over in the corner, the older English couple stands up from their table and the man puts his arm around his wife's waist and they sway to the music next to the fireplace. Sophie says, "Oh. My. God." Iris starts giggling, covering her mouth with her hand. "Girls," I say, giving them what I can manage of a raised eyebrow. "They are so sweet." Even so, none of us can tear our eyes away as the music slides around. When the song ends, the couple sits down, flushed and smiling; the old man is raising his hand to pour them each another glass of champagne. The music changes now to a Billie Holiday song, "What a Little Moonlight Can Do": "Wait a while / Till a little moonbeam comes peepin' through . . ."

Suddenly, Didier is by my side again, leaning on the top of my chair, his apron slung lower on his hips, as if clothes just keep falling off this man as the night wears on. "*Voilà, les filles,*" I hear him say. "Madame, your girls look ready for bed, *non*?" I follow his gaze away from the older couple, now holding hands, to take in Sophie stifling a yawn and Iris resting her head on her hand, her eyes at half-mast.

"Oh dear, yes."

As I put my hands on their backs and turn to say thank you to Didier, he is talking to a woman who has just come in wearing a pale yellow dress that flows like a daffodil around her ankles, her long dark hair rippling down her tanned back. He barely notices me leave, just gives me a short nod and a wave good night.

17.

SOPHIE

After that dinner with the guy oozing—yuck—all over her mother, the old-people music, the dancing old people, Sophie is finally back in the clean room with the warm lights. She looks longingly at the bed, wanting to curl up, hoping that Iris will please just be quiet so she can read her book and forget as much as she possibly can. The gray boards of the walls are shiny in places where hands have touched them for years—maybe hundreds?—next to the beds and beside the fireplace.

"Girls." Her mother is trying to sound cheery, birdlike. "Let's get ready for bed."

Iris asks, "Can we talk to Daddy?"

"Once you are showered, teeth brushed, and in your PJs, lovey. Scoot—let's get you ready. Into the bathroom."

Sophie can hear that Iris is sitting on the toilet, rustling around, likely shredding the toilet paper as she poops. In the room with her mother, Sophie feels self-conscious, awkward all of a sudden. She watches her mother open the wine and smell it, then pour a little into a glass. There is a paper on the table that has the times for meals, cocktails, hikes, swims. Sophie picks it up, reading: "*The chalet has a pool set deep into the mountains where you can swim en plein air. Furthermore, we are surrounded by rushing streams, farms, hikes, and skiing not far away, and best of all, we are a world gastronomic destination.*" Sophie dwells for a moment on that strange and repugnant word, "gastronomic." And then reads on: "*Breakfast 7h to 10h. Lunch buffet 12h to 15h. Apéro 17h to 18h. Dinner 20h to 22h. Local and house-made digestifs served with desserts from 10:30 to midnight.*"

"Look," she says to her mother. "There's a pool."

Her mother takes the paper and reads it. "My God," she murmurs, "does he do all this?" There is an affectionate, even awed, lilt to her voice that turns Sophie's stomach.

"What are those weird 'h's and why are the times written like that?"

"Oh, yes." Her mother sounds distracted, still in the chalet pool swimming through her own thoughts.

"And?"

"Those are the hours—like around the clock with twenty-four being midnight. So, twenty-two, that's ten p.m. And the 'h' means '*heures*,' which means hours. They say it that way here." She still sounds dreamy.

"Whatever. Mom, can you tell Iris to hurry up? I want to get into bed."

Slowly her mother is coming back to earth. "Can't you get into your nightgown over there, in that little nook with the curtain?"

"No. I need a shower."

"Right. Of course. We all do." Her mother is now inspecting a magazine she's found on a bookshelf by the window.

My God, thinks Sophie. She doesn't even realize. Out loud, she throws a line to her mother, giving her a tiny bit more information. "I think I am getting my period."

"Oh. Okay. That makes sense."

"What do you mean by that?" Sophie feels defensive, exposed.

Her mother sighs. "She sighs a lot," Sophie had said to Iris earlier that day when they were alone in the car and their mother was talking to Charlotte. "It's annoying. And she breathes a lot. And chews loudly. And her hair is all wispy, and there's that one breast, so embarrassing." Iris had said, "But Mommy was sick. And she has that pros-tat-ick. And she's beautiful now."

"Alice, please tell Iris to hurry up. I need to get in there," Sophie says now with authority.

Without answering, her mother gets up and knocks on the door. "Iris, honey. Your sister wants to get in there. Can you finish up?"

Lots of watery sounds, water buffalo–type snorting.

Sophie tries again, conspiring: "I'm sure there's water sprayed everywhere on the floor and counters." Her mother gives Sophie a distant smile. Again, it seems to Sophie that her mother is in a room of her own, somewhere inside her heart or head.

Then Iris bursts out, the towel barely covering her, legs moving, whooping and jumping on the beds, making wet imprints. Sophie is sure her bed will be rumpled and damp when she gets into it.

"Oh my God. Alice, are you even going to say anything to her?"

"It's okay—go get yourself ready. She's just burning off steam. It's been a long, trying day. We all just need rest, and tomorrow we can swim or hike. Iris, are your teeth brushed?"

"What about the beach?"

"We can head there after."

Iris is bouncing like Tigger as Sophie goes into the bathroom. "Alice, get her off my bed!" Sophie sounds whinier than she wanted to sound and suddenly feels like she might cry. Instead, she slams the door and whispers, "I hate you!" Iris is laughing and squealing, "Mommy, the beds are so bouncy!"

"Okay, okay. Get down. Not on Sophie's bed. C'mere, I'll get you into these jammies. You can FaceTime with Daddy."

When Sophie pulls down her pants, there is a little pool of dark red blood, that warm wetness, the sticky feeling in her pubic hair. This explains the throbbing pimple that feels as big as a penny under the skin on her chin, the garlicky smell of her armpits all day.

Later, after talking to her dad, while her mother showers, with a clean pad in her underwear, the bed so soft it almost feels magical, Sophie is happy again, expansive. The world can be anything and it isn't all her mother's fault. With the lights still on, she drifts into a doze, her book in her hand.

Her eyes open and close, and she is so warm and cozy and perfectly content. Soon, she sees her mother come out of the shower with a towel held around her with one hand and, with the other, rifle through her suitcase for clothes. The steam has followed her mother out of the bathroom and made it as if Sophie were watching her through netting or plastic wrap. She must have closed her eyes again, because she is surprised to see her mother transformed when she opens them once more; she is wearing a peacock-blue cotton dress and is brushing her hair and putting her earrings back on.

Her mother looks like a vision—so beautiful and young and happy—it is almost unreal, and Sophie wonders if she's dreaming. Next to her in the other little bed, Iris is snoring and making pursing gestures and popping sounds with her lips. Sophie turns back to her mother and now sees she's standing in the doorway, looking curiously at both of them.

"Sophs, are you awake?" she whispers. Sophie notices how long her mother's arms are, and she sees the thick silver bracelet her father bought her mother last year at Tiffany for Christmas.

"Yes," Sophie says uncertainly.

"I'm too awake to go to bed, sweetie. I'm going to duck out to have the after-dinner drinks with the other guests. Can you stay with your sister?"

"Okay," Sophie says. Does she have a choice?

"I'll be back soon. Don't worry, I'm right down the hall and the stairs. You know where to find me, right?"

"I think so."

"I love you." Her mother tiptoes in, the skirt of her dress swaying a bit in the warm rose-scented air. She kisses Sophie on the forehead, and Sophie notices that her mother smells like lilacs. And then she is out the door, and Sophie is lying in the gray wooden room alone with her sister. The light is still burning next to her mother's bed, and the animal pelt by the fire glimmers and ripples as if it were alive.

18.

ALICE

A long, narrow, grooved wooden table that looks eight million years old has been hauled out next to the Matisse and the fireplace. The color of the wood is almost gray, it is so old: The legs are pockmarked and there are scoops taken out of the surface, almost as deep as ice cream bowls in some places. Something about how gray it is makes it look silver in the light. On top is a dark chocolate cake, or more likely a torte, given its crumbly unfrosted texture, sitting on a round silver platter with a silver serving knife that is elaborately filigreed. Next to the platter are a pile of mismatched floral-rimmed plates and a jar of honey with a white label lettered in black cursive: "*miel de notre tilleul.*"

It must be expected that one would take only a dainty slice, I assume, even though I am feeling like I could eat the entire cake at once, despite how full I was an hour ago. My hunger suddenly knows no bounds, like a tap has been turned on. That cake looks so light and friable at the edges and so rich in the center. Next to it are piles of tiny green plums, the mirabelles Iris loves, and a low dish full of glistening just-washed strawberries. Peaches, halved, sit in another long ceramic boat; they look like they have been sprinkled with sugar and then broiled, because they sparkle and sweat. Next to them sits a small dish of crème fraîche or, perhaps, sweetened yogurt. Low bowls and silver spoons are placed next to these offerings.

I cut myself a thin sliver of the cake and pick up the small silver spoon next to the honey and drizzle it over the top, watching the amber liquid soak into the dark dirt of chocolate. I find a fork in a pitcher covered with blue and white ducks and, without any restraint, sink it into the cake with the honey and take that first bite to my lips. I am weak at the knees as the sublime sweetness of the floral honey hits my tongue and the cake crumbles down my throat. I close my eyes and take a moment. You can almost taste the work of thousands of bees in that honey, smell the perfume of flowers on the wind, hear the leaves rustling above, and feel sunshine. This homecoming to food is none too soon, I think again. Wow, it almost feels erotic to enjoy taste again. I make myself laugh with that thought.

When I open my eyes, I realize that, despite my own private honey-cake experience, the real grown-up event is at the end of the table, where twinkling crystal glasses stand sentry to several bottles of clear eau-de-vie, a tall bottle of something lemon-colored, and yet another and even larger bottle of Chartreuse gleaming emerald green. He wasn't joking about how great the French think this grassy, licorice-tasting spirit is. On a smaller table is a ceramic teapot with a patchworked tea cozy on it. It is surrounded by a cacophony of delicate teacups, all different colors. I walk over and stand next to the tea and breathe in: It smells of piney lavender and something citrusy mingled with an earthiness that is another herb, perhaps anise.

The older couple who danced earlier stands just off to the

side of the long table. The husband is holding a small glass of something clear in his hand, likely the eau-de-vie. The wife is holding a bowl with half a peach and is eating it slowly, methodically, as she listens to the young man whom I saw earlier in the blue shirt; she is nodding docilely.

I look around and see Didier smiling and walking toward me, the look on his face for all the world like he has been waiting just for me. Though I am sure he makes everyone feel that way, I'd be lying if I didn't say that I don't feel a little hop-skip inside me and a warm wash of hope.

"Aleese." I hear Didier's voice coming ahead of him as he walks with such confidence, his apron still semi-on. His smile is broad, his hands out. He reaches me and pulls me toward him, which makes me say, "Oh," and then he kisses the air next to both of my ears.

"Are the leettle girls in the bed?"

"Yes. It's only, like, five or something back home. Iris fell sound asleep; Sophie is reading, I think. They are jet-lagged." I am immediately embarrassed for saying so much and I feel myself look away.

The door to the kitchen is ajar, and I can see that the windows are open in there. I can see a tall man, maybe twenty, washing dishes, and a woman who is around the same age as he and is wearing crisp gray Levi's and a white tank top washing the counters down. Another woman with a messy auburn bun on the top of her head is chopping something that looks like melons and arranging the pieces in a low pan. The entire kitchen is stainless steel, and there is a long stone sink that is black and has three basins. Copper pots and colanders hang from all over the ceiling. There are ribbons of herbs and garlic and peppers hanging, almost grazing the heads of the kitchen workers. Huge glass containers with cork tops sit on one counter, and, in one, there appear to be entire lemons floating in a brandy-colored liquid; others hold peppers, olives, tiny peeled onions, garlic cloves, dried flowers, and bouquets of herbs. Under a glass dome is a raft of cheeses, all different colors and in different stages of ripeness.

"Come," Didier is saying. "Try a drink. I have this lovely framboise eau-de-vie—raspberry—it's so smooth, you will hardly believe it."

He takes my hand and walks me to the table with the drinks and serves me a little of the clear liquid in one of the bottles and then waves his hand to a couch near the open door and suggests I sit down. I do and take a sip. It tastes intensely of raspberry and under that something else, maybe manure, which is not entirely unpleasant.

As I sip my drink, I look around. It is hot in this wide room, though bright and clean. Didier is talking to guests, some of whom take pieces of cake to tables or back to their rooms. Others are holding drinks and laughing, going out the doors onto the lawn, where it is cooler. I feel out of place, slightly homesick for my girls and the safety of our room where they are nestled in bed. A wave of missing Pete comes, and I wish for his familiar breath patterns and the way he walks into a crowd, so confident and sure. He'd make this easy, not awkward. I feel silly all of a sudden, for trying so hard, for the dress, the earrings.

So much has happened. Alone, so far away, I feel a sob coming up inside me, and I go outside into the dark and walk to the edge of the garden until I find a seat near some roses. I let the smell take over and then I let myself cry. I don't know how long I sit there, my nose running, no tissue, using the corner of my dress to wipe my face, again and again, but then I feel a warm hand on my bare back, fingers spread wide open, the palm pressed between my shoulder blades, steady. "Nothing like the smell of roses in the night." Didier's voice.

"'A rose is a rose is a rose,'" I try to quip, but he looks at me, confused. "Never mind. Gertrude Stein."

He pulls up another wrought iron chair next to mine, so close we could be touching except for the sliver of nighttime between our legs. We sit looking at the peach-colored roses catching bits of moonlight in the dark, breathing the same air, until he reaches over and touches the side of my face with his knuckles. I turn and then he leans over and kisses me, slowly, one hand pushing back flyaway hair, the other cupping my chin. A sweetness travels through my body like honey dripping into all the places I've stifled in those long years of forging forward, always forward, and simply surviving.

19.
IRIS

Iris is awake before her sister or her mother. She tries oh-so-hard to lie still in her bed so that Sophie won't yell at her. Sophie is lying with her mouth open in an almost perfect O and is making piggy sounds with her nose. Iris giggles under the covers. Through the open door, she sees a blue dress of her mother's slung on a chair, her mother's Birkenstocks on the floor—one by the window, the other by the fireplace, an open bottle of wine, a glass, and a lipstick. Iris guesses she has missed something, but what that was, she is not sure. She often misses things. It's part and parcel of being "the littlest bean," as her mother calls her. Her mother lies on her side, she is still in the big white bed, her face pale. Iris sits up on her elbows and watches the golden sun coming through the slats in the long louvered shutters closed over the windows, the roses beyond, the blue sky, the sounds of birds, and somewhere, distantly, she smells bread and something like vanilla pudding. She lies back down, trying even harder not to wiggle, but the more she thinks about not wiggling, the more she wiggles. Sophie shifts in her sleep, as if a marionette string ties her to her sister: Iris moves, Sophie moves. She does it again. Then she notices that when Sophie shifts, so does their mother. Iris is imagining the invisible lines that tie their family together, pliant like spiderwebs, stronger than you'd ever think, sometimes twinkling with dew, sometimes dusty and shabby or worn down, but always there, nonetheless. "Nonetheless," that word, a word her father sometimes says after her mother says that something is bothering her. Iris is big enough to know that when her father says that, it has the funny effect of erasing what her mother just said. Now Iris is thinking about the spiderweb in *Charlotte's Web* that read "Radiant" and "Some Pig," and how, when Charlotte got old, she was too tired to make another web, and how incredibly sad her mother was reading that book to Iris, how they were both crying so much it was hard for her mother to keep reading.

Iris moves again, slowly, watching to see if her mother or sister will notice. Then she gets bold: She picks up a graphic novel she brought on the plane about a girl who made a camp for herself in the woods in Maine, back behind her parents' house, where she'd go whenever her father was drinking. In the woods there, the girl would feed the foxes and the squirrels, and the birds would perch so close to her, and she would feel a peace alone there. Iris drops the book on the floor next to the bed, then dives under the covers to hide. Sophie sits up, looking confused. Iris peeks out and starts to giggle.

"Iris. What are you doing?"

"Nothing."

"Mama! Iris is waking me up." Iris notices how whiny and babyish Sophie sounds.

Iris hears her mother sigh—those sighs!—and then sit up. "What time is it, Pickle? I mean, Sophie, let me get my phone.

I'll see what time it is. My God, guys! It's eleven a.m. No wonder she's up."

"Mama, I'm starving. That's why I woke you up."

"C'mere, Pickle. Grab an apricot. Come snuggle."

Iris gets up and grabs an apricot and runs to the window, opens all the shutters, da-da, da-da, da-da, and lets the room fill with light. The rose branches tumble in, full of sunshine. Iris's hands are sticky with apricot juice when she gets under the white sheets next to her mother's hot body and cuddles until the heat is too much and she wriggles up again.

"Okay, girls. Let's go eat some breakfast. I need coffee."

"Are we leaving today? For Provence?" her sister asks.

"I think so. I don't know. It's so wonderful here. Let's go eat and discuss."

Eating seems okay, but for Iris, this kind of conversation, which leaves them hovering and not knowing about the day, is worrying. Weren't they supposed to be camping, not sleeping in big white beds? She knows, though, that if she pushes the issue too much, her mother will get grumpy, before coffee and food, and she will say, "Iris, please. I need time to think." Her mother will sigh at her, and she doesn't want that this morning.

So, instead, Iris pulls on her shorts and T-shirt and notices how she, her mother, and her sister all pull their hair back into the exact same kinds of messy knots, and then they go down together, their sandals scraping the wood floors and the smells of the dining room beckoning.

20.
ALICE

To be honest, we should have left that day. But the sun was so languid, and it was so late in the day already.

We eat our croissants and slivers of soft cheese and fruit for breakfast. Then Didier comes to our table, smiling and tanned, suggesting a picnic on the lake, a little hike through the woods, one more night. I say yes. I say yes before asking the girls, before thinking, and then I turn and see the look on Sophie's face. A line from my favorite story by John Updike, when the father tells his children that he is separating from their mother and calls out to his youngest daughter, "You knew, you always knew," ricochets around in my feverish head. They know, they always know, your children.

We go back to our room, and Sophie is angry, anxious. "What about our reservation in Provence, Mom? The beach? Your article?"

"We have time, my love."

"We have an actual reservation, Alice."

"I will call. But we are here, and in the Alps, and Didier's suggesting a hike and a swim? How could we not?"

Iris pipes up from the floor, where she is scrabbling around playing with a LEGO Ninja she's brought from home. "What about Daddy?"

I am pulling out our swimsuits. We've all gotten the same suit for our trip, my usual practical navy blue Speedo with white piping. This time, I've put enough weight back on to get a size up from the last one Pete bought me. I am now regretting this mother-daughter matching and neutered choice. "What do you mean, 'What about Daddy?'"

"Well, doesn't Daddy think we're going to Nice?"

"Daddy is back in New York. He doesn't care where we are, I don't think?"

"Daddy doesn't care?" Iris looks alarmed.

"I don't mean that. Of course he *cares*. He is fine with us wherever we are as long as we're safe, is what I am saying. Girls, your suits." And I toss them each theirs. I go into the bathroom to remove my bra with the prosthetic and to put on my own suit. The odd vacuous place where my left breast should be still startles me: the horrible scar that creates a fault line on my chest. I almost never change in front of a mirror anymore, I am always turning away, averting.

The bathing suit is going to create a conundrum for me this morning. I can't wear a bra under it. I hold the suit out and try to make a plan for what to do. A wet soggy prosthetic is not really an option, is it? Won't it slide around? There's no bra in these suits. Back home in the late spring, I'd tried everything I could think of to make those stick-on prosthetics you can order, custom-made, work. But the industrial-strength adhesive made to keep a fake boob from slipping and sliding on a flat chest for days, or even weeks, created horrible, painful, blistering rashes all over my skin, making my scar boil and ache. I tried every brand, method, suggestion from every cancer forum, group, and online channel. Nothing worked. Of course, back in June, when I gave up trying and threw the entire package of patches into the trash, I hadn't expected an audience. I was so involved, day by day, in the survival part of my story that looking normal was an afterthought. I didn't even care.

Now, in the bathroom, thinking about Didier seeing my missing boob, I want to scream and smash something. I mutter a list of what to expect when you don't expect anything: "*Your husband will cheat. There will be a global pandemic. You will get cancer. You will survive cancer but lose a part of your body with which you nursed your children, a part of your body that, it turns out, is so entwined with your identity that it's more like a limb. You will care what you look like again. You will want to be sexy. In your desperate desire to be wanted, you will be hurting your children.*"

Back when my surgeon told me my left breast was too small to save, given the placement and size of the tentacled tumor buried deep inside my flesh, I decided not to have my breast rebuilt. I had done all the research on implants and recurrences—hurriedly, chaotically, while trying to endure, day by day, the poison of chemo. All I cared about was the tenth of a percentage point added to my margin of survival with a mastectomy. I just wanted the cancer gone. I'd figure the rest out later.

But now, life coursing ecstatically and unexpectedly through me, I feel angry at myself for never considering that one day I might have something to be vain about. Staring in the mirror I try to coach myself, "Okay, you're lucky your breasts are small.

You are thin. It's not very noticeable." I pull on my cutoff shorts and a shirred, loose white top, add some lip gloss. This will have to do. I look away from myself and open the door.

When I come out, Sophie is eyeing me and the breast situation. She seems somewhat mollified by the idea that I haven't tried to hide anything. Perhaps she feels it's safer this way, with me bare for the world to see, disfigured. Both girls have their suits on, shorts slid over them, light blouses on top. "Okay, let's go," I say.

"You forgot the camping place in Provence."

"Sophie. It's just an app. I can do it in two seconds."

"Then will you?" She sits back down, resistant.

This daughter is my penance for last night, for every bad decision I've ever made, I think.

"Errgh. Everyone is waiting. Yes. I will do it now." When I go on the app, I see that we have lost one of the nights we have paid for. And now we will lose another. We are still open for the third, yet I do see some tiny writing about not showing up and how they could give it to a passerby if you aren't there. I send a message to my "host," the person who owns the field: I'm so sorry. We are waylaid in the Alps. We will still arrive tomorrow for two nights. Thank you. If you have the availability and can add another night or two, that would be great. We are coming!

As I close the app, I hear Sophie. "Mom?"

"Yes?" I am wary. What now?

"I'm wearing a pad in my bathing suit. And it's kinda bad."

"Oh no. Okay. You know, I saw some very thin tampons in a box of toiletries in the bathroom they left for guests. Want me to show you how to use one?"

Iris throws herself down on the floor. "Not again! They are going to leave without us!"

"Stop it, Iris. We need to take care of these things." I use my mean mom voice.

She starts crying and yelling, "We will be left behind!"

"Iris! Get ahold of yourself. Sophie—want me to take you into the bathroom?"

"Yeah, kinda?"

"Okay, honey, come on. Iris, stop it. Stop it! Stop crying. Your sister needs help."

In the bathroom with my tender Sophie, she is no longer my adversary. I am her mother, and she needs me. Why does this get lost so often in the do-si-do of these teenage years?

"Will it hurt?" she asks.

"Not at all." My God, if I'd died, I wouldn't be here to do this, I think.

• • •

The hike is hot and damp, with Didier leading the way. A German couple called Sandra and Rolf have joined us. He speaks very good English and has an aspect about him of a cadaver, something about the sinew of his muscles, the ropy veins and arteries, eyes that protrude a bit. Sandra speaks in a bouncy way, her ponytail following suit. I am immediately regretting all of it: the Germans along with us, the hot sweatiness, the bathing suit without a cup to put a prosthetic in, the kiss. My mind keeps tripping over that kiss, and I worry the girls can see it on my face, feel it emanating off my lips, in my hands as I touch them. Sophie stomps as we ascend, her vulnerability from the bathroom gone and her face reset in irritation the moment she sees Didier.

Up on a rise, the hike levels out and we come to a flat part with a path through a field of flowers. As we walk, Didier slows down and walks closer to me, the hair on the lower part of his arm exposed by the light denim shirt he wears rolled up to his elbow. Each time his arm grazes mine, my body is electrified all over again. Around his neck are binoculars, and he carries labeled flasks of water for everyone in the group in a big black rucksack, which he hands around. The field is a carpet of green and every color you can imagine, blooms everywhere.

Didier points out some light blue upside-down-tulip-looking flowers called harebells, which seem to spread across the grass like a wave, and more of those huge pink polka-dotted lilies we saw when we were camping, which he calls *martagons*. There are also orchids that look like big purple cones, and something long and pink with the word "rose" in it that reminds me of the fireweed that will be blooming at our house in Maine in late August.

Didier gets down on a knee, his ripped jeans dirty now, and holds his binoculars for Iris so that she can look at the sleek black birds he calls *choughs* in the trees along the border of the field. He points out his bee boxes, a stack of wooden drawers under a tall tree with heart-shaped leaves. "That is where our honey comes from. That lime tree there," he says. I see no limes on it, but I nod and take in the wide girth of the tree and the shaggy bark: It looks like the sugar maples on the edge of our field back in Maine. Now that I think about it, this tree also has maple-like seedpods dangling between its leaves, the ones that fly through the summer air. "Beautiful," I murmur.

Iris is so happy in that field, she goes running off and, as she runs, she stretches her hands wide, skimming the tops of the flowers and yelling for Sophie to follow her. Sophie stays rigid, softening only a little in her shoulders. But Iris, Iris is pure joy.

We carry on through a thicket of blackberries, and Didier pulls out a metal container and begins filling it with the berries. Soon we all join in, the soft plop of berries on top of berries mildly indecent. When the small bucket is full and a top secured, we walk again, Didier whistling as he leads the way through a pine-needled path under huge, towering trees. We come to a sharp rise through big pieces of gray rock covered with pink flowers blooming out of the crevasses, and then dip down, our hiking sandals rasping against the rocky path. When we look up again, we see the water: a giant canary-blue pool carved out of the rock. Everyone gasps. Didier chuckles.

"*Et voilà!*" he says. Iris starts jumping and clapping her hands. "*Allons-y!*" he says, and we all follow him. We would follow him anywhere, he is like the pied piper, leading us to the promised water. We go down and down and down, beech trees tickling our arms and cheeks, sometimes making us bend to stoop or crawl under their low branches. Beech trees, Didier tells us, are called *hêtre*, which is like the verb "to be," he explains, with a silent "h" in front. As if the trees' only job were to be, to be, to be, and never not to be.

Just before we reach the water, Didier stops us all at a plum tree and pulls off a dozen tiny, raisin-colored plums, tossing them to us, the golden flesh oozing juices all over our faces, juices we'll soon wash off. We eat like savages. Then he tells us all to be very quiet, because lots of "animaux" come to drink at that pristine lake. And surely, just as we turn the grassy bend to the water, we see a herd of ibex raise their heads, and then they are gone in a thundering instant. Everyone gasps. Iris says, "I thought those were only in Africa."

"Ha, *ma petite*!" Didier booms, his voice ricocheting off the water. "Dis one is very shaggy and dark-colored, the one in Africa, is . . . how you say?"—he looks at me reflexively—"It's got the ink brushes all down the sides?"

"Oh! Striped!" supplies Sophie, and then I can see she regrets having helped him.

"Striped. We also have something called a chamois—it's like a goat-pony thing. Whoops, don't step backward, Sophie—I see a marmot hole!"

Sophie turns slowly around and takes in a big hole in the mossy bank. She looks at me.

"Like a gopher, maybe?" I say, shrugging.

"*Le dernier à l'eau est une poule mouillée!*" Didier suddenly calls, and runs to the water, stripping off all of his clothes and tossing them to the bushes, his buttocks emerging, then something swinging in front of him, and then he is gone, only our memory of a muscled back and a tight, tan butt, which indicates to the casual observer that this is a regular occurrence. When his head comes up from the water, he is laughing like a boy. Sophie's mouth goes down into an absolute frown, like the kind you see in children's books. I look away, feeling my face get very hot, and Iris just stares. The Germans are also stripping down to nothing, hooting and jumping into the water.

"Oh. My. God," Sophie says.

"It's a European thing. Girls, let's get in over there." I motion to a little sandy spit where the water comes up to form a perfect triangle alongside a log where we can leave our clothes. Pulling our shorts off, I catch Didier's incredible blue eyes dancing with the hilarity of it all, the girls' reaction, the shock, the Europeanness of everything. He sees that I get it, the theater of it all. Already we are sharing a language. I find myself glancing at my uneven breasts and hoping he is looking away as I slip off my shirt and dive into the water as fast as I can, knowing it will be harder to hide once I get out, once my shirt is wet. But I needn't have worried; Didier is swimming underwater to the rocks and pulling his body out by those muscular arms, and every part of him is dripping water as he climbs onto the shore and pulls a huge cotton-napkin-looking thing out of his bag and ties it in a knot at his waist. Now that he is covered, I can look. But all I can think about is what is underneath.

Sophie's voice speaks next to me. "Mama, the water. It's so clear. Look at the bottom." I turn back to my girls.

Iris is in the water a little way off, splashing and grinning to herself. You can see every limb through the clear water, and the bottom is white. The girls and I laugh and dive, pretending we are porpoises, until we hear Didier call, "*À table!*"

When we look up, we see that he's laid out a cloth with wine and grapes, cheeses, meats, and breads. My stomach growls. "Iris, Sophie—look, lunch!"

We all swim in as fast as we can to the little sandbar and pull our clothes back on. I am so hungry that I almost forget about my breast until I see Didier's eyes. In an instant, I see in his face that he already knows, I will never have to explain.

21.

ALICE

When we get back to our room, Iris starts a list in her notebook of all the animals and plants she is seeing in France. She writes as I spell the words for her, slowly, tediously: "Ibex. Plum tree. Harebells. Blue butterfly."

Then the girls and I nap in the late-afternoon heat and wake up disoriented. Sophie's face is puffy; I might have thought she has been crying. But my daughter has become so hard-boiled lately, so intractable, that I hesitate to ask. My girls are well behaved in many ways, well mannered; they brush their hair and put on sundresses to go down to dinner. They are quiet.

When we get up, we WhatsApp with Pete. "Still here. Hiked and swam, a bit of an adventure."

"Aren't you still going camping?"

"Of course! You're just like Sophie. We still have the plan. Girls want to say hi."

These odd periods when Pete and I pull away, in and out of

connection, holding "us" together with nothing but the flimsiest piece of string—maybe this is all marriages. If I'm honest it never feels great. I shove it away.

• • •

Didier is showered and shaved this evening, holding court in the dining room, handing out bubbly Aperol spritzes, each with a pour of blood-orange soda and a slice of lime, sour just like I like them. I take a glass from him and his hand lingers a second on my fingertips, an electric eel thrashing between us. He turns to the girls and makes each a soda on ice, garnishes them with their own slice of lime, and then wipes his hands on his apron, a smile for each girl. My daughters take their sodas to a nook by a window that looks out toward the drive and is crammed full of books and a tall lemon tree, heavy with green and yellow fruit. I see them pull out a checkers set and begin to play. I'm grateful for this reprieve from my girls' gazes, from the censure of Sophie.

In the kitchen, Didier's jeans-clad staff is cooking away, and I see an enormous bowl of beautiful green lettuce heads on a stainless counter. A young woman with tattoos on her shoulders, a camisole, tight jeans, and enormous hoops in her ears is picking up the lettuces with tongs and plunging them into a huge pot of steaming liquid. Each lettuce head comes out dripping and wilted, and then she nestles it next to other lettuce heads on a long ceramic baking dish. The smells wafting our way are intoxicating. Jaunty music seems to catch a ride on fumes of broth and garlic and travels through the hot July air to my ears, my nose, all of my senses turned on. A song I've never heard, though I've spent the last two months listening to French music on Spotify, makes me want to wiggle my knees. The voice is deep and insouciant: *"Vilaine fille / Mauvais garçon / Dans cette vallée de larmes qu'est la vie / Viens avec moi par les sentiers interdits"* My mind is reaching to try to identify this song, this singer. I am standing still with my drink, smiling at the audacity of the lyrics, which are something like "naughty girls / bad boys / in this valley of tears called life / come walk with me along forbidden paths . . ." And then I feel a warmth behind me, a hand on my back, a voice. "*C'est* Serge Gainsbourg. The, eh, greatest French songwriter, possibly ever."

I turn to find Didier. "How did you know?"

"You had the look of deep thinking on your face." He already knows me, this man whom I know nothing about yet have seen naked, my children have seen naked.

The girls have borrowed my phone to use the timer so that Iris can ponder her next checkers move for a maximum of three minutes, lest Sophie lose her fucking mind. Better her than me. But now Iris is running up to me. "It's Daddy," she's saying. "He wants to talk to you."

My breath catches a bit in my chest, and I move my shoulders away from Didier's hand, which has been resting there. I take the phone from Iris, saying, "Thank you, honey." I turn to Didier. "I'll take this outside."

Out near the chairs next to the roses, the same chairs I sat in with Didier last night, I put the phone to my cheek. "Hey."

A rush of angular, brittle-sounding words from Pete: "What's going on with you guys? Sophie says you aren't going to Provence, you're staying in that chalet? I've barely heard from you. What's the story?"

I sigh and bumble a bit and then say, "I don't know how to explain it. We've fallen into an unexpected world—it's like everything has stopped, *time* has stopped. I feel like I'm in an E. M. Forster novel, honestly. Trying to connect, or maybe I'm finally connecting. We hiked into a lake and swam and then slept. And now we're having drinks—those Aperol drinks you make—and there's this fun, old-fashioned music on the radio. It's wonderful. Like a wrinkle in time, Pete." We've known each other so long, sharing it all is reflexive. Sometimes my life doesn't seem to exist unless we live it together.

I hear him breathe out. "Alice?"

"Yes?"

"Never mind. It's—"

"What, Pete?"

"I miss you. This last year has been hard. Last few years. And—I miss you. That's all."

"Okay." I know I should say the same, but a sourness comes into my throat, and I am hot in the sun and the roses smell too strongly, making me nauseated. And then Sophie is at my side, thankfully, saving me, saying she needs to ask Daddy about a checkers move. "Sophie wants the phone. We will call tomorrow from the road! Love you. Here's Sophie . . ."

I hand the phone over and walk away from my life, back into the chalet.

• • •

Dinner is a pigeon pie and those tender lettuces, which are covered in a garlic-shallot-broth reduction that is a pure distillation of allium, you could never have told me what that was going to taste like. French onion dip has nothing on this. I'll never forget it. Who thought of cooked lettuce? Of course, the French think of everything. I could eat the entire pan.

As I cut into the pie, all I can think about is pigeons making nests on the struts of underpasses around New York, clucking and cooing as you walk underneath, the musty smell of their excrement. But this pie is, in fact, a masterpiece of pastry, onions, vegetables, and a thick sauce that seeps onto the plate. For dessert, after the cheeses, we have a clafoutis, like a huge sweet pancake with blackberries in it.

"Mommy, these are the berries we picked," Iris exults, shoving a large, squishy bite into her mouth, juice running down her chin. I tell myself to breathe; I am rushing, rushing to enjoy the next bite, then rushing to the next thing, trying to get dinner done, and the kids to bed, so that my evening can start, my stomach twisted into a deadly vine of anticipation, regret, shame, self-righteousness.

Back in our room, the girls brush their teeth, get into bed. I read to Iris, Sophie reads to herself. In my mind, I have been preparing: "Girls, I am going back out for the digestifs with the grown-ups. I will lock the door and take the key. Sophie, you may read as late as you want, but Iris, your light must go out."

"You're leaving?" Iris looks shocked.

"She did this last night, too, dummy."

"You left?"

"Iris, you are safe. You have your sister. Any kids here are doing the same thing. I like being out in that room with the adults."

I hear Sophie snort and say, "Okee, Aleese." I shoot her a warning look.

Iris says, "Are there any other kids here?"

"Actually, I don't know. But I won't be gone long."

I give them both kisses, tell them I love them, and then, like an old-fashioned mother in one of those black-and-white movies who just turns out the light and walks away, I lock the door and keep going. Do I feel good? Not really. But I am determined to find a clearing for myself, a clearing where I am sure I am alive.

• • •

The dining room opens wide and bright and clean. Adults mingle. On the stereo, more jazz. I recognize it from an album with John Coltrane and Duke Ellington. My father used to listen to it on Sunday mornings, smoking cigarettes in the kitchen while he made us pancakes. When my parents were split up and he had us for the weekends, there had been something cloying and false and maybe sad underneath the smooth sounds. Now something about the music both envelopes me in the warm sogginess of pancakes and also makes me slightly seasick.

My hands are shaking because I already know where I am headed. I scan the room and see Didier from behind, the shape of his back, his shoulder blades under his light blue cotton short-sleeved shirt. His neck curves out of the collar, and the back of his blond hair is thick and peppered with gray. Watching him from behind undoes me. Outside, in the blue-veined twilight, is a table of digestifs next to the rosebushes. I step out, find the bottle of green Chartreuse, and pour a little bit into a tiny crystal glass and take a sip, the overpowering tastes of how many herbs did he say it was? Too many to remember. I breathe in grass and alpine peaks and beech trees and mirabelles. And then I feel an arm around my waist. I smell musk and sweat and shampoo, and Didier is next to me.

“I am married,” I say, the first thing coming out of my mouth.

“I know. But you are ’ere and ’ee is not.”

"It's not been perfect. Even good. It's been hard." I look at Didier: His eyes are wide and blue, his hand resting so softly, like a butterfly, on my left hand, the one I am using to hold on to a chair to steady myself. "My husband. Pete is his name. He had an affair. He was the love of my life. But then. Well, it wasn't only that, it was all the things that can happen . . ."

His hand leaves my hand and traces, ever so softly, the outline of my lost breast, the edge of my prosthesis. "What happened here?" he asks quietly, and then looks back to my eyes.

"Cancer. After Pete cheated. I had a lump. I was lucky—they just needed to remove the breast, and I did some chemo and radiation, and it's gone—or they say it is."

"You don't believe them?"

"I mean, they tell you they can't proclaim you're cured until it's been five years. And then after ten, they're more sure. But. My doctor says he's pretty sure now. I have a good prognosis. Even so . . . it's honestly"—I feel my breath catch—"You don't stop thinking about it, is all."

"*Oui.* I imagine."

"I just don't want cancer to be the end of my story, if that makes sense?"

"It won't be." He says it with such confidence, like he's a god who could ordain it so, not a mere mortal. I want to fall into this man.

Fighting away tears I say, "Tell me something about you?"

"Well, I have a daughter, too. Her name is Marguerite. Like Matisse's daughter. She lives with her mother in Toulouse. She's sixteen. We never got married. We were too young to make it work."

"Do you seduce all the single moms who come to your chalet?"

"Ha. Only the ones who are, how you say? Vanquishing *le cancer*?"

"Touché."

"Are you seduced?" Quicksand. Pulling me. In.

"We are leaving tomorrow. I have an assignment. For a story I am writing. I need to take my girls."

"Then we have to make the best of the time we have." He leans in and releases my glass from my hand and puts it on the table. He then takes my hand and leads me around the chairs, through an arch in the hedges, and down a rocky path that scintillates in the moonlight. We walk hand in hand like we are a couple until we come to a stream. We cross the stream one by one on a little wooden bridge, and on the far bank sits a small cottage. Didier goes on the porch, opens the door, and turns on the lights. I follow him inside, like there are bread crumbs. Thick Persian rugs cover the floor, overlapping in colors and textures to create a patchwork. The walls are wood-paneled, and there is a large fireplace with a bed neatly made up next to it, and over by the windows, the rugs stop and there is a huge canvas on an easel next to a bench covered with paints and brushes. The whole place smells of oil and turpentine, and when Didier turns on more lights and opens the windows to the rush of stream water outside, I can see the chunky forms of what I assume are impressions of the flowing water and rocks on the canvas. In the small kitchen, Didier runs the water and brings me a tall, (a first of its kind in this country) cold glass, which I drink gratefully as the smell of paints starts to dissipate. I look around and see more canvases on easels and on the walls—many of a blond girl with a red sweater, others of a dark-haired woman with a sad face.

"Are these yours?"

"Yes. I never bring anyone from the chalet in here—but I wanted to bring you." My bullshit meter twangs. He goes on, "I only let Marguerite stay in here when she visits." I see a basket of hair ties next to the bed, an old stuffed teddy bear, a box of tissues. But mostly, I see a man cave, an artist's retreat.

"Do you live back here?"

"No, I am normally at the chalet. Or with my bees. But I spend a lot of time out here—*oui*. Sometimes I need to retreat from it all for a few days to make my own work, refill the well. Did you say you're a writer?"

"I am trying to be. Again. It's a long story. My kids and marriage . . . I've become a person who is mostly mediocre at everything."

He's running his hand up and down my arm now, and the hair is standing up. "When was the last time your husband touched you like this?"

"Um. You go right for it, huh?"

"Hey?"

"I mean, you go right to the nerve of it all. The exposed part. Raw."

He only smiles and laces his fingers in mine. "I seriously doubt you are mediocre at anything," he murmurs.

"Oh, believe me. These days I can barely do anything very well. Mediocre mother; mediocre writer; mediocre wife; even mediocre cancer! Not the kind that kills you. Just the kind that makes you lose your breast." I start laughing, a bit unhinged; it's the wine, the drinks, the food, the place. I'm drunk, though not technically, just drunk on my own adrenaline, nerves, guilt. Do I think I'm doing stand-up? A regular Sarah Silverman.

He looks like he isn't sure if he should laugh.

"No. I once wrote a play that was good." And then I stop.

He pulls me to him, likely glad I'm sobering up a bit. Lunacy is not on his menu tonight.

"What was the play?"

"It was about these girls. In college. Where I went to college—a school in Providence. It's a small city near Boston. And they had this falling-out and then this thing . . ." He's caressing my cheek, rubbing his lips slowly over my jawline. "This thing happened to one of them when they were in New York . . ."

"What happened?" He's kissing my neck, and I have no fucking idea now what actually happened to the girl in New York.

"Ummm . . . she fell. She fell and . . ."

And now he is kissing my mouth so tenderly, so quietly, so full of lips and hunger and wine and the smell of paint is all around us and I can hear the gurgling stream (or was that my heart?). I shiver and try to surface like I've been drowning. I say, panting, "I need to get back."

"Stay a moment." He looks long into my eyes. Pete and I have been sexless for over a year. He treats me, I sometimes feel, as brittle and delicate, and I feel a certain shelter in that, a kind of refuge. Or I did, anyway.

But tonight Didier's strong hand holds the back of my neck under my hair, and the other slips off my dress and then traces my hips. He stops and goes to the fireplace, finding a thick white woolen blanket that reminds me of the felt pads I used to put in the girls' cribs under their fitted sheets. He lays it on top of the mattress, making a smooth white place. He opens two more of the long windows facing the stream so that another gasp of cool air comes into the room; then he turns out the light. Before I can find him in the dark, his mouth is on mine and traveling down my body as I listen to his breath and the rushing water and I feel tears streaming down my cheeks.

• • •

When I get back to our room, my heart is thrumming and pounding. Sophie stirs in her bed and I hope she is asleep. I turn on the hot shower, scald myself, and run the cold water, hoping to temper the fires burning inside me. I've left my nightgown from the night before hanging in the bathroom on an old iron hook. I take it down, pulling the crisp pink cotton over my head, and I tiptoe ever so quietly to the bed. I lie there until the sun comes up, and then I start packing.

22.

IRIS

Iris is in the car and her mother is driving again. She's had hot chocolate, fresh apricots, cheese (the kind she likes, the hard cat kind), and croissants. Her belly is full. Her mother is damp from showering and was packing the car while the girls ate breakfast.

Iris watched her mother, in her jeans and a tank top with thin straps and her bra with the fake boob, go back inside to check the room and pay, she said, while Iris and Sophie waited in the car. The girls sat in the car for a long time, and it was hot, and Salsa came and sat next to the window and whined and put her paws up on the door, sneaking her head inside to pant and lick Iris's face. When her mother came back out, she was out of breath and flustered, her cheeks hot and red. Iris noticed her sister scowling and then putting on her headphones, and Iris felt alone in the back seat as they drove down through the tunnel of trees and out to the winding road and started back down the mountains following the signs for Nice. "A long drive," their mother told them.

Now joy has come back: They are dipping down and up and the mountains are sparkling and whitecapped and there are gorges of water and Sophie puts "Shut Up and Dance" on the radio and her mother is taking her hands off the wheel when the road is flat to clap and they are all singing and bouncing and laughing: "I said: You're holding back / She said: Shut up and dance with me."

Iris feels the day open up to the possibility of a beach and a new place and the tent, their own little home, just the three of them, once again. And that feels right, good, just what she needs. All they have to do is get there.

PART 2

Le Golfe du Lion

23.

PETE

Pete writes and rewrites his text. He almost wants to laugh that Alice has turned the tables on him, and so effortlessly, at that. My God, did she just run away to France and forget him? Weren't they still in process, still rebuilding, still coming out of Covid and cancer, and yes, also his affair? Okay, he and Alice have been disconnected. Yet somehow they'd stayed together, come back to each other, still made their family. They'd been through so much. It used to feel like it was never too late to turn things around. Now, alone in New York in the stultifying summer, Pete is wondering if there was a moment when, actually, it became too late. Jesus, what a terrible thought. What in the hell is she playing at? He'd supported her all this time. She always said he was the game player. But he wasn't the one playing games. Not now, right?

It's early morning in New York. Not yet terribly hot, but the humidity is sticky. Pete wipes his brow and opens a window, leaning over a tippy jade plant to catch any sniffle of a breeze off the river. He starts again:

Hey. So . . . ok. You must be on your way south today? Talked to the girls last night. Sophs said you'd gone out? To get a drink? Some sort of nightly hotel party? Ummmm . . . seems sort of weird, leaving the girls? Alone? You're drinking? So soon after cancer? Isn't alcohol a carcinogen?

Fuck. This was ridiculous. Too many question marks. Plus, it might be perceived as starting a fight. That last bit about cancer and alcohol could be interpreted as shaming, though what he actually felt was fear. And outrage. Shouldn't he also be allowed to express such things? God, by now Alice might know—if she were even paying attention to him (doubtful)—that he was writing something (for over an hour now). That stupid bubble with the ". . ."

Hey. You guys on the road? Sophs told me last night you were making tracks today for Nice. Call me?

Better. Stronger. Maybe not the "Call me?" Seems pathetic. Hey. You guys on the road? Sophs told me last night you were making tracks today for Nice. I'll call later. That was better. He was in charge.

Pete hits send. He runs his hand through his hair. Gulls are flying around in Riverside Park. He needs to shower and go to work. What time is it? Seven a.m. Okay, so like one over in France?

"Nah, I'll go for a run. Fuck the heat." Before he can change his mind, Pete pulls on shorts and a sleeveless shirt and grabs his headphones and laces up his sneakers. He drinks an old kombucha that Alice has left half-finished in the fridge—Strawberry Sunrise. Gross. Whatever. Follows it with actual water. Remembers he has to pee. Then runs down the stairs, banging his fist on the metal numbers which designate each floor as he counts down. Okay, this is a tad toxic male, even he can admit it, but still. Then he is outside in the heat and the sun and he is running and Guns N' Roses are singing into his ear: "If I can't have you right now, I'll wait, dear / Sometimes I get so tense / But I can't speed up the time."

Pete feels like his chest is exploding. He keeps running, pulling off his shirt as he goes. By the time he gets back and is out of his cold shower, after masturbating quickly to relieve yet more tension, he sees there is a text (finally) from Alice.

Hey! 😎 Stopped at a rest stop. The rest stops here are amazing! It's filled with books for kids! Books! And organic yogurt!!! We are about an hour from Nice. But then another hour or two to where we are going—west! Nearer to Marseille than I realized. I thought it was closer to Nice, but the campsite is actually, if you want to look on the map, here. She has dropped a pin somewhat west of Nice, on the coast near a town called Toulon. Call whenever you want. A body of water called the Gulf of Lions is blue and wavy, almost cartoonishly marauding, on the map.

"Okay, slow down," Pete says to himself. Clutching the phone to his damp chest, his towel slung around his hips, he goes to the fridge. He puts the phone down and scoops out yogurt. Pours in granola. Eats methodically. Sets up the coffee maker. Takes his meds. While the coffee is percolating, he gets dressed—khakis, button-down, CeraVe face cream with sunscreen, hair clay, aftershave (organic, German), gray socks, orange HOKAs. "Gulf of Lions, I'd say," he mutters to himself, still fuming. But over what? He can't quite put his finger on it.

With the coffee in his hand, he sits down carefully, breathes out his nose, and dials her number. (God, he feels like an idiot: This is his wife, for God's sake. The wife who needed him while she battled cancer. His own children. I'm a fucking wreck, he thinks.)

Sophie picks up the phone. "Dad?"

"Hey, Sophs!" He is yelling.

"Yeah, um, Dad—we can hear you. We figured out the speaker."

"Hi, everyone!" Still yelling.

"Hey, Daddy." That's Iris.

"Hey." Alice. Does she sound weird?

"Daddy, guess what?" Iris is piping up from the back seat. Also yelling. It's not just him. "We went over this thing that was like the Grand Canyon—water everywhere. So up high and water down below. And there are all these fields of lavender like in the pictures. And we're going to go camp in a field. Maybe one with lavender. It's so beautiful here, Daddy."

"Sounds great, sweetie."

"You getting ready for work?" This is Alice, all business.

"Yup. But . . . gotta say, I'm starting to wish I was in France with y'all."

Volley not returned by the wife. Cringe: y'all? What, was he a Texan now?

Volley returned by teenager: "Yeah, that would be nice. This is: A. Lot. Of. Alice. Time."

"I'm sure you guys are having a blast. So much of a blast, I barely hear from you." He sounds caustic. He tries following with a laugh to pretend it was a joke.

"Mommy's been drinking." Iris spilling the beans. "And hanging out with French people."

Alice's voice. "Ha, drinking. Iris! Everyone in France drinks wine with dinner. Oh my God, girls, look at that! Pete, we're driving along a beach that's as long as I can see—and it's amazing. Roll down the windows, girls." Suddenly, he recognizes his wife, the one who finds excitement and joy in everything, even the mundane; his wife who's always shared what's on her mind. He hears the whoosh of wind, and then their voices are breaking up.

"Guys?"

All he hears now is laughter and then "Bbbb—zzzz—uggggghhhh."

"If you can hear me, call me later. I love you! I love you guys. Alice, I love you. Bye."

He holds on to the phone for a beat too long, like an idiot, a perma-grin pasted to his face, like they can see him. "Guys?"

"BBBBgggggguuuuuwwwww. Whoosh whoosh."

"Okay, bye now . . ." Pete puts the phone in his pocket and grabs a blazer and his bag. Better not to think. Keep moving. Dr. Bruno said it was the only way through a spate of totally understandable, completely normal depression. One foot in front of the other. Walk: out the door, down the hall, into the elevator, out into the heat, sun, smells, subway, okay, he is on his way, he will survive the next minute, the next hour, maybe even the day. Pete sits down in a seat next to the door, the clanging of the train banging through his head; someone smells like armpit. He closes his eyes, takes a breath through the sleeve of his blazer, reopens his eyes, and looks around. "It's okay. It's okay. I'll be okay." He puts Eminem on his earbuds, "Ope, there goes gravity," and he feels his stomach lurch, newly weightless, his body slack as if wrung out.

24.
ALICE

On the drive down the mountains, circling the bustle and heat of Nice, and then west along a highway that went on forever into the shimmering sun toward Marseille, we finally dipped down to the Mediterranean Sea, and all I could think about was the wind buttressing the car and Didier's hands on my body, his breath in my mouth, his smile and heat. We turned up the AC, and Sophie played music for us as the hot sun seared into the car: Queen, Led Zeppelin, the Beatles, Billie Eilish, and My Chemical Romance. Somehow, though you could not have told me how or why, Iris knew almost all the words to the songs. I watched her mouthing along in the back seat, saying things I wished she didn't understand. Maybe she didn't.

After talking to Pete we curve along the sides of cliffs that drop down to sandy beaches and turquoise water. The afternoon is waning. We go up dusty roads with signs for "Goat Crossing" (indeed, shaggy mountain goats stand in crowds on the sides of the hills, which Iris just loves seeing, already telling me she is going to add wild goats to her list of flora and fauna), and through small villages, until we wind around a cobblestone square, past windows covered with wisteria and white and fuchsia bougainvillea and stucco walls painted green and blue. Then we drive out another sandy road with olive groves, the old crooked trees looking so human and expressive, their limbs holding clumps of green fruit like old men at the vegetable market. Fanning under the trees as far as we can see is lavender. Every so often, in the midst of the purple lavender, there are patches of tall blue flowers swaying slightly in the breeze. I stop to open the windows, and the girls and I reflexively close our eyes to breathe in blue sky, sunlight, and the perfume of joy. Out the windows is a high-pitched sound, like thousands of tiny chainsaws.

"What's that sound?" asks Iris.

"Crickets?" I wonder out loud. "Grasshoppers?"

"Like locusts?" wonders Iris, who is always harkening back to the *Little House on the Prairie* books.

"I don't know," I say, and keep driving. The combination of smells and sounds in the car is so powerful now, it's as if our senses have taken over; our minds have been (finally) cowed.

"Where are we?" Iris asks from the back seat, her voice awed.

"Maybe heaven," I say. We can hear waves crashing in the distance. In front of us, a manor appears at the end of the drive. The entrance is flanked by two marble lions, one male and one female, gazing at each other across a ruff of grass.

We park on pink peastones, wheels crunching and announcing our arrival. A small Brittany spaniel comes bounding out from behind a hedge, ears flopping. Hot-pink bougainvillea tumbles down the walls of a stone barn attached to the manor. I see a very tall, thin woman with long gray hair come out of the house to a stone landing that sits high above the drive with two ornately carved stone stairwells winding up to it. Behind her, a huge turquoise door. On either side of the landing is a potted tree covered with miniature green fruits. The woman is wearing a dark blue apron with small white stars all over it. I get out of the car, smiling reflexively, and then immediately remember how, once, a long time ago now—I must have been, what, sixteen, twelve—my grandmother, my father's mother, had told me that I could be prettier if I trained my smile to go straight across my face rather than in an upside-down moon shape. I remember her leaning over and tracing the half circle on my face with her long, intrusive fingers. I remember the cold feeling down my spine, the shame that I wasn't measuring up. "You're almost beautiful, except for that," she said. Aunt Alice! (That's what we called her, though she wasn't our aunt.) All these years later, this has stuck, making me unsure how in the world anyone can retrain a smile, and whether my smile is good enough to use.

"*Bonjour,*" I call, waving and walking toward the steps. As I get closer, I can see a patinaed knocker on the big door shaped like a roaring lion. The woman descends and holds her hand out as she approaches, singing, "*Bienvenue*, welcome. You must be Alice and her daughters, here to camp?"

"Yes, *oui.*"

"We have been waiting for you, haven't we, Circe?" she asks the dog, who is bounding and waggling around in circles. "I am Penelope." She says her name with no "e" on the end, as if that "p" were the end of the discussion.

Sophie and Iris are unfolding out of the car and brushing cookie and croissant crumbs off their jean shorts. They come to me, Iris leaning her little body into mine as they stick out their hands to shake and smile. Gorgeous, perfect smiles, unique to each face. I've never thought about whether my daughters' smiles spread across their faces in the right way or curve up or down; I just care that they smile. Penelope gives Sophie a nice, firm shake and then leans down to look into Iris's brown eyes, and takes her hand gently, saying, "*Coucou ma petite fleur.*"

"She's calling you a flower," I whisper into Iris's hair, pushing her ever so slightly forward, in front of me.

Iris smiles and fixes Penelope with her gaze. "What's that sound?" she asks, pointing to the sky. "Is it locusts?"

"Locusts, oh, dearie me, no! It's cicadas—in the afternoons in Provence, the cicadas come out and make that sound. It's all the boy cicadas calling for females to come join them. They are a very big deal here in Provence. We give little silver or ceramic cicadas to children to hold on to when they first go off to school, or on a long journey, to remind them of home and give them good luck."

"Oh. Okay. Can I play with your dog?" Iris then corrects herself: "I mean your *chien*?"

"*Chienne*. She's a girl. But of course, my petal! Circe loves to play. Here is a little biscuit—I keep these in my pocket—and if you give it to her, she will love you forever. Run to the barn over there, you will find a ball for her." Iris takes the treat and squats by Circe, who pants and gulps. Then Iris runs off with the dog, her long legs knocking slightly at the knees as she goes. My heart breaks, watching her. God, what is this mess I am making here in France?

"So, you are here to camp." Penelope turns to look penetratingly into my eyes and then reaches out a wrinkled but firm hand and grabs my forearm, steadying me. How did she know I needed ballast right then?

"Yes. I know we are late—"

"No bother. I have made some lemonade. It's my son Georges who does *le camping*. You will go down that field there." She points past a grove of olives toward the sea mist. "And there's a big wide area that is mowed, right on the sea—you have the entire Gulf of Lions—*en fait*, the entire Mediterranean"—she laughs now with this joyful news—"in front of you. There's a—porch? For the tent, right there?"

I nod. But I hear Sophie mutter behind me, "Um. A platform?" I turn, shocked. Then I see her face: She is standing a bit off from me, her face registering every nuance to the conversation, her eyes following the line the woman's finger has made down the fields to the sea. She doesn't look at all snarky. She looks enraptured. How can I explain to Penelope that my daughter is not trying—in the slightest—to be rude right now?

I open my mouth to speak but Penelope smiles winningly and turns now to Sophie. "That's it, *chérie*. *Merci*. A platform. There is a grill, too. And a fire on the ground, though it is too dry and the mistral—the winds—are too strong right now. Steps go down to the sea from there. To the side, just there"—she points to some spiky evergreen-looking trees—"is a little path, and in there is a small hut. In that hut, *chérie*, there's an icebox, an open room with hammocks in case you get rained out, cards, checkers, chess, and a loo. All rather primitive, I fear—oh, also a table and chairs, some towels, sheets, blankets. A bar with what you need to make a martini or a spritz. A sink. You know, a place to retreat to. A turntable with some of my husband's old records—mostly American jazz, actually."

"Wow," I hear myself stammer. "We may never leave!"

"Ah, well, Georges takes care of the calendar—here he comes now."

Across the field, I can see a tall man in pants walking through the flowering grasses. "How do you speak such perfect English?" I ask Penelope, turning away from yet another dangerously handsome French man coming my way.

"Oh, boarding school many years ago—in England. Mayfield, in Sussex. Do you know it?"

"Oh, no, we're American!" Immediately, I realize that was idiotic. Of course we are American. "How did you end up there? In England?" I peek over her shoulder at the house, which is taking on more the ambiance of an actual castle than a mere manor. I notice that behind the low building Penelope has called a barn is a larger, modern structure, all windows. Another pink peastone walkway I hadn't seen before curves around that barn and disappears under an arbor of wisteria, ostensibly making a path to this next building.

"My father was a diplomat, so it was customary to send the children away, England being the best at that sort of thing. My parents lived here"—she gestured behind her—"and in Hong Kong, in Russia, if you can believe it, and Japan. When you come in, you can see, the house is full of so many curious things my parents found. When it was my turn, I sent Georges to Eton. He speaks very good English, too."

"Hello, Mummy." I hear a British accent behind us with only the tiniest lace of French on the edges. Georges has dark hair and a beard and is wearing riding boots. He looks like he has spent a good part of the summer outside. He leans over and kisses the air, once, twice, next to his mother's cheeks.

"This is Alice. And here is her charming daughter, Sophie." Penelope is beaming. "There's another little girl, Georges. Iris is her name."

"Bonjour," he says to me, and takes my hand in a firm shake, olive-colored eyes twinkling.

"You ready to camp?" He turns to Sophie.

"Yes, I am. Thank you." Sophie gives her most radiant smile. I am bubbling with pride.

I call to Iris, thinking that we should get down to the campsite, late as we are. "Iris, yoo-hoo—come on—"

"Georges." I hear Penelope switch to French: *"Rien ne sert de courir, il faut partir à point."* She turns back to Sophie with a bright smile. "Come have a lemonade first, dear." We follow Penelope up the marble steps, and Sophie goes in with her as I stand waiting for Iris, who comes out of the barn covered with straw, a red chicken squawking ahead of her, Circe grinning and bounding along, drunk on chicken clucking and little-girl attention. "Iris, come on, honey. Lemonade?"

"Mama!" Her hands are clasped in front of her face, beaming. "It's amazing in that barn! So many things: There are shelves and shelves of old blue bottles, and then there is a carriage! An actual carriage. It has red velvet seats! And horses, Mama! And one of them is pure white all over, with a pink nose! He has his own doorway with huge doors, and he goes into that field over there." She points. Now she is clapping her hands, her face so bright and open I think I might weep right then and there, this feeling coming over me, as it does, the same realization over and over, a CD that is stuck: My God, I almost could have lost all this, been gone from this picture, done. I still could be. It can always come back, do me in.

I shake my head, pushing that terrible, indelible C word away, and put my arms out as she comes up the steps to me with the dog. "Mama? Are you crying?"

"No, no, of course not. Just tired, and the pollen—so many flowers!—it's intense."

Inside, the kitchen counters are filled with various cooking instruments, magazines, bowls of lemons, bright green pears, and several trays of plums that have just been washed; someone (likely Penelope) is in the process of dunking them in a hot-water bath to loosen the skins and then core. There is a big glass cheese dome (does cheese never go in the fridge here?) with an array of cheeses, and a dining table covered with toast crumbs, and that morning's *Le Monde* still open. A painting in blue that looks awfully Picasso-ish hangs over the table. As we pass it, I lean over and, indeed, see the famous signature. Sophie is too far away from me to say anything; I'll have to tell her later.

"Come, come, out to the patio." Penelope beckons, then says, *"C'est un bordel ici!"* She gestures around the kitchen, which I take to mean that she thinks it's a mess. She pulls a glass pitcher of lemonade out of the fridge and holds a stack of glasses in the other hand.

Outside, we sit at a low table surrounded by potted lemons and limes, the sea breeze heavenly in the hot sun. From a planter, Penelope picks a sprig of rosemary and drops it into the lemonade before she serves it, running back in for ice, which she passes around in a silver bowl with little toothy tongs. Georges appears again, taking a heavy breath as he sits down, scents of hay and barn steaming off of him, his pants dusty. He and his mother talk quickly in a singsong nasal French that is so fast I don't understand it, and then he smiles and says, "So. Your great French odyssey has begun, *n'est-ce pas?*"

"Yes."

"What inspired it, if I may ask?"

"Oh, I am writing an article. And many years ago I came to France and loved it. But honestly"—I feel myself glance nervously at Sophie, wondering if she thinks I should tell them; she gives me a small, encouraging smile so I start to explain—"I was sick recently, and I'm better now—"

"She had cancer," Iris pipes up, deadpan, from where she is

crouching almost under the table, patting Circe. I see Sophie roll her eyes. She's my friend right now, and I am grateful.

"I wanted a trip with my daughters." I rush in, trying to frantically drown out that terrible word. Jesus, I must be tired. The Didier thing, the leaving, Pete's phone call earlier, the hot sun, Sophie on my side for one second there, I am a basket case all of a sudden. Thankfully, I am saved by a female voice calling, "*Coucou?*"

"Ah, *c'est* Marie—my wife." Georges smiles and stands, calling, "*On est là, chérie, sur la terrace!*"

"*Mais oui, j'arrive.*" A tall woman appears in a pair of high-waisted white jeans that are punctuated at the feet by some almost nonexistent sandals, which somehow manage to make her whole body seem nude, though it is only her lovely feet. Her top half is semi-covered with a short, square white T-shirt that shows a perfectly toned stomach, deep brown against the white ensemble. It's hard to take my eyes from her, and for a second, I am grateful that Pete is not here. I find myself turning to watch Georges, who, I noticed, blushed like a schoolboy when his wife appeared. I am taking in her long black hair swishing like a horse's mane down her back, colorful wooden bangles up and down her arms clacking like castanets. Now Georges leans over and kisses her on either cheek, his hand lingering for a second too long on the small of her back. This small gesture tugs me, like a drowning woman, back to Didier, his hands, his breath.

"Ah, Marie," Penelope says, patting a chair next to her. "Come meet my new friends."

"Hello." Marie looks at us all, beaming, her voice heavily accented, her lips puckered in French red. The white jeans make me think of the horrendous bed-soaking periods I've been getting since cancer, since chemo, since Tamoxifen—yet another volcanic game changer in the long slog of chemically hastened perimenopause. And yet here is this woman, ostensibly my age, her jeans as white as snow, her body so lithe, she could have just bounded from the pristine tops of the Alps, a handful of daisies in her hand and a look of *"what next?"* on her face.

"You ah-re *les campers*?" she asks.

"Yes," I respond, feeling ridiculous, American-car-and-life-rumpled, and very pasty. Perhaps I was childish to want to tent in a field, like a teen on an Outward Bound program. This is not a woman who camps, I imagine.

"Georges and I take our sons to camp every summer in the Alps, near Chamonix." She surprises me.

"Oh, we were just there!" Now I am relieved. Maybe we are more alike than not. "Are your sons here now?" I look around, half expecting one of them to leap from a hedge nearby.

"Oh, you know." She waves her hand in the air like I would actually know. Of course, I have no idea where little, or big, depending, French boys go off to, but I nod anyway.

Penelope gets up and comes back to the table with a fresh pitcher of cold lemonade and a chilled bottle of rosé. She refills the girls' glasses and then hands around a plate of plums, each cut in half with a tiny dollop of what looks like some sort of goat cheese in the center, drizzled with honey. I take more lemonade instead of wine; it's only three p.m., and we still have our tent to set up. But that plum! The filling is something like ricotta in texture, but with the lusciousness of whipped cream, and the honey has the sweet earthiness of nectar.

Marie takes a bite of a plum while carefully holding her glass of rosé in the other hand. Cheese spreads over her top lip in an almost obscene way. I look away, then look back, enthralled.

This woman is unfussy, grounded, unperturbed by the messiness of life.

"We need to go set up." I turn to Penelope. "I'm worried about the time."

"Yes, my dear." Penelope is distracted and shading her eyes to look out beyond the terrace to her vegetable gardens, her eyes on a fat rabbit that appears to be mowing down some tall leafy-looking things. "Georges!"

Georges looks up languidly. I think he honestly might have closed his eyes for a second there, so pleasant are the sun and wine and female conversation around him.

"*Le lapin—vas-y!*" His mother shakes him to attention with her voice.

"Ho!" Georges gets to his feet and shouts from the end of the terrace, clapping his hands, as much to wake himself up, I think, as to get the rabbit's attention. The rabbit, as far as I can tell, is used to this routine and looks up lazily, still chewing on some frondy piece of green, maybe a carrot top. It doesn't look too concerned if you ask me. Georges yells again and steps off the terrace in its direction, only tepidly menacing. The rabbit lopes off to a field of sunflowers and disappears between the tall stalks, perhaps to play outside its warren with Hazel and Pipkin and Bigwig and Strawberry, I think, smiling. I'm remembering reading *Watership Down* to Sophie when we were in Maine. How we both wept. I'll never forget that time together. Will she remember it? I hope so. Most of our times were good, weren't they?

There is a flurry of French words between the family, and then Georges gets up, turns to the girls and me, and says, "See you later." He is gone, out the door, his feet distantly crunching on the stone drive. Marie yawns and murmurs to Penelope. "*Il va à la quincaillerie.*"

"*Mais oui,*" says Penelope, "*Tous les temps.*"

It's time for us to go. "Girls, let's go set up our tent." Am I shrieking? Control yourself.

Penelope turns her face, bright and smiling again, a balm to my erratic behavior, and says, "Come back for dinner. The boys will be home."

"Oh, no, I wouldn't want to impose. There's the grill." Every word I utter sounds overwrought.

"Silly girl! No imposition 'tal. We will eat at eight p.m."

"Okay," I say, though aren't we supposed to be camping and female-questing, not this woman's guest? The lines are blurry all of a sudden. Do they invite all their guests for dinner?

As the girls and I depart, Marie and Penelope fall back into a conversation begun hours, days, months, years ago; whenever it was, it's ancient and picks up wherever it left off, the two pouring each other more wine, pulling their chairs closer, bending their heads together like Macbeth's witches. Their laughter follows us to the car, where I ask Iris to pull out her backpack; Sophie grabs the tent bag, and I take the duffel with the sleeping bags. My phone buzzes just as we start out across the field, the path narrow and winding through the heady smell of lavender, the din of cicadas, wind swirling around us. On the edges of the path are little wild strawberry plants, which makes me remember our one full summer in Maine, when we got to be there from spring on through, long enough to see things unfurl. There were strawberry plants that bloomed along the sides of the barn and made a white and yellow carpet of flowers. What I remember most, though, isn't the flowers or the fruit, it is the way the leaves looked like crumpled babies' faces until they opened up. I loved how innocent they were, how they reminded me of my babies.

Alice. It's Didier. Not much to say. But . . . I am glad I met you. I found this in my bed. He's sent a photo of a black hair band, the kind from Rite Aid. It is tangled with strands of my hair. Then: I'll hold on to it until I see you again. 😊

My whole body trembles with wanting. But I know it is foolish at best. At worst . . . well, I don't even want to think about it.

I put the phone back into my jean shorts and keep following my girls to the tent site. My eyes are fixed on their straight and long backs, their soft, shiny hair. The lyrics (I can remember) of that Kinks song in my head: "You've been sleeping in a field but you look real rested . . ." I hum along and then I whisper: "This is your chance, this is your time / So don't throw it away / You can have your day."

When I arrive, the grass is bent in supplication around the platform. What was it Penelope called the wind? She was talking about the heat wave, the *canicule*, she called it, and, oh yes, she said these hot, dry winds that come in the spring, that's the *mistral*, she said. It comes every year, she said, only this year it's never left. She told us it's fanning the fires to the west.

25.
SOPHIE

Sophie is watching her mother on the phone, and she knows it's that French guy Didier, back at the chalet. Everywhere Sophie looks, people here seem to pulse and tremble with good looks and sensuality. It's a lot to take in; a lot to witness your mother taking in. Sophie is relieved her father isn't here. But if he were, her mother would have stayed smaller, more restrained, more jumpy and moody. This expansive, sensual, slightly reckless mother is not a person Sophie is okay with right now. It's annoying. Actually, no, it's scary. And then some other squishy feelings Sophie is not interested in naming. She looks back over her shoulder at her mother's irritatingly placid face as she follows them down the path. What is she thinking about? Sophie feels a burst of rage. She decides to run the rest of the way, carrying the tent bag like a sack of potatoes over her shoulder. She is leaping, she is flying, she is winning a gold medal at the Olympics.

And just as suddenly as her rage appeared, now like a butterfly touching down, Sophie forgets she was mad at her mother at all. There is too much to see, take in, wonder at. She is busy marveling: The grassy field has come to an abrupt stop and then it disappears down a steep cliff to a turquoise body of water unlike anything Sophie has ever seen in her life. Iris arrives now and is squealing. When her mother joins them she is pointing to the stairs and the cliffs and telling both girls that "Georges called these limestone cliffs *'calanques,' caah-lonk.*" The word makes her sister laugh, and even Sophie, in the wind and the sun and looking down at that sea and those cliffs and not a soul to be seen, has to admit that the word sounds hilarious, clunky, like from a children's book, maybe something from *Madeline* or *Blueberries for Sal*—"Kerplink, kerplank, kerplunk."

"Mommy," Iris is screaming into the wind, "can we go down there?" She's pointing down the endless winding stairs, which fall in switchbacks down and down and down as far as the eye can see and then seem to disappear, as if you might just fall into the sea, never to return. Sophie imagines silently that there must be a ledge or a beach under there. But she doesn't share that idea, out loud, anyway. Many ideas seem to stay on the inside lately.

"Sophs!" Her mother is trying to get her attention, she realizes in that distant way she absorbs or, rather, doesn't absorb; her mother's voice is like waves receding and pulling the sand back with them into the breach: rhythmic, ever present, sometimes just noise.

"Sophie. Are you listening? Let's get that tent up, even though it's windy. Then put on our suits?"

Sophie nods, vaguely wondering what the sons will be like, whether it will be "a thing" having boys, French sons, waggling all around the place. She goes back to the platform to open the tent bag. Iris takes off into the wind-torched pine trees and disappears, likely to go check out the cabin. Their mother is following behind Iris with their food bags.

Before she gets to work, Sophie looks up one more time, taking it all in. It's not yet "the golden hour," a term Sophie learned when her mother was planning this trip. But Sophie can already see how this entire world will look in an hour or two, like it's been dipped in golden paint, the stuff of dreams and myths. She is starting to understand why people like her mother talk so much about France.

26.

IRIS

On the drive that took them halfway across the country of France, on their way to the big house on the edge of the sea, with the fields and the little cabin with the hammocks and the flowers all around, and the tall gray-haired woman who welcomed them as if they had been on a long voyage for years and years and she had been waiting *just for them*, her mother had stopped at a little store and found cold foods for them to eat over the next few days. There was a word on the top of the store that looked like "traitor," but Iris figured the store itself wasn't the traitor, maybe there had been a bad guy who came once, like a pirate, or a robber, and somehow the history was etched in the name. The three had gone in together, sweaty and sticky from the hot car ride, and found all kinds of things like a sliced mozzarella and tomato salad, sandwiches with butter and ham, yogurts with plums and honey, and marinated strips of steak in a container along with long thin slices of endive and blue cheese on top. They were so hungry. In the end, they bought many things, and her mother put them all inside the insulated shopping bag she had brought from home, and back at the car they pulled out the sandwiches and more Oranginas and sat in the hot parking lot and ate. As they drove, they ate a box of tiny cookies shaped like elf's ears and then opened a container of tiny potatoes that had been roasted with salt stuck all over their skins and you ate them just like that, in your hands.

Then there was the yellow lemonade from Penelope and those plums, and now Iris is quite full and happy, even sleepy, though she'd never admit it, in the sun. When she feels sleepy, Iris likes to move her body, to run and jump and shake out the woozy wiggles of being tired. While she runs with her arms airplaned out over the grasses and lavender, she can hear her mother calling to her. When she finally stops, her chest heaving and the unpleasant feeling of tired dissipating, she hears her mother's voice coming through the winds and asking her to help put the little containers of food and brown-paper-wrapped cheeses and extra Oranginas into the little fridge in the wooden cabin.

After, when they walk back from the cabin over the pine-needled path, back through the loud din of the cicadas in the trees, once more to the platform, they find Sophie standing triumphantly next to a tent that is all set up. Inside, Sophie has arranged the pillows and sleeping bags and duffel bags, and she is already in her bathing suit, looking hot and damp but proud, too. Iris watches her mother high-five Sophie. And then her mother says, "Just a second, guys. I gotta write some of this down, right? I mean . . . for my article." And she pulls out her little white notebook with the white pages and the scrawly writing inside.

"Don't forget the cicadas," says Iris.

"Or the wind!" says Sophie.

"Yes, girls—right. Thank you. You are so right!"

Then, Iris and her mother shimmy their own bathing suits over their sweaty bodies in the tent, laughing at how hard it is to get them on, and they all three start down the steps to nowhere.

No one could have prepared Iris for a sea like this, or a beach covered with so many tiny smooth pebbles that do not poke or stab at your feet. It looks to Iris like millions of lentils piled on the shore, all the dusty taupe color of putty and so easy to walk on. And the water! It is so shallow that Iris could go on forever without her mother and not worry about being swallowed. Even with that warm wind tearing across the field where their tent is and skimming over the surface of the sea beyond, the cove remains calm and clear. When she looks down, Iris can see a white powdery bottom, wide bacon strips of kelp brought in with the tide, and her own feet, even her toenails. No mucky murk like what lies beneath the roiling tidal seas in Maine.

The cove is theirs, Iris decides, along with those white cliffs all around them and the pebbly beach sneaking its way around one of the cliffs and vanishing. In the distance, Iris can hear laughter and screeches of joy, splashes and mysterious French words that Iris wishes she could understand. She dives back into the water, opening her eyes and letting the salt sting them.

Quietly, the three of them swim together, their own laughter and enjoyment subdued and shy. When her mother is swimming and Iris can't see the empty space where her mother used to have a breast, she is relieved. When her mother's hair is wet and Iris can't see her gray hairs, she is relieved. When her mother and sister aren't fighting, she is relieved. When Sophie is happy and diving like a porpoise, she is relieved. Her own body is relieved because the water is cool and it is so hot in France.

27.
ALICE

Marie is standing at the edge of the water wearing no top, her beautiful breasts exposed, her nipples dark as chocolate. She is waving at us, her breasts swaying. Despite being my age, the woman has the abs of a twenty-eight-year-old, and you'd never think those breasts nursed four boys (who knows, maybe they didn't).

"Hey, Marie," I call from the safety of the sea, the salt water grazing my chin. Somehow I want to come out less with Marie, with my lost breast situation, than I did with Didier. She is waving her arms and pointing to the *calanque* and the noise. "My boys! Come sweem with us, around dere." She points again, breasts waggling. "We'll walk over in a moment," I call back, cupping my hands to my mouth to enunciate, smiling to my girls, who are at once unsure and interested. "Okay, Sophie, Iris—do you want to go around that cliff there? And meet their boys?"

Sophie eyes me like a strange specimen. "Why would we do that?"

"I don't know. Be sociable. See the French boyz." I put a "z" on the end of the word, trying to be lighthearted.

Sophie rolls her eyes. "Fine."

"Iris, you okay to come?"

"Ugggh. Okay. But can we swim here again before we go back up?" Iris is always mourning old things before she tries new things.

"If we aren't too hungry, yes."

Out on the beach, I reach for the stack of towels, which aren't really towels in the way I think of towels, but large tablecloth-like things that are only minimally absorbent. Didier wore one at the lake. And I saw them for sale on clotheslines all along the coast as we drove here, with the word *fouta* printed in black marker on pieces of cardboard. In the cabin here, there was a huge stack of them, all in bright colors with differently sized white stripes. Now I wrap one tightly around my chest, making the knot where my missing breast used to be, should be. The girls grab theirs and walk holding them. We all put our sandals back on, our hair draining puddles into them. We begin the slog around the cliff, the scrubby green rosemary and gray-green lavender crawling up the rocky dirt above our heads. My thighs are damp and salty/sticky and rub together the slightest bit, which reminds me of when I was pregnant with both girls and how that huge stomach made my thighs stick together and how hot and miserable it was and how I thought that if the thigh rubbing continued for much longer, I might be completely undone by it, the horrible shame of it.

When we come around the cliff, there are *foutas* spread out over the pebbles, and someone has erected a badminton net. There are, as advertised, four boys, all of them enormous teen-boy-man-chimeras, their legs hairy, their noses protruding, and their parts bulging. There is also a flock of girls/women who come with the boys, I presume, and not a single one of them is wearing a top. One, with long auburn hair, has a thong that perfectly bifurcates her round bottom into two grapefruit slices. Farther down this straight part of the cove, I can see other families clumped together on what looks like, maybe, a more public beach: I see a lifeguard chair and floats in the water. No one there seems to be wearing a top, either. I look at Sophie to get her reaction, while a wet Iris sticks herself to my leg, her hand finding mine. Sophie ignores me.

I take an extra *fouta* next to Marie, who is slathering sunscreen all over her breasts and laughing with a teenager who looks like her twin but has a cigarette in his mouth. "Hello," I say as cheerfully as I can manage given that I suddenly feel we are a long (very long) way from home. Niggling underneath is a sudden pang of homesickness. I miss Pete. How can I miss Pete and also be betraying Pete at the same time? This is a caustic mix of emotions that don't even make sense. But, if Pete were here, everything would be different: the night before never would have happened, my stomach wouldn't be in knots while my brain slips through the events with Didier. If Pete were here, I would have slept in the car as he drove, I might not be so tired and hungry and adrift in a place that is, well, so foreign. Also, Pete has this way of making people feel, oh, relaxed, I guess, and fine about their difference, our difference, like it's all just one big party. He's pretty gifted at that.

Marie turns to me, her well-oiled tits jiggling in the sun, and gives me the warmest smile you could ever see, which almost distracts me from her chest. "Come, Aleeese, come sit. *Les filles*, come sit." She pats the *fouta* rumpled next to her. But I spread my own yellow-and-white-striped one down, still keeping the other *fouta* knotted at my (non) breast firmly in place. When I look back up, she is holding out a paper bag with the sides rolled down. Inside are bright red raspberries, all perfectly succulent and not at all mashed. The boy who was next to her has gotten up and now has his hand on the ass of a blond girl standing facing the water in tree pose, her face upturned to the sun in a beatific smile, as he kisses her neck. What is this like for his mother? I wonder. Blatant son sexuality in her face? Maybe this is how it goes now . . . how would I know? I am only just at the beginning. There is so much (always) I don't know about how my (and our) story will turn out.

The girls and I each take a raspberry, and then Marie hands me a small glass filled with something from a long, thin bottle I saw peeking out of one of her baskets. Inside is a lemon-colored liqueur that is sweet and sunny at once and tastes like essence of lemon but hits my head like a hammer in this heat. Sophie asks me if she can taste it, and though I should have said no, I hand it to her anyway, saying, "A tiny sip." I watch her adopt a look of grave maturity while she tries the alcohol. I continue hopefully, "But in the bargain, I need you to take your sister to that sandy spot over there and make a castle or whatever with her."

"No, Alice, I'm not making a castle with Iris." I look down at Iris, curled next to me in her own *fouta*, her wet hair streaming down the side of her face, with a raspberry on her thumb. She is muttering under her breath the old rhyme about Tom Thumb.

Marie has turned to her boys, who are horsing around with the badminton, which they have turned into a game that involves someone always falling into the water as they leap to hit the birdie. "*Ho—Alain. Viens ici—oooh—la-la—viens! Viens inviter les petites filles à jouer avec vous. Claude! Arrête une seconde!*" The boy I assume is Alain plunges into the water and then surfaces, his body rising out of the sea like some sort of Bernini sculpture, his dark hair slicked against the back of his head and dripping. He is older than Sophie, at least by a year or two, only missing a trident. Oh dear, I think.

He comes to stand in front of us, all bulges and biceps, making eye contact for a moment with his mother, and between them some communication that only mothers and children understand was given and received, with nary a word spoken out loud. Then his voice, deep and British, asks Sophie, "'Ello. Want to come 'ave a game with us? We're just playing badminton. Do you know it?"

"Um, yeah," says Sophie.

"Want to have a go, then?"

"Okay, sure."

"This eees Sophie," Marie instructs. "Sophie, this is my son Alain. He is the middle child. There's a younger one over there, Iris, but he tries to be older." We turn to look at another scantily clad young man, tight shorts, holding a racket. He looks maybe twelve? Anyway, eons older than Iris, who is still apparently into nursery rhymes.

"More drink? Hmm?" Marie is holding the bottle in front of me as I watch my elder daughter get up; her modest navy Speedo is cut to accentuate her strength but now it's seeming oh-so-very naked to me. She is following Alain, pebble lentils stuck to her butt, which she, I am sure, has no idea are there. I notice from this distance how beautiful she is, as if I'd forgotten, and I get this pang of fear that she will be stolen from me by Alain, right in plain sight. She wades delicately, like a nervous filly, into the shallow turquoise water and takes a racket from a girl who I hear introduce herself as Rose. Sophie stands awkwardly, both hands clutching her racket. Alain, a natural leader, smiles at her, and I can feel her stomach flip and flop as if it were mine. "Ho, Adele," he's calling to an older brother, twenty or so, leaning against a copper-colored rock, his bottom half in the water, his chest out, and a cigarette in his mouth. I hear the girls titter and Marie chuckle next to me. "That's my golden boy, Adelard. Alain is our family pain in the ass. He calls him Adele, like the singer, you know?"

I nod vaguely, having a hard time picturing Adele all of a sudden. Marie picks up on my fuzzy margins and chastises, "She's veery fay-mousse in la France.

"Yes, and that one there"—she continues, pointing to the boy who was fondling the blonde—"is Claude. He's sixteen. He and Alain are—how you say?—Irish twins. And then my baby is the one I show you earlier. Theo."

"Wow. Four boys. You are brave."

"Yes, four boys. They are all like aliens. But. You know . . . that was how I kept Georges."

I laugh. And then see that Marie is not laughing at all. Warily, I turn my head to see where Iris is as I realize we might be getting into "married women territory." With relief, I see that Iris has peeled off and is quietly talking to herself while making a cairn in the shadows thrown off the calanque.

"How did you and Georges meet?" I am hoping to veer the conversation to small talk so that I don't have the wrong reaction when we get to the actual meat of the story.

"Georges came to Senegal, where I am from. He was doing a stage"—she pronounces it "staaaaj"—"you know what this is?"

"No."

"It's a sort of thing when they are in college and they go work somewhere, do something useful."

"Oh, an internship?"

"Yes, dat. These diplomatic families, the blue bloods of *la France*, they all go off and do dis. So Georges came, and I was working in a gallery on the coast there, where we showed the best modern art in all of Africa. Georges was 'elping to build a school after the problems with Casamance. He came in, and I saw 'eem and said, 'There he ees,' like I was always waiting for dat guy.

"We spent all of our time together there, and then when he left, I cried for a month. But he came back. And when he did, he had a ring and a plane ticket, and I said goodbye to my parents and my brothers and sisters—I have six brothers and sisters—and came to France. Now my two sisters live in Aix, and one brother is in Marseille, another is in Paris."

"And are your other siblings still in Senegal?"

"No. One of my brothers is in Belgium and the other one died in the fighting. It's just my mother and my aunts back in Senegal now. My father died."

"Do you ever go back?"

"Yes. Once a year. We go to the beach in the winter."

"The beach? Wow. What is that like?"

"Beautiful. Palm trees and horseback riding, zebras. It's good for my boys. You know, all this," she says, laughing, "this is *charmant*—how you say?"

"Charming?"

"*Ouais.* Charming. And all—it's an amazing life, dis. But dis is not the real world. Senegal is the real world, or it's their mother's real world." She laughs again, this deep—is it happy?—laugh that kind of disarms me. Rather than joy it radiates something more nuanced, like tolerant and enormous love.

"Do you miss it?" I am shaking all of a sudden with a little bit of anxiety.

"Absolutely not." She snorts through her nose and pours herself another drink. "Africa is too *compliqué* for me now. My kids are European. And I am French now, more French than African."

"You have a beautiful family." Envy flows through me. Marie seems so centered, this matter-of-fact life, at home on two continents, a strapping husband wearing riding boots, that insane hair, tall body, gorgeous sons, and a manor on the Mediterranean Sea. Also two breasts. No cancer. No fear, it seems. Who is this woman?

"Wayyy . . . it's not all as perfect as it looks. Come on, let's go jump in the water." And then she is up and striding with her long legs down to the shore, our conversation over.

I look around, realizing I haven't even thought about my girls, I have been entranced by Marie. Iris is wandering along the side of the calanque now, leaning down and touching, ever so gently, the lavender plants, her hands cupping the blossoms when she bends her nose to each one, the scents teaching her something important about her life. Her devotion is almost monk-like, intense.

I think of her in Maine, running through the tall grass at night chasing fireflies. She is dirty and free when we are there, letting the fireflies land on her hands, holding still with not one second of fear about the dark, her concentration on the primordial creatures flying around. She takes my breath away, her courage, her love of life. I often think about my younger one, this child who started life in the NICU, who almost drowned once, and her insatiable will to survive! But it's her stillness that always surprises and amazes me. When she is still, when she is homed in on the natural world, I am in awe. Sometimes I watch her and I think, Maybe I've forgotten how to be still. Maybe we all have. The world no longer allows it; we are pinged and messaged and terrified, daily, minute-by-minute, with dispatches from near and far, our brains reacting like popcorn in a hot pan.

I turn my head and I can hear my older child laughing. She is leaping and plunging into the water, a racket in her hand.

I'll close my eyes just for a moment, I think. All is well right now, I can be still, I can let go.

28.
IRIS

At dinner, Iris sits in between her mother and sister at a long table that stretches under some trees. Iris has never seen such a long table. It's covered with an endless tablecloth that is yellow with red pomegranates all over it, and by each plate is a large ceramic cicada, greenish with eyes bulging. Penelope tells Iris that those are *porte-couteaux*, where you are meant to "park your knife" as you are eating. Iris has no idea what Penelope means, but she likes the creatures sharing the table like that. Iris's mother says to Sophie, "Stop hovering, Sophs—come sit down." The teens are standing in clumps, like deer in the middle of the road, all huddled in the wrong place, bumping into each other. Georges and Marie and Penelope are carrying out platters of food and having to maneuver around their large bodies.

Iris is watching the food: There are enormous meatballs on a platter, and chunks of eggplant shiny with olive oil and dusted with large flat salt crystals that you can see glittering like mica. There is an entire fish with fennel and lemon slices, so thin they are like little pieces of translucent paper. There are tomatoes in a bowl, sliced and without peels; layered in between are huge leaves of basil and thick slices of creamy mozzarella. There is some kind of yellow-colored rice in a bowl that has a top on it, and when Georges lifts it, the smells of spices and raisins and onions mixed in with the rice waft up tantalizingly to Iris's nose. And then a large plate of steamed artichokes surrounded by lemon wedges. Georges brings out wine and serves everyone, even Iris, a little bit in a tiny glass. Hers is only a sip, but it is light pink and tastes like bubbly grapefruit.

Georges raises his glass and says something in French and everyone else raises their glasses and clinks and then the food is passed around and the setting sun is hot on Iris's back. Iris notices how pretty her mom looks in a white sleeveless cotton dress, and underneath Iris can see her mother's white bra and she knows her mom has put one of those fake breasts inside, because she can see the faint flowered pattern of it through the fortress of the dress and the bra. But to Iris, on the outside, everything looks like it is all okay, normal, fine, happy. She sees more of that every day: her mother getting tan, the dresses, the hair less and less thin. That all feels so important to Iris. As they start eating, Iris's mother taps her shoulder. "Pickle: your napkin, on your lap. And see how everyone's using both the knife and their fork upside down. That's called the European manner—try it, it works so well. And check your shoulders, honey. Nice back."

Penelope has been telling a story during dinner of going to Japan with her husband, Georges's father, named Pierre. Iris gets the sense that Pierre is somewhere else now, not dead exactly, but almost. That sounds weird. She'll remember to ask her mother later. But in Japan, Penelope had given Georges ninja classes—this story perks Iris up. She is listening now. And Georges had learned to be a warrior and wield a katana, a samurai's sword,

Penelope said. Georges is chuckling as his mother tells about how he'd taken his sword and cut down a white gardenia that belonged to the old woman who was hosting them, and then how the woman took Georges with her to the market and had him pick out a new plant, then dig a hole and plant it for her. The woman showed Georges how to layer seaweed into the dirt for fertilizer and how to soak the roots. Penelope is claiming that it was then that Georges started to appreciate growing plants, and that moment turned him, eventually, into a farmer. Georges chuckles at the word "farmer" and pours himself some more wine.

Dinner lasts so long that Iris starts to get tired. She tries hard to sit up straight, her napkin on her lap, her neck long, but little by little, she is starting to deflate and slump against her mother. Her mother puts her arm around her, and Iris leans in, feeling the crocheted breast ball rub against her cheek. Her eyes must have closed for a second, because when she opens them again, she sees that all the platters are gone and they are being replaced by even more dishes being served. "How are we going to eat any more?" she whispers in her mother's ear. There are cheeses—so many cheeses—and long sticks of bread on the table that people just grab and rip apart; there are lettuce leaves with the slightest dribble of vinaigrette and a little blizzard of chopped herbs, each person taking a single large leaf and eating it with both fork *and* knife; there are tiny cheese soufflés which come out in little earthenware dishes and are flecked with black pepper. How do these people eat so much? Iris wants to know.

After all the dishes have finally been cleared and the ends of bread are gone, Penelope brings out a deep ceramic dish of cold chocolate mousse and more little glasses to serve it into at the table. Iris whispers to her mother, "Mama, they have *endless* amounts of tiny glasses!" Her mother shushes her as Penelope serves a clear liquor to the adults. To Iris, it smells like fresh raspberries, and her mother seems to know that it is called *framboise.* Then there is coffee for the adults and even some of the teens. Penelope goes back inside and comes out with a steaming cup of something for Iris and says, "*Tiens, ma chérie.*" Iris looks at her mother and asks, "What is it, Mommy?"

Her mother gives Penelope a questioning look. Then Penelope says to her mother in her singsong voice, "It's tilleul. We make a tisane from the leaves and flowers here in France. Some people call it lime, but it's not a citrus lime tree. Have you ever heard of it?" Iris sees her mother shake her head. Penelope goes on, "Maybe you read *Swann's Way*? Proust dips his famous madeleine in tilleul tea?"

Her mother shakes her head again and says, "I confess, I only read the beginning of *Swann's Way*. I can't remember the tea part of it, but of course, yes, I remember the little madeleine."

"Ah," says Penelope. "I have several of the trees around. The bees love the yellow flowers, and we make honey that we sell at the market—just in the town there." She points back toward the road. "Mostly, in Europe, we call it linden, my love. I think your species in America is different and . . . Georges, what do the Americans call tilleul?"

"Basswood," he booms, as if he were waiting for this question all evening.

"Ah, is it called basswood? Have you ever seen one?" Penelope asks her mother.

"No, I don't think so . . . well, wait—I think in Minnesota, where I grew up. But the flowers were whitish." Iris is curious now about what her mother saw in Minnesota that they also have in France.

"Here in France, we think it's a very good *digestif* and terrific for sleepy children who need a good rest. In France, we also say the linden tree brings protection and healing."

"Will I have protection if I drink it, Mama?" asks Iris.

"I think so, Pickle. Or at least a good sleep! Which is a kind of protection!"

Penelope winks at Iris and says, "On the *lendemain*, dear, you will feel perfect." Then she passes a bowl of salty caramels around, and Georges lights a cigarette and blows the smoke up into the leaves of the tree with the peely bark that towers over the end of the table where he presides. By then, the older girls and boys have retreated into the shadows, and Iris can hear giggling coming from behind the tall hedges and see plumes of skunky-smelling smoke. There is a splash and then another, loud laughter and shouting; some of the teens are jumping in a pool, Iris thinks. Iris is glad that Sophie has stayed at the table. At least she thinks she has. She does hear her mother say it's "time," and she remembers later that the three of them walked down the path, through the field, almost to the edge of the world, the waves crashing into that Gulf of Lions beneath them, the moon high above.

The last thing Iris hears before she drifts off to sleep on top of her sleeping bag, the warm breeze coming off the sea through the tent, is Sophie asking her mother, "How much longer will we be here?"

"A night after this."

"No. I mean . . . France."

"Oh. Let me think. A little more than a week is all."

Her sister is quiet. Which makes Iris wonder what this sister, whom she knows and doesn't know, is doing just on the other side of her mother, against the other side of the tent, all the way across the world in this country called France where everyone speaks a language none of them really understands. And then she hears Sophie say quietly, "I miss home." Iris lies as still as she can and waits for her mother to answer.

But the tide is so deep, and her body is sinking as if weights are tied to her feet, and she can't make the sound come out, even as she thrashes about in her mind, calling "Mama—Sophie! Don't forget her! Are you going to answer her?"

29.

ALICE

The girls are still sleeping when I wake up, the sun is hot on my face, my cheeks are burning, and the tent feels tipped, like it could be sliding into the sea below. It is late, I can tell. I pick up my phone and see it's after ten.

My mind is roiling: Didier tracing my lost breast that still—for me, anyway—hovers like some kind of maddening ghost, just off my body, never quite gone, never quite back where it should be. Who knew I'd want—so often—to touch my absentee breast, feel its comforting softness go slack against my body when I lie down? Sometimes I wake with a start and I remember the surgery, the waking up, the whole surprise that any of this had actually happened to me, to *us*.

When I was in the recovery room after the surgery, I had been screaming for Pete, they told me. They called him in and said, "She's very upset." It was only Pete who could calm me down, only his voice. Only when he told me I would be okay, that he was there, did I quiet. I don't remember that—I have the story of it.

Us. When that word comes into my brain this morning, I feel my heart seize under my lost breast. Pete. Who *was* "us" anymore? What had I done?

I take my notebook outside to write. First, I walk to the cabin to use the bathroom and make myself a coffee. The coffee is bitter; I deserve the most bitter coffee in the world. My nightgown is damp down the back like I have been sweating. I feel a toxic mix of sensual and also shamed. Since chemo and radiation and Tamoxifen, my hot flashes are nothing like I expected. These are dry chemical fronts of heat, originating in the most lifeless deserts of the world. I feel like one of those space heaters lined with asbestos.

A little distance from the tent I find a large rock in the field and I sit to scribble:

> *Lavender fields are just like you've seen on Pinterest, only you can't imagine the smell.*
>
> *Olive trees look like old people, much wiser than any of us humans thrashing around. The wind is constant, hot, loud sometimes. The sea can seem calm one moment and savage the next.*
>
> *The thing about traveling with girls is you need to show them things, be open to anything, talk and talk and more talk. Especially in the tent at night, when they are vulnerable.*

And then I remember what Sophie said the night before. Did I answer? I must have. She missed home. Well, of course. She is a child, and missing home in the summer when you go away is totally normal. I used to miss home even when I went on a sleepover. But I had my mother's silence and anger. My father moving out. The coming back. The upheaval. It was hard to feel safe enough to leave. Is this what Sophie feels, too? I have tried so hard to create something better. But there have been failures, mistakes.

I pick up my phone and text my friend Betsy, back home in Minneapolis. She will already be up, even though it's barely after four a.m., making coffee, doing her eight-minute abs, which somehow she's managed to sneak in for years and years, looking as fit as Jennifer Garner. She's a single mom and makes the Shackleton-like endurance test of raising twins on her own seem orderly. We don't talk as often as I wish, lives get crazy, but we are always there for each other, tuned in. A month can go by, and we'll pick up like it's been one second, so much history behind us it's effortless.

I write: I think I am blowing up what is left of my life. I have no idea what I am doing here in France. I seem to be completely lost. Sophie is homesick and I am thinking maybe this was all a huge mistake.

Blowing up . . . how?

Well, for one, I slept with another guy. A French guy. A hot French guy.

. . .

. . .

. . .

Okay, this is going to be a long thing, I think. What is she writing? I swallow a lump of phlegm in my throat.

Oh Alice! She writes that first.

Then: You have been through a lot. I read that and tears start flowing down my cheeks. There is more coming. More of those three dots.

. . .

I'm not sure what my role as the girls' godmother and your friend is. Did you want to do it?

Betsy, of course I wanted to!!!!!

Were you trying to hurt Pete, I guess I mean? Like get back?

No.

Nothing in response. No dots. She isn't responding. So I write more. His name is Didier. He was in this chalet. And he looked at me like . . . he looked at me without pity, like totally clean of everything—the cancer, Pete. People are different here. They don't care about all that backstory as much. They see you as a person first. Or something. I can't work it out.

And?

And, I don't know—he just SAW me. He saw the hole in my chest. He saw my pain. He got me. And then . . .

He fucked you.

Um . . . yeah?

Honey, I think we need to talk on the phone. Texting won't unpack this.

Are you mad at me? I say it out loud as I write it, and my voice sounds small, unsure.

For cheating on Pete? Absolutely not. For doing it right under Sophie's nose, a bit.

I feel a pain in my temple. Can we talk now?

Not now—I am just finishing my exercises and I have to shower this morning and I still have to clean up the kitchen from last night and make the kids' lunches and breakfast and then I am taking Willie to the vet—he stepped on some glass. I am running late and can't really focus like I need to. Text me when you can talk again later? In the meantime, just be careful, Alice. Make sure you talk to Sophie.

It's hard.

I get it. But she needs you to talk to her. Gotta go. I promise I am here for you and we'll talk later today. I love you.

I put the phone down, dissatisfied. Somehow Betsy has made me feel worse, more alone, though I am sure that's not what she intended. It's the limits of texting and her available time and a time zone change which create this lack of warmth, of resolution. I try hard to concentrate on the grasses in front of me, the sun on my shoulders. I take some deep breaths. And then I remember a yoga class I took sometime just after we got back to New York, before the surgery, and before I started all the treatments. It was online, in the evening. I was in our bedroom, facing the river out beyond our magnolia tree, and I could see lights coming on in other people's apartments to the right and left of our building. Out my window, I could see the blurry gray outline of "my tree" (as I liked to call it, though I certainly didn't own it) and the Hudson beyond. And I could also see myself reflected back in the lights from my bedroom. The teacher was hairy, named Rob. And I remember this one moment: We'd just gone into tree pose and Rob was playing that song, "There's something happening here / What it is ain't exactly clear . . ." And I had my foot wedged against my groin and my fingers were stretching up to the sky and Rob said, "There are only two rules today: Show up and breathe. Show up and breathe." And I was stretching my fingers and I was breathing and for a second I felt like maybe they were leaves at the ends of my arms, maybe I was a tree, like in *Runaway Bunny* when the mother is the tree, or maybe I was Daphne changing into a tree, and I was crying and I was looking at myself dead in the eye in my reflection in the windows and I was telling myself, "Just breathe. Just breathe." The body, I read once, no idea where, is just a vessel for the soul.

There is a sound of low singing nearby, and when I turn, Marie appears in the field. She is wearing a long red tunic with wide sleeves and there's beautiful gold and blue stitching around the neck. She is carrying a colander that she is filling with what appear to be berries from along the taller hedgerow of bushes. Something pangs inside me, this wish that I'd never been sick, a wish that I wasn't currently blowing up my already-blown-up life, a wish that I could just escape to France for good, grow back my breast like a fat cucumber in a garden, gather berries and wear tunics and forget everything that has happened before.

But my children. My children. They are tied to me, pulling me backward, "ceaselessly," as the great book says, "into the past."

When I wave, Marie doesn't see me at first, and then, when she does, her smile makes everything seem okay, manageable. She comes across the field, stopping to pick more berries, and then, finally, sits next to me on the rock, the breeze tousling our hair. She is wearing those clacking bracelets, and she has the thinnest gold necklace rippling like a tiny snake across her clavicle and then on around her neck. Her colander is full of perfect red raspberries.

"The sun is so hot already." I point to it, in case this isn't translating. "And . . ." I hold up my notebook. "I need to work a little bit."

"Aha. You Americans are always working."

"Yeah, well. I am here in order to write. And . . . I haven't written anything like this in a long time, so it's like . . . I sort of have to . . . try."

Marie gives me a smile then, at once wistful and compassionate. Somehow just sitting with this woman, her soothing voice, her steadiness, I feel like I'm in an Esther Perel session, cared for, held, in the presence of greatness.

"Do you work, Marie?"

"Yes, I do." She smiles into the sun. I'm not sure if she's going to tell me what she does or not, but I realize that maybe it doesn't matter. I've just done this American thing of needing a label to connect with a person. As if our jobs define us more than anything else. Aren't we all just imperfect humans knocking into each other on this fragile earth?

After a long beat she offers, "I design clothes. For women. I have a studio in one of the barns." She tilts her head back up the field. "And I go up to my atelier in Paris once a month. But mostly I get to be here." She stretches her hand out to the sea then to the field and olive trees, all around us is this empty space where it seems like it's just us and only us, two women working out the problems in our lives and perhaps other lives, too. She closes her eyes and tilts her face back into the warm sunlight and pulls her hair back from around her ears.

"You know—all this—this place, the beauty of it, it's only part of my story. Georges, he is a good father. But he cheated on me in the beginning. Addie was only four. Alain and Claude just babies. My father had died. I was alone in this country with Georges and three boys. I was just finishing my fashion apprenticeship. She was a French woman. White. Her daughters were in the nursery school with Addie. I say to him, 'If you don't stop it, I will go back to Africa with the boys.' So he stopped. At least he said he did. And I gave him one more boy as punishment." And then she laughs.

I try to smile. But I have questions, lots of questions. Something about this woman, her statuesque features, her self-possession, her intention in the world, her lack of flailing around, makes me hesitate, like any interrogation would be wrong, unseemly.

"I cheated on my husband here in France. Just two days ago," I blurt. Surprising even myself. I hear her inhale. I don't want to look at her. "At a chalet we found in the Alps. That was why we were late here."

"Why?"

"My husband cheated on me. For years. And then we split up. And I was alone in Maine . . ."

"Le Maine?" She turns to me, breaking that fourth wall that separates the audience from the stage in a theater, when the actor just simply speaks right to you, like an angel touched down from up high. Marie and I have confessed our truths while looking out at the sea. Similar to how Sophie and I used to talk when we watched a show, little bits she'd share about herself while watching *Gilmore Girls*, never making eye contact.

"Oh, it's a state. North of Boston? Country. Ocean, like this—but cold. Fields, like this, and pine trees instead of olive trees. During Covid, we went there."

"Wow. We came here, from Paris. And moved into the carriage house and created my studio here. We sold our house in Paris, kept only my studio in Le Marais. So much changed."

"And then I got cancer." We both look out at the sea again, the fourth wall back up, our shoulders brushing. I feel the warm heat of another woman next to me, her breath, her softness.

"And then?"

"And then he came back to me. We did the entire thing—I lost my breast. And then some of my hair." I start to cry now, unexpectedly, in front of this woman I barely know. I feel her arm come around me, and when I turn back to her, I see she has tears in her eyes, too. Oh to have a friend cry with you!

"Come with me. I have some oil for your hair. To help it grow strong again."

"The girls?"

"*Oui*. You have paper! Leave them a note. Tell them to come up to the garden in the big house. I'll meet you there. Okay?"

I do as Marie says, pulling a piece of paper out of my notebook. I watch her holding the colander full of berries and going back up the field ahead of me. I write the note, I go to the cabin and splash water on my face and throw on a sundress and press a knitted ball where my left breast should be, muffling my beating heart, hiding the hole where the phantom lurks. I brush out my thin hair and put some mascara on.

In an hour, the girls find me outside on the patio under the lemon trees with Marie massaging a thick lemon rosemary oil into my scalp and hair and neck and rubbing my shoulders and head with her strong hands. As she kneads, she is singing a catchy song I don't know: "*Oh, Djadja / Y a pas moyen, Djadja . . .*"

"Mama," Iris squeals, and climbs onto my lap. "I didn't know where you were!"

"I'm right here, Pickle. Marie is taking care of me." Iris beams at Marie, who continues to massage the lemon oil into my hair and sing. Sophie hovers, awkward, until Penelope comes out, dressed and ready for the day, "*Allez, les filles! On n'a pas mangé?* Have you eaten?" The girls shake their heads, and before I know it, Penelope is serving them fruit, juice, and croissants under the lemon trees and everything smells of citrus, rosemary, fresh bread, and berries.

30.
SOPHIE

That morning, Sophie had been writing in her diary while Iris was still sleeping in a sweaty mass, mouth open, sunlight making the tent boiling, salt air drying their lips and making them crack:

I remember this feeling from when school would get out, or when we were in Maine and driving in the car and my parents were playing music and laughing, or when all the doors and windows were open in the summer and the air was coming through the house and there was nothing planned and it felt like freedom but also a bit like falling and it was scary and ok at the same time. If I were to tell you how France feels to me, it is that. Falling and free at the same time. It feels like pages in my life are getting turned faster than I can read them, but there is information I need on those pages . . .

When she read back over what she had written, she felt proud of it. It felt profound. True. When Iris woke up, they got dressed and meandered, together, slowly up the field in the sun and to the manor as if they were born there.

Alain comes out as the girls are eating breakfast. He looks tired, puffy, his blue-green eyes shining like a cat's. He looks over at Sophie, then away to his grandmother, who hands him a plate with four croissants. Sophie's brow is suddenly sweaty. She bends her head to her food, focusing on the bowl of strawberries in front of her.

Last night in the dark, while her mother was talking with Marie, and when Iris had dozed off leaning against her mother, Alain had asked Sophie to come join a game of Frisbee next to the "maze." He told her that the maze had been planted who knows how long ago and that if you were high above in a plane, which he has done in his father's small Jodel (she gathers this is a kind of small plane), you can decipher the pattern. Down on the ground, trying to find your way through just gets you hot, confused, angry, and stung by nettles that grow on the edges of the privet, he said. Though some of the other teens milled in and out of the maze, going off to smoke cigarettes or pot, or to make out, then laugh and splash in the pool, Alain and Sophie had thrown the Frisbee back and forth. A huge lighted candle stuck onto an iron pyre at the edge of the maze showed them where to leap and which direction to throw. And so the two had settled into a silent conversation, the only medium being the Frisbee. Sophie couldn't help but notice his chest and arms and the way his hair bounced about his face, sometimes getting tangled in a leather necklace he wore that had black beads separating three white shells which dangled, making a small triangle on his chest. And then her mother had called from the other side of the hedge that they had to take Iris back, and when she turned to hand Alain the Frisbee, had she imagined it or had he touched her wrist, just the tiniest bit, a small glance, like from a sword, that zinged right through her.

Of course, like all kids, Sophie had thought about whether she liked boys or girls, she had thought about sexuality, she had fantasized about Paul McCartney when he was young, she had liked other boys in New York, maybe even liked girls, too, she wasn't really sure, as the rushy-ness of her hormones was so confusing it was hard to figure out what she felt about anything at all. The only solution to her confusion she could think of that might make the intensity of the feelings stop was to go home, get out of France. So she had told her mother that.

Often, Sophie felt her stomach slip and slide between intense emotions, which seemed to bleed like the way her period soaked into the cotton nighttime pads her mother supplied her with, staining outward and making a thin, dry line at the edges until the next warm, unprovoked rush of blood. When she'd told her mother she missed home, she had. Missed home. Missed her dad. All of that she felt strongly. But she also felt hot and wet in between her legs when she thought of Alain, and she felt her breath catch, too. And the idea of just that Frisbee, the way it was still warm on the edges where he had touched it, made her anxious. Lying in bed that night, her mother smelling faintly of raspberries and alcohol, the wind from the sea coming through the netting and caressing their faces, Sophie had felt this intense *wishing* that she were small again, young enough to curl against her mother, and that her mother would explain to her that all these feelings were okay, normal. But something had happened to Sophie in the last few years, some strange curtain had closed. And even if she wanted to share more about her life and her thoughts, her feelings, it was like the words couldn't find a way out, as if her voice box had receded somewhere deep into her neck, too far down for retrieval. She felt that she had to sort her feelings out on her own, and she figured that maybe growing up meant you handled it all by yourself, all the time.

Now it is morning, and she doesn't ever want to go home. It surprises her that this is just as intense a feeling as thinking the night before that she wanted to go home. There are strawberries now, and this tall giraffe of a woman, Penelope, to fill every need, and Marie is massaging her mother with lemony oils, and there are croissants. Her mother seems happy, peaceful, healed, normal. And then there is Alain.

Soon there are more teens in the kitchen, all hungry, giggling, talking in French, the boys grabbing unabashedly at the croissants while the girls pick up solitary strawberries. The girls are wearing shorts that start just under their breasts and end before their legs begin. These girls wear bralettes, which leave a strip of tan rib cage. The boys smell like smoke and bleach from the pool, and they are all bumping into each other and smiling secretly.

Sophie eats slowly, listening to her mother with Marie, watching her sister pull her croissant into little bits, watching the teenagers. Sophie wonders if she should be eating as much as she is, which makes her touch her stomach nervously and feel the edge of it pushing into her jean shorts.

The more she watches these French girls, who seem more like women to her, she feels herself get smaller. But then she hears a voice, deeper than one might expect, behind her: "Eh—Sophie, *viens à la piscine?* The pool? *Avec nous?*" It's Addie, not Alain. Claude and Alain stand a bit off to the side. She looks into Alain's blue-green eyes. He nods, ever so slightly.

Sophie turns to her mother and says, "Alice. Can I go swim with them?"

Her mother looks up. "Yes, Sophie. But not Iris—Iris, you need to stay with me. After lunch, we will swim in the Mediterranean. We leave tomorrow morning, you know." And off Sophie goes to find her bathing suit in the hot tent, to fix her hair and apply some lip gloss in the small cabin.

Then she is sitting on the side of the pool, her golden legs hanging into the blue square, quietly taking in the teens smoking, playing music on their speakers, and laughing. Though invited, she feels lonelier than ever sitting here, a part but not a part.

Adelard has strung a net across the pool and brought out a volleyball. Then with quick and officious masculinity he divides the teams, putting Sophie on the girls' side, the boys on the other. The game begins: diving, punching the ball, laughing, heart thumping inside her chest as she tries to parse language in French, water, sport, boy.

31.

ALICE

Marie has invited Iris to help massage the oil into my scalp, and soon I feel my daughter's little hands on my head, my neck; her tender, knowing touch. In the distance, I can hear the older kids laughing and shouting, splashing and the hard thwack of the ball. For a moment, newly confessed, I feel the happiest I've felt in a while, my anxiety no longer crawling through me like a demon. Then the phone dings, once, twice. Then it rings. Pete. I've totally forgotten about Pete. I've not called, not suggested the girls call, nothing. It's like France has swallowed us into a totally different life, some sort of place where my real life and this trip aren't even connected anymore, as if we've not just gone through the wardrobe but arrived in a parallel universe, and everything we do or feel in this other world might have no bearing on our real lives. My heart sinks when I see it is my husband. There are real implications to all this, the phone reminds me.

"Excuse me, Marie—Iris, stop! It's Daddy. I need to get this." I pick up the phone, my fingers oily on the screen. "Hey."

"Alice." There is a firmness in his voice. "You're doing the thing again, where you fucking vanish."

"Just a second, Pete." And then to Iris, "Honey, I am walking over there to the trees for a second to talk to Daddy, okay? Marie, will you be here for a second more?" Marie nods and beckons to Iris to go with her while she picks up plates, bits of napkin, and strawberry tops from the patio.

I launch in, unabashed, angry already, spewing fury with no humility. "Really? Me? You think having an affair wasn't vanishing?"

"Jesus. Will we ever get past that? Haven't we been on the rinse cycle here for a couple of years? You've just dropped out. It feels aggressive, Alice."

"*I* drop out?"

"You have no idea what I've been through, Alice."

"You? What *you* have been through?" I roar back. And then I start crying. I have no idea why I cry when I'm angry, cry when I'm sad, cry when I'm overwhelmed, cry when I'm scared, cry when they're all rolled into one. Outrage smashes like glass inside me, a million dangerous pieces, everywhere. "It always comes back to *you*. No matter what happens. I'm just living, Pete. Trying to find myself again. Trying to think about writing. Trying to be alive. Not dead. Not dead! You don't know what that's like!"

"I understand. I mean, I do." His voice softens, sickeningly. A crack.

I take a breath in and then hurl more into the opening: "No. Actually, you have no fucking idea, dude." I choke. Then, more softly I say, "I am just trying to totally be here in France and, fuck—Pete, I—" Oh my God, what am I about to do? This is napalm. But I can't stop it.

"I—I did what you did."

"You what?" He's caught off guard.

"I slept with someone else, Pete."

"What? Who?" He's been slapped when he thinks we've just connected.

"At the chalet. The guy who owned it."

"The guy who cooked all the food, played the jazz on the stereo, *that* guy?" Pete's voice sounds strangled and high-pitched all of a sudden.

"Yes, that guy." I stop crying then. I feel angry again. Defensive.

"What the hell are you doing, Alice? Our daughters were there with you."

"I know. They don't know. They were sleeping."

"You think Sophie doesn't know?"

"Jesus, Pete, you weren't exactly subtle. She knows about you. Don't you even try to turn this around on me."

"Well, you got me, Alice. Jesus fucking Christ. I've been there and been there and been there for you. Through cancer. Fuck. I feel sick. You've made me feel sick. I knew it."

"Are you hearing yourself? Do you have zero humility, Pete? Zero self-awareness?" I'm enraged all over again now. I can feel hot tears on my cheeks, and I'm stomping my feet. I want to kick something, smash a branch of a nearby olive tree, gnash the grass with my teeth.

"Well, I guess we're fucking even then, Alice. Does that make it better?" Do I almost hear victory in Pete's voice? It's like, finally, though he is angry, hurt, appalled, he is aware that now, if he plays this right, he is vindicated.

"Maybe. I don't know."

It's quiet on the end of the line. I think I hear him shatter, like maybe he's crying. I hear him give a jagged breath. Then, "Is it *a thing*, Alice? Like a thing you want?"

"Of course not. It's France. I've left there. I don't—" I stop. Slow down. Did I dream of it being a thing? Did I want to reconnect with Didier? I'm not sure. Was this what Pete felt? Wrong and also like he wanted more? God, what a toxic fucking purgatory to hang out in. So I say, "I know it was wrong. And we've left now. And we are leaving here. We are going west. And I can think when we do. And I am sorry. I really am."

"Were you trying to hurt me? I mean . . ." His voice trails off.

"Do you actually think people do that? Have affairs to get even?" I sound whiny, pathetic.

Silence. He's back in charge, on top. He knows it. His voice gets officious: "We'll have to figure it out when you are back. I have to go to work now. I want to talk to the girls."

"Not right now. Sophie is playing volleyball, and Iris is with Marie."

"Who the fuck is Marie, Alice?"

"Our friend. Here at the house. I can't explain."

"Alice, you can't keep our kids from me."

"Jesus, Pete, I am not trying to. I promise. I'm barely—" I realize I am sobbing, snot on my face, trying to use the hem of my dress to wipe it off. "I am barely recovered. I am so scared all the fucking time. I am trying to not feel and also feel and be alive and not die. Do you understand? I'm lost. Really lost. And I'm trying to find some path back to not lost, to whoever this new Alice person is, this one with one breast, hot flashes, moods, a husband who cheated, a tiny desire to be a writer, and a bigger desire to be a good mother—I am trying to find that new Alice. Does any of that make any sense to you?"

Then it's Pete my friend, the guy who has known me a long

time, with whom I share two daughters, who has been there during cancer, who cried on my shoulder when both his mother and his father died earlier than either of us could have expected. It's *that* Pete who reaches through the line and takes my hand, looks into my snot-covered face, and has mercy: "Alice, I understand. I do. You did the right thing, telling me. I was too much of a coward to tell you. If we want to, we can fix this."

"What if we can't?"

"That will only be because we don't want to. Because we decided to keep smashing everything. We can choose the other direction. To fix it."

"Are you sure?"

"I think so." I hear him take a deep breath. I can hear the physical effort this all is costing him. Then he says it again, less sure: "I think so?"

"We will call you when we leave to go get lunch. Okay?"

"Okay." He sounds like he is exhausted, a paper bag crumpled at the bottom of the recycling bin. "I need to go."

"Okay," I say. But just before I hit end, I hear him gasp and then the call is over.

There was this interview I heard once with an Irish writer, I don't remember his name. He was talking about Irish women leaving their families to move to America. And how there was a tradition of women getting aboard the boat and their mother or father or loved one was on land holding one end of a ball of yarn on the dock or beach and the other end was held by the woman on the boat. That yarn would unravel and get wet as it touched the ocean, and finally, the parent or loved one back home would let go, and then the woman on the boat would roll up the wet yarn and take it with her, holding on forever to their connection, and a bit of Irish sea.

I sit there against the olive tree and cry about the yarn tied around my heart, the yarn that still attaches me to Pete, and how, no matter what you do sometimes, that yarn is still there, stretched between you, fastening you to each other. I can almost feel it tug inside me, pull and stretch, the knot tighter, about to burst apart if I yank a tiny bit harder, or if I simply trip. My breath feels squeezed out of me, and I have to lean down and put my head on my knees.

When I go back to Marie, she is sitting on the patio and playing checkers with Iris. I take one look and I realize that I just want my kids to myself, to get back in the car. I need to get out of here.

My mouth is dry when I say, "Iris, hey. Go find your sister. We need to go get lunch and do a few things before we leave tomorrow."

"Okay," Iris grumbles.

When she is gone, I follow Marie into the kitchen where she is slicing long green zucchinis for dinner. Penelope has gone off to write letters in her office, and Georges is managing the estate in his tall boots, olive-colored jeans and lavender T-shirt. Marie drinks a glass of water and fixes her gaze on me at the kitchen sink.

"You will go home, to your husband." She says it like a statement, no question mark. Maybe she's the kind of woman who always speaks with periods at the end of her sentences. She does seem *that* self-assured. I feel my mind wandering for a second as I think about that. I am a person who speaks in questions, circles. I turn to look into Marie's eyes. I want some of her sureness, her strength. I want her to bounce-pass whatever it is I am missing from her to me. Her eyes are large and the color of cashews burnished in a warm oven. My breath is catching in my throat and tears are streaming down my face again. Those darn tears!

"You love your husband. I can see it in everything here—with these girls, with your body after that phone call." She takes my hand and sits me down, her soft shape close to mine, her leg warm against me.

I feel myself whisper another question: "How am I ever going to fix this?"

"You will. You will go home and fix it. People can fix anything. Trust me. I am African—we have fixed so many things, even when the whole world laughs at us and judges us for being the most backward place. We know how to fix a tin can. We know how to patch a bucket. We can find value in anything, even your American trash. You can, too. It just will be different, that's all."

I feel myself nod, snot streaming, shoulders quaking. Marie's hand is on my shoulder, rubbing. Then I am leaning against her, breathing in her lemony smell, and I feel so small. As she holds me, I hear Iris come back, scuffing the floor, dirt on her little knees like she's been crawling under a hedge or a rosebush, leaves in her hair. "Mama, she's not there."

"What do you mean she's not there? Of course she is." I blow my nose on a paper towel.

"Nope. She's not at the pool, Alice." Sometimes Iris holds her ground in an unnerving and very irritating way.

"Okay, let me go." I look at Marie, wipe my face, try to smile, and go off calling, "Sophie, Sophie!"

• • •

The pool is, as Iris has told me, devoid of the teens. Someone has left a speaker pumping American rap music on a glass table. Next to the pool is a sort of cabin or pool house. I can hear muffled laughter inside. I ask Iris, "Did you go in here?"

"No. You told me to look at the pool." I take my daughter in for a second. She's this weird bird I am sometimes miffed by. "Iris . . ." I am about to argue, but I remember that this is always who she is: literal, distracted, probably found a butterfly or an ant to chase.

When I open the door, I see couches and a pool table and teens sprawled around, smoking cigarettes. The girls are still wearing their bathing suit tops and have pulled on jean shorts. The boys wear only shorts. Some are playing pool, others just lounging, laughing, whispering. At first I don't see my daughter, everything else is so distracting, all those bodies on display, the red lips of the girls, the abs of the boys, the pumping candy-shop sexuality. And then I see that Sophie is sitting with another girl and is quickly extinguishing a cigarette. My mouth opens and closes. I know enough not to say a thing. Yet.

Iris, behind me, is whistling under her breath, "Oh dear. Oh dear. Oh dear."

All I say is: "Sophie Anne. Now." Looking back, I will say that I was very calm. Later, Sophie will tell me I screamed at her and was "so embarrassing." I stand outside and wait. I don't give two flying fucks if those French teens think I am a disaster. I want my daughter out here, now.

When she comes outside, the door barely closed, I take her shoulder and say, rougher than I should, "Come on." As soon as we are a few feet away, I pull up, Iris knocking into me and staring. I say, "Sophie. You are not even fourteen. What the hell are you doing with a cigarette?"

"I barely tried it. I mostly just held it."

"Let me smell your breath." I lean in. She closes her lips tightly and looks defiantly right back at me. "Sophie, I can smell it."

A thin bolt of honesty zings across her face: My daughter is no liar. "I did try it. But it was gross. So I just held it."

"I am so disappointed! In *you*! Sophie!" I glare. I want to point my index finger at her but think better of it. Teenagers are sort of scary, I don't care what anyone tells you. We are standing now in a little shady alley behind some hedges, a path back to the house stretching in one direction, the pool house in the other.

Sophie smirks. "Yeah, and I'm not, like, at *all* disappointed in you, Alice." The look on her face is fierce and infuriating; honestly, it's riot-inducing in its impudence.

"Sophie. I. Am. Your. Parent." I punctuate these words, ridiculously, with my finger pointing at some mid-zone—not exactly her face, but not exactly the ground or the sky, like I can't make up my mind. "I am here to keep you safe. You also need to keep *you* safe."

"I was perfectly safe, Alice."

"Why are you being so rude?"

"Just chill, Alice. Chill, my God, chill." Her armor is locked, soldered, fallen into the salty Mediterranean.

"I'm not going to *just chill*, Sophie. Why are you acting like this?"

"Because."

"Because?"

"Because you never do anything I want. You took me to Maine. You bring me here. You make Daddy leave. You got sick and you didn't get an implant so you look gross and weird. Oh, and yeah, you almost died, or did you forget that part?"

I start laughing. It's a reflex born out of shock. But my laughter makes her red-faced and furious. She hurls her final blow: "And then? What about here in France, Alice? You fucking abandon us. For a guy. A French guy. And what about us? What about Daddy?" She lets that all sink in and then her coup de grâce: "And I." Suddenly, she is sobbing. "I just. Hate. You."

I know I should want, in this moment, to comfort my daughter. But I somehow can't. Her list of gripes on top of the conversation with Pete, the hot sun, the smell of the dusty privet hedge, the feeling that we've gotten lost in someone else's fabulous French life, all of it becomes too much. I look from my older daughter to my younger one. "Come on," I say. "Time to go." And walk away.

• • •

That afternoon, the girls and I go swimming after getting things for our own lunch in the small town. The girls talk to Pete in the car while I do the shopping. Later at the beach, Sophie rolls the top of her suit down. I tell her to put it back up and she says no, her eyes leveled at me, challenging. "Girls here do it. No one is looking. I like it."

"Sophie Anne."

"Look, Alice. In America, nudity is stressful. But here, in France, it's not." To punctuate this thought, she smears sunblock on her perfect, pale chest.

I want to say something about what a philosopher she has become. I want to jump up and yell and scream and stomp my feet on that rocky shore and roar like the lion this gulf is named for.

Instead, I watch and remember having two breasts. And I

close my mouth and don't say any more. I walk to the water and wade in and then dive under and swim as long as I can, the water cool through the bathing suit on the one nipple I still have. When I finally come up, I see my daughters on a French beach, cliffs above them, and above that, the bluest sky I've ever seen. I think about Pete crying and how I felt when I found out he had cheated on me. I feel my stomach drop and I dive back into the water, lost to my girls, to myself, to my husband.

Iris is in the shallow water as I swim back to my girls. She is diving over and over, spluttering up, pushing onto her forehead a pair of goggles I bought her at the *tabac* in town, talking to me, then pulling them back down, diving again. When I come near her, I say, "Hey, Pickle, can I have a hug?" She reaches for me and wraps her wet body around mine. Just as I am about to put her back down into the water, to let her swim away, she says into my ear, "It must be hard to be a mom." I feel tears again on my cheeks, or maybe it's just French sea, I don't know anymore.

Sophie stays topless on the shore in the sun while Iris and I share her goggles and paddle around. We see kelp and shells. And then Iris leaps out of the water and says, "Mama, an octopus!" "No," I say, incredulous, laughing, amazed. We both look down and there, pretending it's a pile of sand, eyes bulging, is the shiest-looking creature I've ever seen. We watch it creep away, look back at us, creep some more, until it disappears in a cloud of silt under a rock. Our joy at seeing this wonderful creature is so huge, we fall into each other, hugging and hooting. Sophie calls from the shore, "Guys, what?"

"An octopus, we saw an octopus, Sophie!" I look to the shore and try to read my older daughter's face. Does she feel left out? I can't tell. I just wish she had been with us, also laughing.

That night we eat sandwiches while sitting on the grass, and we all go to bed when it gets dark. I am ready to go to the next place, to be in motion once more.

In the morning, the wind is insane. It's so strong that it's blowing us over as we try to pack up the tent, the mattress pads, and the sleeping bags. It dries our eyes and our mouths. When we take one last swim in our little cove, we are tossed around, thrown up on the beach, chucked left and right, and it makes me feel nauseated, vulnerable, scared. I want to get out of here. The girls laugh and bodysurf. Iris, especially, loves the chaos of it. She argues with me when I say it's time to go.

When we finally pack the car, our hair almost dry from those mistral winds, we go back to the house to say goodbye to Marie and all her sons and Penelope and Georges. Marie presses a jar of cherry jam into my hands; Penelope puts her hands on both sides of my girls' faces, cupping them for a second, her gaze firmly on theirs, and tells them to come back to her one day. Without my seeing, she presses a small silver cicada into each girl's palm, which they show me as we drive away. We are going west, toward the Pyrenees. Just the two girls and me in the car, and no music. The windows are open and the only sound is of the wind and more wind. We are all lost in our own thoughts.

PART 3

Les Pyrénées

32.

IRIS

Iris has the windows open, and her skin feels tight and her body exhausted from one last jump into that salty, crazy Gulf of Lions. Her mother is driving through oil-tank farms, along the sea, and then through salt marshes with flamingos standing in pools of water. They drive through a small town with cobblestone streets and buildings covered with strawberry-flowered cacti. There are so many things to see. But Iris has fallen asleep.

At some point, from deep inside the hot sticky haze of a car nap, Iris can hear her mother and Sophie whispering.

"Is she asleep?"

"Oh, yeah."

"Okay, I can go in. Can you stay in the car, Sophs?"

"I wanted to get out. I need to pee."

"Okay. Let me wake her."

And then Iris hears the car door open, and even though it feels so good to keep her eyes closed, the hot sun on her T-shirt, the seat belt swaddlingly tight across her chest and her mother rubbing her shoulder, she hears, "Pickle. Pickle. Can you wake up? We are in a town. And Sophie needs to pee and I need coffee or a Coke and we have more driving to do. How about an Orangina?"

"Mama?"

"Yes, sweetie."

"I was dreaming." Her mother smooths her bangs off her sweaty forehead and answers, "Hmmm?"

"I was dreaming about sleeping on a beach in the calanques and there was lavender all around me, as far as you could see, right up until the water started and Sophie was there, but she was really far away and she had forgotten I was there. I was waking up and trying to call to her, but every time I called, the wind took my words away and the wind was warm . . . And she vanished, like, I don't know, around the corner, or into the wind?"

She hears Sophie's voice now. "Okay, we get the point, Booby. Let's go."

"Come on, Pickle, should I carry you?"

"No, I'm okay." Iris bounds out, pulling her navy and white checked shorts down from where they have bunched between her legs, shaking out her sandals so they aren't stuck to the bottoms of her feet, and rubbing her eyes, her satchel slung across her chest and full of important little things like a rock she found in the Alps, a lavender stalk from the field by their tent in Provence, the silver cicada from Penelope, and a small seashell Marie had pressed into her hand, saying, "This is from Senegal. It's called a *cauri*. I think in English it is 'cowrie shell.' It will bring you good luck."

In the bakery, Iris holds her mother's hand while her sister uses the toilet and her mother orders three *jambon-beurre* sandwiches and two blood-orange Pellegrinos and one Coca-Cola. And then they are driving again and eating and Ed Sheeran is on the radio singing: "But darling, just kiss me slow / Your heart is all I own . . ."

Later, Iris will remember how she noticed that they were all quiet, almost holding their breath, the three of them, listening to these words sung so sincerely about love. And even though it seemed like a reach to understand, Iris got it, somewhere deep inside her, she got the dancing in the dark, she got the longing, she got that her mother and her sister were hearing it differently than she, and that they were both feeling something older, more complicated, more mysterious, and so she felt something, too, because where they ended and where she began was never exactly clear, even though she was the lone passenger in the back seat, the same seat she used to share with Sophie until Sophie got older.

And then they are in the mountains, and Sophie and her mother are pointing and saying, "Oh my God, look at them," and Iris looks out her window and can see trees burned like matchsticks rising up mountains that loom, and she hears her mother call back to her, "Pickle, on the other side is Spain!" They are heading up along the side of the mountains now, and there are cows grazing under the burned trees, and Iris is wondering what in the world is happening to the planet with fires and viruses and heat and tsunamis and floods and wars.

"Mommy, what happens to the birds when there's a fire?" she asks.

"I guess I imagine them flying out," says her mother.

"But lots of animals aren't that fast. Babies."

"That's true. But sometimes, I think, maybe it's often, I don't know, somebody gets out."

Iris thinks about that for a second. She is picturing a book she used to have with pictures of Noah and his ark. What would a person take to get out of a fire? she wonders. A hot-air balloon?

"What about the ones that don't get out, Mommy?"

"Jesus, Booby," says her sister from the front seat.

Her mother is silent, and Iris knows she is thinking. She also knows that on some level these kinds of questions hurt her mother, leave her mother feeling skinned. Iris just wants to know, that's all. Later she'll wish she hadn't asked all that.

"I love you, Pickle. Trying to understand something as big as a fire like this is hard. There's a line I heard Michelle Obama say when I was listening to her a lot while I was sick. I think of it all the time. Maybe it will help you like it helps me? She said, 'The world will remain both beautiful and broken.'"

"God, you guys. Too much. All the time." Her older sister again, intolerant of the ways she and her mother shovel into the wet pooling layer beneath the hot, dry beach sand. Just leave it be, is all her sister wants.

• • •

"Okay, we are almost there!" Her mother is trying to sound bright now.

They pull off onto a dirt road and the burned trees give way to short, squat olive trees. They finally come to stop at an old rambling building made of crumbling stones with flowers growing all over it. Iris can barely see outside the car window, it is so covered with ash and soot.

"Okay, girls. Next stop," her mother says. They all sit and peer. "Looks dry," says Iris.

A wide wooden door opens and a big white dog with long hair and huge ears comes galloping out, and then comes an old woman onto the stone veranda dressed all in black, her white hair tied in a bun on the top of her head with an orange ribbon. Her tan arms are covered with silver bangles. She is motioning to them and saying something they can't quite hear, and then her mother opens the door and is smiling and saying in beautifully fast French (It has come back! thinks Iris), "*Bonjour, bonjour. Oui, je m'appelle* Alice*! Oui, je suis avec mes deux filles. J'arrive . . .*"

33.
ALICE

The woman is named Nanette. Her words sound different than Georges and Marie's, her R's roll like the drum section in an orchestra. She motions with a craggy hand to a brown field and a bald, dirt-covered area where I can see a rickety blue metal table under an almond tree. "*Amandier,*" she says, after all, an easyish word to understand. There is a firepit there, I can see that. But no logs, a rusty grate over it. She windmills her hands and says, "*Pas de feu!*" over and over, pointing to the firepit. "No fire," I say, nodding.

Not far from the field, along the edges of the mountains, are more charred trees. The sun bakes down, and I know immediately that I need to get more provisions. We stopped not far from the mountains and bought some jugs of water, baguettes and butter, sliced ham, a cheese, and plums. But the heat and the scorched look of this makes me think these supplies are not going to be enough. I thank Nanette and make a lot of motions with my hands to indicate that we are going to go set up our tent (my French can bubble and flow one moment, then trickle through my brain, barely retrievable, the next), the girls peering out the windows of the car at me like "Oh my God, is this hell?"

Nanette goes back, muttering, into the low stone house. Beyond the house, I can see black cattle and hear them lowing in a wide field with sheep meandering in between, munching on field flowers and reaching into the low branches of the greener trees here and there. Beyond the animals, I see a wide, rocky stream. There are two white horses drinking; wild, as far as I can tell.

"Girls," I say. "Let's set up the tent. This place is exciting. Different."

"Is a fire coming *here*, Mommy?" Iris asks, her eyes very wide.

"No, not right now. That was weeks before. Before we even came, I think."

"It smells smoky, burnt," says Iris. Sophie is scowling. She has been scowling since we left Provence, except when she sang along to Ed Sheeran. Snark takes over before I can even think. "Sophs, you must like that smell. Familiar, right?"

Iris looks at her sister, a combination of humor and empathy playing over her face. I've put her in a funny position; I'm making her choose allegiances. If she were to ask, I'd say, "Always choose your sister." She doesn't ask.

"Shut up, Alice." Sophie kicks herself out of the car, grabs some of the camping gear, and takes off to the field, the big white dog trailing after her. I see her turn and glare at the dog, who stops, sits, then follows her once again when she starts walking. Iris starts to giggle. "Mama," she whispers, "that dog is following Sophie!"

Nanette comes back out and hands me a green bottle with no label, and a round of what I assume is cheese; it is cold and wrapped in fig leaves and smells pungent. "*Merci, merci,*" I say, and Iris smiles shyly from behind me. She whispers, "Can you ask her the name of the dog?"

"*Um, le chien?*" I point to the dog. And then say belatedly, "*Nom?*"

"*Eh?* Manou." She says *manou* almost like "manure" but missing the "re." "*C'est un Patou. Comme le chien dans Belle et Sébastien! Les patous sont partout ici. C'est le chien des Pyrénées.*"

"*Merci.*" I smile. She's said a lot of words.

"*Il est très gentil,*" she assures us, smiling and nodding at Iris, which I take to mean the dog won't bite.

"Manou? *Oui?*" I ask again.

"*Mais, oui.* Manou. Manou, *viens!*" she calls to the dog.

But Manou has other plans and is still dutifully following my daughter on rickety large-dog hips. He lazily stops, turns his head back to his owner, then continues on after the angry Sophie. "I think it's Manou, sweetie," I tell Iris, as if she hasn't already understood that this word Nanette has said several times must be the dog's name.

When we get to the campsite, carrying our mats and bags, Sophie has the tent almost set up. She is angrily shoving the stakes into the ground, pounding them with her heels. Her long, tan biceps and her streaked blond hair make her seem terrifyingly powerful and goddess-like. She looks twenty-five, not almost fourteen. She has a little tool she is using to attach the tent and winch it tightly to the poles; she is already an expert at it. I am grateful to have such a strong girl/woman with me. I try to catch her eye. She ignores me. Manou, on the other hand, is entranced with Sophie. He has no knowledge of attitude, or cigarettes; he only sees her powerful beauty. He sits watching her every spellbinding move, panting and whining, begging her to give him a glance, a pat, anything at all. She doesn't oblige, and eventually, he yawns and lies down, putting his face between his paws. But he keeps his eyes on her.

I know what that feels like. I used to drive Sophie around to nap when we were in Maine and she was a baby. I'd play Ray LaMontagne and Woody Guthrie and Nick Cave. I'd steal looks at her in the rearview mirror, just amazed, like every mother is, that someone so beautiful had come out of my body. I was in love with what I saw as her perfect nose and freckles and the soft golden curls around her ears. There was a line from a Nick Cave song that always reminded me of her, "And I don't believe in the existence of angels / But looking at you I wonder if that's true." She was my angel. And then Iris came along, a second angel, and I had to split my time watching, noticing, adoring. There was so much amazement and wonder in my heart for both girls, just not as many minutes anymore. It was hard to feel there was enough of me.

Iris, not to be outdone by Sophie, squats next to Manou and plays with his ears. Soon, he lies on his back for her to rub his very fuzzy white belly while licking her hands. A gray cat comes picking over the patchy field to us. Its green eyes gleam and it meows as it gets closer, then starts rubbing its head and ears all over Manou's tummy. "Mommy!" says Iris. "It's a kitty!" She is laughing with joy over these two animals. The cat gets excited and starts biting Manou's ears, and Manou lets out a long howl of pleasure-pain. "C'mon, Manou," Iris says, and she and Manou start running in circles in the field. The cat wiggles some more in a dusty patch near the tent, purring loudly. Sophie watches Iris and Manou cavorting and then grunts, "Iris finally has a friend." The cat rubs itself on Sophie's left calf and purrs. I want to say something about how all the animals love her, too. She is so lovable! But I just smile. I am not sure I'm allowed to say anything right now.

Having a teenager, I'm starting to realize, is more about

knowing when to shut up. Everything we say is an affront, a criticism, a mortal wound, a rash. They have so much power, or at least my daughter does. And yet they are so fragile. It's all so confusing.

After we are set up, I put out the fig-leaf-covered cheese on the metal table and pull out a water jug. I open the wine. I give Sophie a tiny swig from the bottle and then drink a swig myself. We eat the cheese with a baguette. We are hot and the ground is dusty and my nostrils feel singed by the burnt smell.

"Last one to that stream is a rotten egg," I blurt out, and start running, my one breast flapping and the phantom breast as still as a Michelangelo statue in the Uffizi.

Iris squeals when she sees me take off and starts running. Then she is in front of me, her sandals slapping the dry earth, her brown braids flying behind her back, her checkered shorts and pink T-shirt dusty, and the long line of at least fifteen friendship bracelets she's made so far—braiding and knotting the bright threads in the tent, in the car—seems to glow in the hazy air.

I don't wait to see if Sophie or the cat will come. Manou is up with Iris, yelping. Soon I hear the lithe footsteps of my powerful huntress, my own goddess Diana, behind me, then she's in front of me, then surpassing Iris, she's up with the bouncing Manou, then she passes even the dog. Her speed is indomitable. She's in the water, dipping her long arms in before we get there. Manou and Iris and I arrive, all panting. Iris and I start splashing each other in the cold, clear water, and then we notice a flock of sheep standing on the edge of the stream, watching us, chewing, and discussing our antics. Iris and I sit down and pee in the water through our shorts; Sophie laughs about this, tells us we're gross, and then sits down, too.

When we get back to the tent, we pull on dry sundresses and

dry sandals and find Nanette in the back of her house making sangria on a stone table next to an outdoor sink. She's mashing fruit into a big glass pitcher. I tell her, as best I can, that we are going to town, and she nods, then hands me a glass of the purple drink, sweet and cold. When I have drunk it down, she points which way I should go to the village.

There's a handful of houses that make up this border town, which has only one tiny bistro for everyone to share. We are given a table in the cool back, near a damp stone wall. We order Bayonne ham and bread and cheese and olives. Then crispy potatoes cooked with garlic confit and a spicy sausage and also a clay dish of chicken legs that are perfectly crispy and salty.

Later, when we go back to our campsite, I let Sophie have another swig of the wine, and I have some, too. I cork the bottle and leave it on the small table, we all pee in the grass, look up for a moment at the dark, dark sky, where only stars and the moon are up above, and then we get into the tent and don't even bother with our teeth.

In the night stillness, we can hear the animals coughing, breathing, chewing, sneezing. They seem to be right outside our tent. I hear a horse whinny and snort. I find myself wondering if maybe the animals have come closer to our tent in order to feel safe. Or is it just that sounds in darkness always close in? Iris is asleep immediately, her mouth is open, her friendship bracelets all damp and stringy on her wrist. Her breaths are deep.

Sophie asks, "Are there, like, wolves here?" I put my phone flashlight on and angle it to the side of the tent and sit up to look at her. Her face is vulnerable, open, thank heavens.

"I doubt it. Maybe coyotes. But I don't know . . . I think

they killed everything in Europe, sort of like the American West."

"That's sad."

I reach across a sleeping Iris to put my hand on the outside of Sophie's sleeping bag. I say, "Hey. I'm not mad at you."

She's quiet. Then, "I'm sorry I smoked that cigarette. It was gross anyway."

"I understand why you wanted to."

"And I'm sorry I took my bathing suit top off. I just wanted to see what it was like."

"I understand. It's okay. You should be proud of that beautiful, strong body you have. Show it off however you want. It's not my choice, really. Sometimes I feel like I need to help you. Probably more than you need or want my help. But your instinct to love your body is good." I've chosen my words haltingly, slowly.

Suddenly, Iris pipes up from the dead, listening, always listening, with those Harry Potter "extendable ears," even when she is asleep. "Mama, your pubic hair shows out the edges of your swimsuit. It's all like, 'It's party time!'" She spreads her arms out wide and wiggles her fingers to show us, I suppose, what it's like to be pubic hairs partying, and starts laughing hysterically. Now we're all laughing and I say, "Iris, you little devil! I thought you were asleep."

When both girls are heavy and unmoving, I cry. For everything. I have been waiting all day, holding it in. I cry and cry and cry. I let my tears run down the sides of my face. They make my sleeping bag wet. I am thinking tonight that having a teenager is this long, painful, pulling-off-a-Band-Aid-stuck-to-your-arm-hairs process of losing a child. You realize this with a shocking clarity one morning, then relearn it over and over and over, daily needles in your heart, your throat, your eyes. Ah, yes, you tell yourself, this is what we were always doing: preparing to say goodbye.

And then it is morning and we run to the stream again, where we rinse ourselves and then race back to the tent to put on our sandals to hike into the mountains. Sophie is ahead of me carrying the heaviest backpack; she wears only a sports bra and a light pair of Patagonia shorts, and she looks strong, robust, in charge. Something is changing here in France; she's crossed some line I didn't see her cross, or didn't want to see her cross, or was too stuck in my own disappearing act of marital and life crises that I didn't expect to see it so soon. My girls are on their own timelines, there's no date for this or that, it just happens. This scares and thrills me, both.

Iris bounds after her sister then doubles back to look at bees and moths hidden low to the ground. There are sheep and goats that have wandered way up into the mountains, eating purple flowers and sagey plants. When we get to the top of a rise, we see charred trees for miles and miles and then, like something from *The Lord of the Rings*, right in the middle of the char, there are these deep blue pools of water, lakes or ponds, that look so close, you could almost jump to them from here. I feel a crazy yen to tumble, throw myself.

All day I have been a wreck inside, I was a wreck all yesterday on the drive, that piece of yarn that ties me back to Pete feels like it's snaking through my heart, tugging, asking me to find my way back, reminding me of what a shit I am. And somewhere buried under that is a small voice that repudiates my shame by saying, "Live your life. You don't know how much is left." I don't know which voice to choose.

When we get back to our campsite, there is an old man at

our rickety table. The cat is meowing around his ankles. His name, he tells us, is Émile. He is Nanette's husband. From what I gather, he's telling me that his family has had sheep on this farm for two hundred years, sheep going up into the mountains, crossing the border into Spain, and coming back down. His arm fans out to show me how far his animals go into the mountains and I see how brown his wrist is as it peeks from his black cotton shirt. He has brought us a sheep sausage, he says, and more cheese wrapped in leaves that are damp and green. Nanette comes out of the farm then, and she is carrying more wine, and a boule that is dark brown on the bottom. She hands the bread to me and plunks down some more of those categorically small glasses. It's official: No one in France has regular-size water or juice glasses, everything is miniature. These have gold designs on the sides. She pours all of us, but Iris, a bit of a light pink/orange-hued wine, even Sophie, and she smiles at *"les filles"* and hands Iris some water.

Nanette harrumphs back into the house and comes out again with a yellow plastic colander filled with purple grapes. She pulls one of the plastic chairs from under the olive tree over to the table and heaves herself into it and begins cutting the bread right on the table and smearing the thick creamy cheese onto it. The cat springs onto her lap, sniffing at the cheese. "*Oh, va-t'en,* 'emingway!" She picks the cat up and puts him back down on the ground. ("His name is Hemingway, like the writer," I whisper to Sophie.) He jumps up again. Nanette laughs and takes a small bit of cheese and lets him eat it off her forearm. He is purring crazily.

Nanette calls to Iris, *"Ho—ma fille, viens, tiens,"* and hands her some cheese and bread. I look sternly at Iris—no creamy-cheese tantrum allowed, I am warning. Nanette reaches over with one of her thick, wrinkled hands and gives Iris a handful of grapes and says, "*Mange, ma petite.*" Just eat, my dear. Iris obeys, thank God.

Nanette does the same with Sophie and me and Émile. She is the center of our wheel as the air grows dusky and the charred smell moves in closer with the dark. Hemingway-the-cat jumps down and starts small-game hunting in the taller grass, looking for a mouse or a bush cricket, who knows. Manou sighs, heaves himself up from his spot by the firepit, and comes in closer, lying on Iris's feet. The girls and I put our hands out, over and over, and Nanette fills them again and again with food. Even Iris eats and eats!

There are so many things I wish I could ask these people, and half as much I'd like to tell them, but I don't have the language, the words, in French. And they don't have the words in English.

Bats are zipping through the air, and I look up through the craggy ancient olive tree at the dark blue sky, and despite everything that feels like it might cleave my chest in two, crush it into splinters, and then burn it to ashes, I also feel so lucky to be alive, so lucky to be here right now, it takes my breath away. Life pinches and pokes. Pokes and pinches.

Soon Émile and Nanette stand up and make their way back up to the house, their ongoing conversation wafting behind them, their feet scuffing. Manou and Hemingway follow, obedient. When they are gone, Sophie wanders off into the dark and comes back with three perfect pears from a tree she must have spotted earlier in the day. We eat them together, the juice fresh and sweet in the night air.

When we are done, we pee together in the darkness and look up at the stars. Iris says, "Mama, what if there's a guy who takes the stars across the sky and puts them into their spots every night." And I say, "I love that idea." Even Sophie is content enough tonight not to say anything cruel or insulting. When we get into the tent, Iris whispers, "I thought I would hate it here. But I love it here."

"I love you both," I croak, my voice faltering. I hear Sophie sigh; I am annoying her again. But Iris pipes up and says, "I love you, too, Mama." And then everyone sleeps, because we're just that tired and there's nothing more to say, anyway.

34.
ALICE

Sophie is up with the first rays of sun, I hear her unzipping the tent. I see her back and the long muscles on her arms, then the backs of her legs as she stands. I hear her putting on her sandals, opening her water bottle, taking long gulps, and then running away from the tent—to the stream? I am guessing so. Even though I know I shouldn't, I doze for a few more minutes as the hot sun spills into the tent. Soon the sun will be scorching and reheating the charred trees. I feel a raw knot of anxiety in my stomach, which suddenly makes me feel like I might have diarrhea or throw up. I push the sleeping bag off my sweaty skin, see Iris, mouth open, deeply asleep in her too hot cocoon, and I creep out of the tent, sliding into my sandals and making my way to the rickety outhouse we've used only when desperate so far.

When I emerge and go to wash my hands at a setup of a hose hung by a hook on a post, dangling over a galvanized tub, a big block of olive oil soap on a shingle next to it, I see Sophie jogging back to us. In the haze of morning, I straighten out and watch. Her hair is wet and flowing, her face is open.

I meet her at the table. Her sports bra is wet and the water drips down her back. Her shorts are stuck to her legs. I hear a tractor starting up and see Émile heading off to do who knows what in a far field. He turns and sees us and waves, still wearing that long-sleeved black shirt and a black straw hat on his head. He is smoking, and Manou is trotting along behind the tractor, also off to work. I see Nanette in the doorway and she waves and then steps out with a bowl. She makes her way to us, Hemingway trotting behind her; she calls, "*Bonjour, bonjour,*" like it's a song, and then hands me a bowl of green furry . . . what are they?

"*Merci,*" I say. "*C'est quoi ça?*" What is this?

"*Des amandes fraîches! Mange.*" She picks one up and bites into it, her shiny teeth flashing against her leathered skin. She shows us the inside of a pearly white almond, the green softness of the barely ripe skin. This is, apparently, edible. Sophie takes one cautiously and puts it to her mouth, making a delicate crunch. "Wow," she says to me. "It tastes like grass and almonds and something almost flowery."

I eat one. And agree. Nanette trundles back to her house and then comes haltingly back out with a small cup of pitch-like coffee and hands it over. I drink it, then some water. She stands beaming at us and seems unsure of what to say this morning, as we understand only about a third of what she utters, mostly gathering meaning from the accompanying gestures. We have experienced a little time together, though; how to give this the benediction it deserves is puzzling for me, too. When she lumbers away again, I go back into the tent and start rolling up my mat. Iris, feeling the commotion, wakes up, her eyes slowly focusing on me, a smile crossing her face. "Mama! I was having the funniest dream. There was a sheep and it was letting us play with it and it kept running away and then Sophie and I would run after it and it would pop out from behind a bush and be like 'Baa-ha!'"

"That's a funny dream, Pickle. Now let's get up and get going. We have a long drive today. There're some green furry almonds outside on the table that Nanette brought us." Iris looks at me quizzically but is curious and bounds out of her sleeping bag and goes straight to see the green almonds. I love how curious kids are; everything is an adventure.

"Sophie: Can I hand you out the mats and bags?"

"Sure." I hear her feet scuff closer. She takes the sacks and piles them next to the tent, then sits down. It's uncanny how unlikely she is to help without direction. When she was younger, she often wanted to help. Now she wants to sit, walk away, sigh, scowl. "Okay, Sophie. I meant—can you please take them to the car? We need to get things to the car, on our way, tent down."

"Fine," she says with a heavy helping of annoyance. "You never said that, Alice!"

"Iris, go carry a few."

While the girls are gone, I get out of the tent with all of our backpacks and stuff random hair ties and ChapSticks into the pockets. Then I pull up the stakes and shake sand and dirt out of the tent as best I can before I start pulling out the poles. The girls come back with greasy brown papers in their hands. Sophie hands me a slice of what appears to be eggs and potatoes cooked into a flaky crust with a lot of thyme. Both girls have their mouths full. "From Nanette, Mama," says Iris. We eat the eggy potato-thyme tarts in gulps, wrap up our last bits of gear, pick up our tin cups, and trudge together back to the car. Nanette and Hemingway come out of the house, and she says, "*Bon voyage!*" and hugs us all. Iris picks up Hemingway and squeezes him until he meows and shakes his ears, sneezing in annoyance. We pile into the car and wave once more.

A few more days, a few more places to go, a castle at the end, and then back home to whatever awaits. Just as I am about to drive, my phone dings. I look down and see it's from Didier.

PART 4

La Dordogne

35.
SOPHIE

The road from the Pyrenees east is like passing from one mythical world into another. From the charred and scrubby foothills that border Spain, the three of them tumble like marbles, it feels to Sophie, into the lush Dordogne River valley, full of dark forests, open fields of sunflowers, old stone farmhouses, and castles with topiary cut into all kinds of shapes. As they put down miles between themselves and Didier and those sons of Provence, Sophie tells her mother she can see why all those princesses in the books she read when she was little were French. "I can just imagine long dresses and veils and crowns of daisies, and look at all those tall turrets. They'd be pacing up on high balconies, pulling apart flowers to do whatever the French version of 'He loves me, he loves me not' might be," she says. Iris loves it when Sophie talks like that and perks up from the back seat. "Oooh, yeah Sophie, you are so right!" She's a tad too enthusiastic for Sophie. "Okay, Booby," says Sophie.

There is something about the way the hills go up and down in the Dordogne and the roads turn in these long, graceful curves that is very glamorous, even to an American teenager wearing her only clean pair of shorts and a tank top, and who is stuck in a car with her jittery mother and her dirty-kneed sister.

They are listening to *Let It Be*, the Beatles album that made Sophie fall in love with Paul McCartney, the young one, not the old dude (gross). It occurs to Sophie, as they drive away from the afternoon, that they are, actually, on their way home. The song "Two of Us" is on, and Paul is singing, "We're on our way home / We're on our way home." "We are, too," she whispers.

When "Let It Be" begins, her mother is singing along, "When I find myself in times of trouble, Mother Mary comes to me," and her sister is in the back with Big Bear buckled into the other seat, and she's whispering to herself or maybe telling Big Bear about castles and moats and armed guards and princes, and Sophie is thinking, Well, this is like it should be. She smiles to herself and then her heart pounds. She misses everyone and loves everyone and wants to run through those fields of sunflowers until she can't tell if she's the wind or still a girl, she wants to go home, she wants to live in France forever, she wants to fall in love. All of it.

Soon the car is winding around narrow streets and there's a towering castle with a small town built around it on the left and a river on the right with people in canoes and kayaks. Google Maps is telling her mother to turn up a narrow street that barely fits their car, and they drive up and up and up, only to come back down and down and down to a campground that sits in a field along the side of the bendy river, smooth as glass, widening, narrowing, then widening again. Along the edge of the river is a wooden rack stacked with colorful plastic canoes and kayaks; from this distance they look like pickup sticks. The field is covered with small white flowers, and the camp road is dark brown dirt. Sophie sees a few other small tents and two people sitting in a hammock together, head to toe, reading those white-covered-intelligent-but-boring-looking French books. The air smells of grass and something sweet, almost like whipped cream. And when her mother comes to a stop, they all sit for a second looking out at the round hay rolls at the edge of the field. There is a stone house with a small red sign and an arrow painted in white that reads "*Bureau.*" Sophie notices her mother picking at something on her head and then smoothing her thin hair over and over. Her mother has been jumpy all morning, her hands shaking the tiniest amount as she leans to put on her blinking light, or stops to get gas, or pays for lunch in a small sandwich shop or when she buys coffee and treats in a bakery. There is still so much about her mother that she doesn't understand. So often her mother seems to get lost to her. When she thinks this, her stomach lurches and she remembers the cancer, something she hopes she will never have to think about again. A tiny guilt to feel that, as she knows that her mother thinks about it. Out loud she says, "Mom, want me to come in with you?"

Alice turns to look at her daughter, her eyes far away until they focus on this unusual circumstance, her daughter offering to help. "Oh, Sophie. Thank you. Yes—would you? You, too, Iris?"

"Yes, Mama," says her sister, and they all get out, breathing in the deep green smells of the hay and muddy smells of the river and deep lushness of the forest. Together they climb the stairs and go to look for a person who can tell them where to camp.

36.

IRIS

Iris awoke in the misty haze of French summer, steam rising off the fields. The plan was to visit some caves called "lass-coh" deep underground where ancient people once lived; her mother told her that the caves had been discovered by a French boy and his dog. Then they were going to spend the afternoon in kayaks on the river, castle-hunting from the water. Iris felt it was a day for a dress, the castles and all, even though her mother told her that they would need their bathing suits to kayak. She opened her duffel bag and pulled out her pinkest of confections, the one with the light pink background on which darker pink and yellow flowers seemed to almost pop from the cloth, their detail in such fine and distinct lines, they were mesmerizing. In the bag, Iris found her new pink Crocs and checked the placement on her arm of her many friendship bracelets, assessing their various levels of dampness and stinkiness, as they never quite dried out, and the stringy ends seemed to get covered in butter or mustard while she ate.

For breakfast, they wandered through a market in a stone

town and ate so many colors of olive, more of the little green plums they were so fond of, shared a baguette that was still warm inside, and each ate a yogurt mixed with chestnut "cream," her mother called it, though it was more like jam that had the earthy nuttiness of almonds but none of the crunch. Iris had decided that she loved French yogurt. Now, she ate it everywhere, all day long. Her mother bought a small tin of something made from goose livers, she explained, for their father. And then they got back in the car and wound down shady forested roads, the river in and out of the window, as Iris watched the world go by. Suddenly, her mother came to a complete stop and Iris jerked forward just a bit, her seat belt tightening across her chest, shaking out the dreaminess. She heard her mother say "Turtle" to her sister up in the front seat. Iris asked, "A what? A what? Mama—Sophie, a what?"

Nobody answered her, and she saw her mother open up her car door and get out.

"A what, Sophie?"

"Shut up, Booby."

Her mother was out in the middle of the road, putting up her hands as cars stopped. What on earth was going on? Now her mother was walking back to the car with a small turtle in her hand. A man rolled down his window: *"Ho! Vous allez manger ça?"* He laughed a throaty chuckle, and Iris could smell the cigarette he held in his hand out his car window.

"Manger?" Her mother looked confused. *"Eat it? No."*

The man chuckled. *"Il y a un étang, juste là."* He was pointing.

Sophie asked, "What is he saying?" She looked at the river.

"I don't know," said her mother. "I don't understand." The man was becoming more emphatic. He was pointing away from the river to the trees and speaking in more and more rapid French. *"Pas le fleuve! L'étang!"*

"*Oui,*" said her mother. "*Merci, merci, merci.*" But it sounded like "Mercy, mercy, mercy."

Before Iris knew what was happening, her mother was handing the turtle to her through the open window and saying, "Iris, here, hold this little guy until we can put it back in the river or a pond or whatever comes first." Her mother was holding the wiggling turtle in one hand and was now on her phone with the other and saying, "Ohhh, guys. I think '*étang*' might mean 'pond,' that way, right, Sophie?" Iris looked at the turtle paddling its tiny legs in the air. Then she took a look down and thought about how her pink dress was so clean and pristine, despite the few dribbles of olive oil from those fat olives at the market and maybe the tiniest smidgen of yogurt on her lap. But no one would ever see those. Here was this muddy creature coming toward her through the window while cars started up and meandered past theirs, and her mother, irritated now, said, "Come on, Iris, take it, there are cars, I need to get back in, it won't hurt you."

Iris balked. "What about Sophie?" she said.

Her sister barked, "No way, Alice. Don't even think about it."

Iris took in its tiny little claws and black little eyes. She hesitated; of course she did. Then she saw the little yellow dots on its legs and face, and she reached out with her finger and felt the cool nails on the ends of its feet, which were rowing like crazy. She stroked the shell, noticing how hard it was, and she decided that it might be interesting to hold the turtle, pink princess dress be damned. So she took it from her mother and put it on her lap and held on to the outside edges of its shell with her fingers. It immediately put its little head inside its shell. She stroked its feet and its head came out and started to waggle around, straining its neck. She turned it toward her, so it could see her face, and held it up to eye level, which made it shrink back into its shell. She decided to pretend it was flying. "Zoom," she said. And then "Zoom" in the other direction. She had retreated into her own private turtle-flying world, until her sister punctured it.

"Booby. What the hell are you doing?" Sophie had turned in her seat and was watching her sister and the turtle, the latter of which, Iris could detect, her sister had the tiniest bit of interest in. "It's not an airplane, Iris."

"I know," said Iris. But its shell was slick, and because she was holding it in such an awkward way, it flipped out of her unsteady hands and landed on the floor and started to go under the seat.

"Mom! This thing is going under the seat."

"Hang on, sweetie, trying to find a place near the river—I mean the pond—where is this pond, anyway—to pull off and let it go."

"Iris, grab it," her sister screeched. "It's coming under my seat." Sophie brought her feet up on the dash in front of her. Iris unbuckled (knowing this was a bad thing to do) and dove for the turtle, picked it up, and tried to grip it tightly. The turtle, meanwhile, was craning its surprisingly long neck all over the place and seemed to be having a mini turtle meltdown; its mouth was hanging open. Was it *panting*? Just as Iris clamped down on the turtle, hoping that the harder she held it, the prouder her sister would be for saving her, Iris felt something warm spreading all over her lap. "Mom! Oh my God, Mama, I think it's peeing on me!" Carefully, she picked up the turtle's hind end, its tiny tail wiggling around. And there on her pink dress was a reddish-brown, sopping puddle of turtle pee, making a large stain, right in between her legs. "Mom, it's peed all over my dress." Iris knew she couldn't let go of the turtle. But she started crying. "Mama!"

"Okay, honey, I know, I know. Hang on." They were on the side of a lily-pad-covered pond, like the ones in that painting she has a poster of in her room, and her mother was unbuckling her own belt (so SO slowly, it seemed to Iris), and then taking the turtle from her and walking with it in her hands, and Iris was out of the car, screaming and crying, and the pee was traveling in one long line down her leg and into her brand-new pink Croc.

"Pickle, come here—watch it. Ugh, poor you." Her mother took her by the hand, and they waded into the clear blue water, and Iris was quiet for a moment while they watched the turtle swim away. "You did that—you helped save that little guy," her mother told her.

Iris turned to her and said, "Mommy, my dress. My favorite dress."

"Let's rinse it off." Her mother helped her out of her Crocs and had her stand at the pond's edge and splashed water all onto the dress and rubbed at it with some sandy pebbles to get the pee out. The dress was sopping and hanging heavily with the weight of the water in the front. Her mother kissed the top of her head and said, "It's okay. We fixed it."

When Iris looked up, her sister was standing by the car watching the entire pond-washing scene and laughing.

"Mama, Sophie is laughing at me!" Iris was outraged all over again.

"Sophie, stop it." But now Alice was laughing, too. Iris was bewildered by both of them. Did they not realize what she just went through? She stomped back to the car and yelled, "Sophie! You were too chicken to even hold it!" As she got to the door, she found that she'd started laughing, too. It was all so outrageous she couldn't help it, and that made her angry and start to cry again. When she turned back, her mother was next to her and gave her a hug, and then they all buckled up again and her mom said, "Okay. Caves!"

They drove on to a low building built right into the edge of a mountain and got in line to see the caves. But then something happened that Iris would think about years later. All of a sudden, out of nowhere, it seemed to Iris, who was busy watching people and leaning into her mother's legs, someone familiar appeared. It was a man, and he was wearing jeans and had a pair of sunglasses like her father's tucked into the V of a white flowy shirt, which her father would never wear. (Iris could see some hair on this man's chest, tangled and gray/blond.) And he was walking right toward them, a huge smile on his face like they were expecting him, and her mother was wriggling against her legs a bit, and the man was saying *"Salut"* and kissing her mother on both cheeks and tousling Iris's hair. Wide-eyed, Iris looked at her sister, and just as she did, she saw the look of scorn and shock on her sister's face, and she realized who this man was: It was Didier, aka Mr. Tumnus, from the place beyond the wardrobe.

• • •

Iris worries now that their trip is ruined. Inside the caves, Iris looks at all the paintings, she puts one step in front of another. But the feeling that things are going on that she doesn't understand, that no one's even bothered to ask her opinion of, this feeling, well, she can't get rid of it, no matter how hard she tries to swallow it down. I just want to go home, she tells herself.

37.
ALICE

The minute I see Didier, I have measles, I have a fever, I am on fire. I feel myself blush all the way down to my toes. Iris will understand, somewhat, I tell myself. Okay, not understand, exactly, but forgive or just work around, I am hoping. It's Sophie. Of course I've known he was coming. We had texted, he had told me he was visiting his mother in the Dordogne when I said we were headed there after the Pyrenees. I had told him about Lascaux. I had said late morning. I had been thinking about it since the night before, holding on to it, this private room where my kids couldn't find me, where Pete couldn't find me. And now he was here, kissing both sides of my face, and it was his touch on the soft underneath of my arm: that place that stops being touched once you are married, stops being caressed. I felt his hand slide down my wrist, and it electrified me.

When your husband has cheated on you, you have only a few options, as I have lived it:

Option 1: Struggle through it, do therapy, try to understand, get him to understand the pain and shame he's caused, then go on a quest for this elusive (and, IMHO, bullshit) panacea of forgiveness, which I think may be a contract of religion, not reality. I think *time* just happens, not necessarily forgiveness. Time passes so the nervous system can calm down and the body can calm down and the heart can calm down. People want to believe they've done some sort of Olympics inside themselves, seen God, whatever, been that incredibly magnanimous. I don't buy it. Time just heals things after some soul-searching, and the sting gets lessened because distance is the great emollient. But you always know it could happen again, and you wait for it, and the scar never quite fades. That's option one. This might feel like what they call "Forgiveness." I just call it "The Great Dulling of Oneself."

Option 2: Get angry, never accept it, and leave your marriage, whether you physically leave and go to another house, or mentally are perpetually MIA, never reconciling, shoving the pain and anger into some rat trap deep inside you that is primed to snap. In this case, your gaping wound is bubbling over with red-hot anger.

Option 3: Never really commit any which way and hover in the middle of those first two, still angry, still hurt, trying to connect, making strides, going backward, circling in a stormy sea while you try to figure out if you can be happy or not, if you can forgive or not, if this affair is a function of so many other things and how to tease those apart, and then, from that, how to come to some new plateau on the river of life (forgive me, I had to get a little woo-woo).

That last one is where I am, neither here nor there. If I am honest, during cancer, I had so little fight in me, I cleaved to Pete. Pete talked so much about everything he'd repair, and I realized how much I still love him; more than love. We are so entwined, so knitted together, so attached, that our lives are like a cat's cradle, with the kids, our house in Maine, our apartment, Ingmar, all the experiences we share—it's never just one thing or a couple of things that connect people. It's a whole lifetime of things; your kids' whole lifetimes. That's the crazy part of marriage, actually. Lives get so intertwined, and it's really hard to undo them. And yet I still carry this resentment, like in a little fanny pack. It came with me to France, and then I met Didier.

And here he is, and here is Iris, waiting to go into the caves, and there is Sophie, watching, reproaching, hurt.

We buy our tickets. We all go in. We see the animals on the walls, and I see Didier explaining some of the history to Iris, and I look at the swimming deer on those walls and feel so intensely what they must have felt, swimming against a current, that I want to sit right down in that cold cave and never leave.

Sophie is distant. If she had her own phone, I imagine she might be calling Pete. Or a friend. Or someone.

When I think back, later, I will realize how alone and powerless this must have made Sophie feel. She just knew too much. Our actions as parents are felt in the bodies of our children.

We leave the caves, and I invite Didier to lunch with us in a café back in Sarlat. I honestly don't know what I think I'm doing. To anyone on the outside, we might look like a family, except we aren't. It's all so reckless. And I know it. I know we've missed the castle I promised Iris we'd go to after Lascaux; the day has been upended by this surprise (and not a surprise) visit. I feel guilty, sick, scared.

And yet. I leave the girls at the tent; I ask Sophie to be in charge, and she looks at me wild-eyed, afraid. I walk with Didier down the road, I kiss him and press my body into his, we grope and go into the bushes and fondle each other, the heat of our bodies pressed together in the damp of the Dordogne, his hands inside my underwear, his teeth on my one nipple, my mouth on his, then traveling down his chest, both of us heaving and panting. After, I murmur that I don't know when I'll see him again, and he says we will see each other again, of course. When I watch him walk away, his white linen shirt rumpled, his American Levi's, his blond hair glinting in the sun, I feel like I might throw up from want, from shame.

Like a teenager coming home to her parents after curfew, stoned or drunk, I slink back to my girls and say, "Come on, let's go swim. We still have a castle to see this afternoon."

And we do swim. We do go to a small castle. Though I can't tell you anything I see. Except I will remember they had a private chapel, where, under a painting of eels, I make every prayer to whatever God there ever was to help me fix the chaos I'm causing so flagrantly.

In bed that night, after Iris is asleep, while Sophie lies awake reading, I say: "I'm sorry."

"You're a mess, Alice."

"I know."

"You'd hate yourself if you met yourself."

"I know."

"Daddy."

"I know. I will fix this."

"I will never like him. Ever."

"I know. It's just—Sophie, I can't tell you how lonely I've been."

"I don't care. I'm not your friend."

"I know."

There is a long, excruciating pause. Has she fallen asleep? No.

"You have us."

"I know."

"Yeah. Do you know? You're just. You're canceled, Alice."

"Meaning?"

"Just. I'm canceling you."

"That's fair." What I don't say: I've felt canceled for years. This whole trip is my attempt to un-cancel myself.

Early the next morning, we roll up our sleeping bags and stuff the tent in the bag. The camping trip is over. I have a special thing planned for the girls to end the trip. But everything might be too messed up now to enjoy it.

PART 5

La Confluence des Fleuves

38.
SOPHIE

The road to Lyon is long. When Sophie looks at the map on her mom's phone, she traces the country of France with her finger. It doesn't seem that big. Her mother says it's as big as Texas, which is, like, just a state. She can see on the map that they have made a huge circle around the country and now they are going back the way they came. She travels the screen over rivers, the green spots of country, and brown summits of mountains. She thinks, looking at the map, that they should be able to practically hop from the Dordogne to Lyon in no time at all. But that isn't the case. They drive through national parks and through woods and across fields with small villages with walls around them and even through Vichy, a town where a book Sophie once read takes place, about a boy who helped the French resistance during World War II by delivering messages to the Allies on his bicycle.

The car is quiet and Sophie doesn't want to play any music. A few times her mother clears her throat and says Sophie's name like she's calling to her, but each time Sophie is saved by Iris, who pipes up with an observation or "I need to pee" or "Can I get some

Camembert at the next gas station?" She has become addicted to the little foil-wrapped Camemberts—"Which, FYI, definitely are a soft cheese, Booby"—that the gas stations sell, along with books and multiplication tables and organic salads and yogurts (*"Vive la France!"* their mother keeps saying, trying too hard).

They aren't technically going to the city of Lyon, though Sophie knows that they will fly out of there at the end of the trip. Instead, they are going to stay in a castle somewhere nearby, somewhere their mother went for a weekend many years ago, "back in prehistoric times," Sophie mutters. Her mother has told her and Iris that in Lyon there are two enormous rivers, the "Sewn" and the "Rown," and that they meet at a "conflewance," she calls it. The château, she says, is just up the "Sewn," in a small town that is having an arts festival right now, too.

Sophie must have fallen asleep for a little while, because when she opens her eyes, they are traveling along a big, wide river and then taking a little bridge over what appears to be a moat to an actual, very big, for-real castle with a turret and a fortress and chimneys all over the place and windows that are way up high in the turrets and even one of those high balconies that you can walk on and, like, survey your kingdom.

When her mother parks, Sophie hops out before her sister or mother. Everything inside that car, all the words unsaid and said, are too much for Sophie to handle anymore. She is relieved that they can leave their sleeping bags and the tent in the car, all she needs is her backpack, and her mother can get their duffel of clothes.

This castle is cool and damp-feeling inside. An actual footman opens the door for them. Sophie smooths her hands down her shorts and tightens her ponytail. When she glances at her sister, she thinks how ridiculous Iris looks in her jean shorts, her Laura Ingalls braids, her stringy, damp friendship bracelets. Her mother . . . well, she hates her mother.

The entryway has a long red rug with potted trees on either side—trees, inside!—and gives way to a wide room with an enormous chandelier twinkling with pieces of cut glass that refract the light all over the gray stone walls. There are red velvet couches and chairs and dark wooden tables along the walls. Under the chandelier is a gurgling fountain of a naked man standing over a naked woman who is lying in the water, holding a small fawn and a hare. The water emanates from the tips of the man's fingers as he gesticulates, and the woman looks passive or just like she's tolerantly tuning him out; the light from the chandelier dapples the water.

A woman approaches them in a tight black suit, with very high red heels and red lips. She says she will guide them to their room, but first do they need help with their bags? Or would they like to wait in the dining area, as lunch is still being served? Perhaps a swim in the pool? Sophie isn't sure she has ever been anywhere quite like this. Outside the floor-to-ceiling windows Sophie can see a pool surrounded by red umbrellas and black lounge chairs and, beyond that, horses grazing, barns, fields, kingdom stuff.

They follow the woman to an elevator and then down a stone-floored hall that has tiny lamps made to look like lighted candles perched along the walls on both sides. Soon, they come to a blue door. The woman opens the door for them with a key card and says, "*voilà.*" She hands one key card to her mother and one, thrillingly, to Sophie.

When they go in, Sophie sees that her mother has gotten them a room with two enormous canopy beds, one for her, and the other, she assumes, will be for her mother and sister.

There's an entire wall of windows that look out over the valley and into the hills beyond. In the corner, with a curtain that can be pulled around it for privacy, is a deep white tub; next to it is a wooden pyre on which is stuck a gigantic white candle. There is a fireplace, a rug and a couch in front of the fireplace, and on the mantel a large white porcelain vase filled with crinkly hot-pink roses. Two chairs and a small table are in the middle of the room, and there is a chess game set up, ready for play. Large dark wooden antique creatures roam the room, maybe naiads or dryads, Sophie can't remember which is which, but one of those or both. There is a white muslin curtain on an iron rod; this curtain can be pulled to obscure the hundreds of tiny diamond-shaped windows that survey the kingdom. Off this main room is a wooden door that leads to a small room with a door that opens to a toilet; just across is a door to a shower. In the middle space between the two rooms is a sink. Sophie thinks, We have one room for a bathroom back home, and these people make three rooms for one bathroom.

Sophie hears Iris gasp when she opens the ornate tapestries that serve as curtains on the canopies—they are covered, Sophie sees, with a story about a princess and a unicorn, and Iris is already talking the story through out loud, always out loud. Sophie has to admit, it's all pretty impressive, and so she says, "Wow." Sophie goes and stands next to Iris and they take in the story together. Her mother smiles. Then her mother says, "Sophie, you and Iris are going to take a riding lesson today, and then see that pool over there? We can go swim there. But first let's eat lunch?"

Iris announces that she is going to put on her pink dress for the occasion. Sophie looks at her sister, alarmed. That dress is now stained with turtle pee and tarnished by the day Didier had, once again, broken into their tender female world. Sophie knows it's crumpled at the bottom of the duffel bag. She opens her mouth to say so, but her mother gives her a look and speaks over her, saying with a wide smile, "Great idea, Pickle. Let me help you find it and smooth it out for the occasion. Sophie, do you want to stay in your shorts?" Sophie feels a tinge of criticism. She has noticed that, lately, every single thing her mother says feels like it comes with a dagger. Even when her mother tries to reassure her by saying, "Sophie, I was trying to help," her body takes it as a blow, a rash, a rasp, a whip.

"I'm fine," she says. She watches her mother stripping out of her sundress, right there in the middle of the room, and pulling on a black linen jumpsuit, still folded and clean. Sophie sees her mother shoving her knitted prosthetic breast in where the real breast should be, used to be, and sliding her sandals back on, and the three of them tiptoe out into the cool, dark, hallway, Iris in the wrinkled pink dress that smells like turtle pee, which smells somewhat like the underside of rockweed when the tide goes out.

In the restaurant, with windows that part thick red velvet curtains and reach from floor to ceiling and look out over gardens filled with a topiary menagerie of a horse, a Totoro, a cat, a monkey, and more Sophie can't see, there are enormous bouquets of flowers. The vases themselves could hold Iris, maybe even Sophie. Sophie is, of course, used to the odd fancy dinner out in New York with her parents or, more regularly, when her grandparents were still alive: 21 Club, Daniel, Peter Luger, Le Bernardin, Atomix (Atomix was Sophie's favorite because she could eat pineapple flowers and seaweed to her heart's content, with no one telling her she wasn't eating enough).

Sophie sinks into a tall, plush red chair and feels small again, while her mother orders a plate of *gougères*, some pâté, grilled anchovies, and a cherry tomato gratin. When the food arrives, Sophie dutifully tries all the dishes, finding herself drawn to the slightly charred, sweet taste of the tomatoes with a crisp cheesy crust and, of course, the puffy *gougères*, which her sister is consuming with an alarming rapidity. "Iris, you're taking them all."

Her mother says, "Iris, slow down. You'll make yourself sick."

"It's okay," Sophie surprises herself by saying.

Maybe a year or so ago, when they'd come back from Maine to New York and Sophie had started hanging out with her friends again, the girls had started talking about "getting fat" and what was "fattening," and one girl, Hannah, had said of the ice cream they were ordering, "I might as well just shove it in here," and she had taken the ice cream and pretended to ram it into her slim thighs. Sophie remembered feeling shocked that Hannah's thighs might be thought of as fat, and if that were the case, then how did hers fare? Cheese, pâté, would these make *her* fat? Sophie is afraid her mother would be weird if she asked, so she keeps her mouth closed and stops eating the amazing *gougères*, even though she wants to eat the entire basket herself, could eat another basket after that, even though she is sure her mother would order them if she just said the word.

Her mother orders, instead, a salade Niçoise for Sophie and one for herself, a mozzarella and tomato salad for Iris, and a basket of thin, crunchy breads for all of them. When the salads are mostly consumed, Iris wants dessert and gets a *pot de crème*, which she languorously eats, oohing and aahing. Sophie watches, wishing she had one, too, but then thinking of Hannah and her ice cream thighs and decides it's more mature to refuse, as her mother has. She regrets it the entire way up in the elevator to their room to change for riding. She wants that *pot de crème* even more now, which makes everything more irritating, especially her mother and sister.

"What are you making us do, again?" she asks her mother.

"I signed you and Iris up for a riding lesson. They will give you helmets, you just need jeans and sneakers. I will sit by the pool and read or whatever. They're going to take you around the grounds."

Her mother has adopted a breezy tone since they arrived at this castle. As if she were one of those remote, inscrutable mothers in a storybook, the kind who often ends up dead.

"What if I don't want to go riding with Iris?"

"I want to go riding," her sister pipes up unhelpfully, energetically changing out of the turtle-pee dress and into a pair of boyish jeans, tucking in her T-shirt, which makes her look ridiculous, her dangling, disgusting friendship bracelets all mayo-ey on her thin, sap-stained, and dirty arms.

"Sophie Anne—you will enjoy it. Let me give you an experience."

"Um, trust me, Alice, you've given me *lots* of experiences."

Her mother looks at her for a beat. A beat of restraint, because no snark leaks out, even though it's swinging ripely in the air. "Sophs, you will ride. I bet you enjoy it."

In a handful of hours, Sophie will remember this conversation as one that she wished had gone differently, with less attitude from her. She will wish that she had eaten more. She did as she was told in the end, though, dragging her feet and rolling her eyes, pulling on jeans (God, so hot and sticky), and tucking only one corner of her tight white tank into the waist right above her zipper, fixing her hair into a loose, flowy ponytail, dropping the sunglasses her father had given her as a gift when they left for France onto the bridge of her nose, applying a tiny schmear of lip gloss.

39.

ALICE

If I am honest, yes, when I saw the young man, Marc, who was teaching riding, something did stir inside me as a vague, if distant, warning. He was a few years older than Sophie, maybe seventeen, maybe twenty, hard to tell, his polish was so pronounced, and he spoke perfect English, which he would use for the riding lesson with my two girls and one other girl.

Marc had brown hair slicked back like Elvis's, mirrored aviators, a Cheshire smile worth ten thousand dollars, and he was impossibly fit in his Levi's and black T-shirt. Of course, Sophie noticed. I saw her posture next to me lengthen, her breasts perk up just the tiniest bit, her expression go from sullen to sensually pouty, her blond ponytail swish. And I do believe I thought somewhere in there: Oh, dear.

Instead, I kissed Iris, touched Sophie on the arm, said, "Take care of your sister. I'll be right over there reading," and took off for the pool to be alone finally, finally, blessedly, alone for the first time in almost two weeks. How can it be that you simultaneously want to run away from your children, rid yourself of them, and also, at the same time, never want to let them out of your sight?

Later, I would want to undo my need for time alone, I'd want to change the plan, the order, make myself take the riding lesson, too, anything. Later, the benefits of an iPhone for a teenager would occur to me, the tracking apps, the trade-offs of my child's brain for parental surveillance, the constant contact. But on this clear French day, I tried to push aside all of my anxieties, I tried to sublimate any sexual impulses that made me want to go up to my room and think about Didier or wish to find him there in my bed while the girls rode away and my husband went to work an ocean, nay, a whole world away.

What I wanted to do, wanted it so badly it reminded me of when I was a girl: I wanted to get off my phone, sit down by the pool, not have to listen to Iris talk at me, not have to worry about the emotional life of my teen morphing into a woman right in front of me, her bare midriff and tight white tanks and short skirts, I didn't want to think about my guilt or my desire, I wanted to read. When I was young, up until my twenties, I spent entire Saturdays, entire summers, even, reading. Now, more than anything, I wanted everything to just stop. I wanted no texts, no emails. I wanted to read so that I could stop thinking about own life, my own survival, all the complicated layers and messes I'd made.

But first, a memory came unbidden, as they do: I am back in New York and we're doing all the tests for a second time. Everyone wants their own version of the same tests: the horrible mammograms where your breasts get squished, the ultrasounds with the cold goo.

Then I need to have an MRI. They ask me what music I want to listen to, and I remember that my father, who had a heart attack several years ago, told me he had requested Beethoven when he had an MRI and could barely hear it over the clanking of the machine. I ask for Led Zeppelin. "Start with 'Fool in the Rain,'" I say. Now, Led Zeppelin I can hear above the clanking. Lying there, I am trying so hard not to take deep breaths, as they told me not to; I am trying not to cry, not to panic, not to throw up. I am holding on to the little balloon I can use to call them, and I am alone in that room while my water molecules get rearranged or whatever it is that happens—*don't even explain it to me.* After a half hour or longer, who knows, just thank God Led Zeppelin wrote long songs, I am dizzy and nauseated. The way the tech looks at me when she says goodbye: She reaches out and touches my hand and says, "Take good care, Alice." All I can think on the way home on the subway is, This woman thinks I will die.

• • •

Lying by the pool, set up to read, silence is all around me (No one else is even at the pool! They must all be at the festival we will go to later.) I shake my head and try to get that memory to go away. Sometimes these thoughts, they feel so dangerous. Ack. These things happened, they are over, I am here. I'm considered a survivor. But still. Every time my mind starts sliding back, I get scared. Once it starts I can't stop it. It's a loop of fear, an eyes-wide-open kind of fear. It makes me think of something my mother used to say: "You are walking into the jaws of the lion." God, the anxiety that would instill: the yawning pink of a lion's mouth, how small I felt in comparison. These days, memories feel like jaws to me. All I want to do is *not think*, especially in France.

Desperately now, I try to stop myself. I try to remember something, anything, else. Okay, swimming: I banish the screaming Gulf of Lions in Provence. Not there. The ocean in Maine? I can only picture it in a storm right now. Then I start wondering about pools. We never really went to a pool in Minneapolis, growing up. We went to lakes and ponds with my mother carrying a picnic basket of cheese and onion sandwiches and our books (our books!). I do remember languid days, the way the ponds smelled sweet, the soft sand, the freshwater clams. Suddenly I find myself thinking, Pete certainly went to a pool at a country club in Westport. He probably did not sit there reading. As I imagine Pete playing as a boy in the pool at his country club, I start to feel calmer. I watch his back, hear him call out to his brother, Dickie. I see floaties and smell club sandwiches and root beer on ice. Now, I am calmer and I feel tired.

Stretched out in the shade, a beautiful crimson umbrella over me, a true lime tree laden with green little fruits right next to the patio, so close I could eat them as I read, I open my book, try to remember the plot of *David Copperfield* so I can follow along with *Demon Copperhead*. And then, before I know it, I have fallen asleep.

When I awake, my daughters are standing in front of me, dusty and smelling of horses, and Sophie is saying something about going to the arts festival in town, with music and theater and tricks and clowns, and Iris is jumping around, excited. At first I think, Who are these people? Where are we? And then I realize and I say, Oh yes, these are my children.

40.
IRIS

Iris will forever remember every detail of this afternoon: She'd been watching out the window as they drove away from the castle and into the French afternoon heat. The outskirts of the small, walled town were full of cars and people and noise. She saw stone and wooden-framed houses that were secretive and quiet. Her mother parked near the river, the "Sewn," she had called it, which sounded almost like "Song" but no "g" on the end, as if you were waiting for some hard consonant to hurry up and end the word, make it finish. But like lots of French words did to Iris's ear, it just sort of trailed off into the ether, dangling. Her mother explained again how it was spelled, and Sophie said, "That's how it's spelled? With an A? That is so weird!" Iris and Sophie had changed out of their jeans and since it was so hot, Iris had agreed to wear a little purple terry-cloth sundress, which looked almost like a towel and was tied at the shoulders. Iris had noticed how Sophie had dressed that day: a short miniskirt with ruffles, a shirt that showed a very long bit of her naked stomach, and five silver bangles on one arm; they were clanking and clicking as they got out of the car. Her mother was wearing a straw hat, and Iris was wearing her San Diego Padres cap. "I'm thirsty," Iris immediately complained. "And hungry." Her mother hadn't even locked the car yet.

"Again?" asked Sophie. "We just ate, Booby."

"It wasn't enough. The portions were tiny. Besides, that was ages ago."

"Okay, okay, Iris." Her mother sounded grumpy, which put Iris on edge.

Iris grumbled under her breath, "What is the problem, guys! I'm hungry, that's all. What's wrong with that?"

"Iris, what?" asked her mother.

"I'm hungry, is all I am saying." She swung a kick at Sophie.

"Jesus, Booby," said Sophie.

"Boo—Iris—stop it! Okay, I will find you something." Her mother sounded frantic.

After walking in the hot sun for a few moments, they found an outdoor café called a *brasserie*, which, when Iris asked about the difference, her mother said she didn't really know, honestly. They sat under an umbrella and both girls ordered a lemonade and then they had some bread and pâté and a small endive salad that they shared. Iris ate a cold chocolate mousse while her mother went into the bathroom, and when she came out, Iris could see that her mother had applied some red lipstick she'd bought at a pharmacy back in Provence and was trying only now, after her nap at the pool, her hair mussed, her skin no longer so pallid, her bottom lip crimson. Iris asked Sophie if she wanted a bite of her mousse. Sophie said no and turned away.

"Sophie, may I order you one?" asked her mother.

"I said no," said Sophie.

"Okay. So, girls." Her mother pulled out her phone, and

after sending a quick text and smiling, she said she was looking at a schedule of events for the festival. "Okay. This seems like it could be very fun. Everything is happening in the little square just over there—we have a mime starting soon, and then some sort of fire-breather, then magic tricks, dance—hip-hop, I think—tightrope walking, a hot-air balloon, and a troupe called Guildenstern, Rosencrantz, and an Elephant. There's more here, like photo shows and street food, but we should go and see. What do you think, guys? Pickle? Sophs?"

Iris was definitely interested in the elephant and the tightrope walking. The hot-air balloon, sure, as long as she didn't have to go up in it. She said, "Good." Sophie said nothing. She yawned and looked away.

Sometimes Iris really didn't understand why Sophie was so mean to her mother; she didn't understand why everything her mother said or did was so annoying, why Sophie pulled away when her mother tried to hug her, looked angry when their mother was actually being fun. Iris tried to stare at Sophie as if to say, "Come on, be nice." But Sophie wouldn't take the hint.

"This all seems really stupid," Sophie grumbled.

"But isn't this the festival you wanted to go to?" Iris noticed her mother sounded shrill.

"Don't blame this on me, Alice."

"Sophie—my God, I'm not."

"Fine."

"Okay," her mother said, now trying for Mary Poppins–bright: "Well, let's see. Maybe you will enjoy it." They gathered their things, and for a moment, the girls waited while their mother disappeared again into her phone, texting, her face shiny. Then, she put her phone away in the cotton bag she'd slung on her arm, and they all went off together toward the town square.

The square was not quite a square, Iris observed. She looked at the lines and the angles and thought, This is a trapezoid. Or is it a rhombus? Iris had some flash cards with shapes and little facts on them. "Sophie, which one is a rhombus and which is a trapezoid?" she asked.

"Never mind. Shut up, Booby," said her sister.

In the middle of the square was an enormous tree. Her mother told her, after reading a plaque, that it was a linden tree, the largest linden in France, no less. Her mother said, "I think this is the tree you had in the tea, Iris. From Penelope. Do you remember, Sophie?" Sophie stepped a few feet away like she didn't know them. Iris remembered that. So her mother read out loud to Iris that this linden had been there for hundreds of years, since before Shakespeare, and through wars and famine and bad years of farming and good years of abundance, and the Nazis, too.

Her mother read, "'It is believed that you cannot tell a lie under a linden tree.'" When Iris looked up, she could see that in its leafy topmost branches, there were hundreds, maybe thousands, of sparrow-size brown birds. Her mother told her that they were starlings. They were chatting in high-pitched voices, and they sounded so happy. The air smelled softly sweet, like when you stuck your nose inside the honey jar at home. Next to the linden, all the buildings and people looked small, miniature, like they were bit players in a drama where the tree ruled the court.

Many of those "players" were half-dressed tourists milling around everywhere, eating large slabs of dough wrapped in paper and covered in something yellow and sticky, with powdered sugar on top of that. Music was playing, loud rap music that was so deafening, it was hard to tell if it was in English or French as it boomed through the speakers. All around them, all kinds of languages were being spoken, and people were taking selfies. Iris held more tightly to her mother's hand and then cried out, "Mama, look, there's Marc!"

"Who?" asked her mother.

"The riding teacher, Marc!"

Iris felt her mother stop to turn, and she saw her sister turn, too, and then she knew—something about the look on Sophie's face—that her sister and Marc had already caught each other's eye, even before she had called out. This was shocking to Iris, how far ahead Sophie always was, how she didn't share her timeline anymore.

"Sophie, it's Marc," Iris said, knowing it was inane, because clearly Sophs had already seen him. This moment, along with so many other little moments, would, later on, come into hyper-focus.

"I know, dummy," said Sophie. When Marc saw Iris and her mother joining Sophie's gaze, his smile changed, not exactly kinder and more inclusive but almost sarcastic. Iris would think of that later, too. The three of them moved along to the center of the square and found a man dressed as a clown, a very thin clown, with a red plastic bauble on his nose and green hair, riding a unicycle across a wire while people clapped and oohed and ahhed. A cart pushed by a man with a beard who was yelling "*Limonade*" ("*lee-mon-ah-ud*") to the crowd passed by. A person dressed all in black with their face painted white entered a low wooden stage. They seemed to come in an invisible door. "Mama, is that a man or a woman?" Iris asked. "I can't tell," said her mother.

The mime demonstrated the door by peering in, looking around, shutting it closed. Then the mime was in a room by themself, or at least they thought they were by themself, until they noticed the audience with a jolt, which made the audience laugh. The mime went on to pretend that they were using a toilet, stuck in a box, eating an apple, had caught their sock on a snag in the floor; they were petting a cat, lighting a fire, going to sleep, with nothing more than their hands to show all these things. Iris found herself narrating along to her mother and saying things like "Mama, they are using the bathroom!" Or "Oh, it's a cat." Or "They are climbing a tree now."

Sophie said, "Jesus. We know, Booby."

People all around them were laughing, and Iris and Sophie and their mother felt the hot sun beating down on them and laughed, too. Next were a man and a woman who did the usual magic tricks, the ones Iris had seen in books, of the woman being cut in half, a dove appearing in a hat, a coin vanishing behind an ear. Then came a theater troupe, dressed as gypsies and jesters, one leading a patient old elephant that plodded doggedly behind them, its eyes downcast. The heat seemed to stretch into the corners of the afternoon, invading the shadows and sucking the square of joy.

The jester was wearing a tight one-piece harlequin outfit, like what Iris had seen in picture books, and he juggled six balls while sitting on the elephant's shoulders. The gypsies shook tambourines and danced around the elephant and said words Iris didn't understand.

"What are they saying, Mama?" she asked.

"I don't know, it's in something Slavic—or Russian—I don't know."

"This is boring," said Sophie. "I'm going over there to stand in the shade. By that tree." Sophie pointed to the linden with the starlings boiling all over it, rising up in one dark, arcing crowd like they were mosquitoes or smoke, touching back down into the branches. Iris could see the shady coolness under the tree, almost feel it, from where she stood.

"The elephant looks dry, Mama," observed Iris.

"Sophie—stay right there, okay? We'll find you shortly."

A princess came onto the stage wearing a high-waisted pink dress, and her long hair flowed out from her golden paper crown. There was a story being told about the man on the elephant dressed as a harlequin and the princess, something about lost love and heartbreak, Iris could tell that much. The elephant had something to do with the melodrama, but it wasn't clear what, exactly. In this fairy-tale hodgepodge, the elephant was being used as some sort of beanstalk and Iris started to also piece together that the story was about a beautiful princess and the wily ways of men. Her mother whispered, "There's some Shakespearean gender-bending being thrown in," and Iris nodded, though she didn't understand. She assumed that was meant for Sophie, even though Sophie was under the linden tree now.

By the end of the skit, the woman was on the elephant with her legs spread wide, as if the trunk of the elephant were her penis, and the harlequin man with the very obvious bulge in his tight spandex suit was wearing the long blond wig, busy spinning wool at a spinner and singing the Dolly Parton song about love being like a butterfly, with a slight twang. Iris's mother had that album at home, and sometimes they put it on the record player in their living room. Iris liked "Coat of Many Colors" the best.

The skit embarrassed Iris and she hoped her mother didn't get it. When it was over and people were hooting and laughing, Iris turned, red-faced, to her mother with a questioning look and her mother said something like, "Well, that was certainly avant-garde, wasn't it?"

Iris nodded. But who knew what the hell her mother was talking about. Why are mothers so hard to understand sometimes? She could hear her mother's phone buzz and then her mother said, "One second." She was smiling—privately—as she wrote a text.

Iris tugged at her mother. "I want to go, Mama," she said.

"I know, hang on." Her mother sent another text, then put the phone away, brightened, and said, "Yes, okay, let's go find Sophie."

The two of them turned, looking expectantly to the church on the far side of the square, where the linden tree grew. That whole end of the square was shady now, as the sun was behind the tree and also behind the church. The shadow cast by the tree was deep and cool and went on forever and ever. Iris noticed that the birds were gone from the top of the tree. At least this was how Iris would tell the story for the rest of her life. Because it was the moment when the eyes saw what the heart and brain had already perceived that she would remember what she somehow already knew: Sophie was not there.

41.

ALICE

At first I thought, Well, of course she's there. I mean. She's here. In the shade of that linden tree. Or she's gone into the church. Or she's wandered off to look at a fresco or a statue.

When Sophie was a baby, she would crawl away from me to play with a toy. But it wasn't the moment of crawling away that mattered, really, it was when she turned back to me. She was out in front, taking risks. But she was also always checking back in to make sure our woolly yarn was still tied.

When she was around one, she started to hold on to me when other people were present. Most babies are like this; she didn't want me to hand her to anyone else. She would turn her little body to mine, burying her face in my neck, looking away from the other person, willing them to cease to exist. The way she held on like that, giving her to a babysitter was torture. Not even worth the whole wrenching thing. Also, I liked to be with her. It was like that for years and years.

Thank goodness, I often think, for all those years when Sophie and I did everything together before Iris, before the time when she'd start to individuate—a process that hurt my body physically. You don't expect that, things to all happen at the same time, when everything is some sort of grueling survival test, your husband and your kids and your body all turned on you, enemies all at once. I'm saying you just don't expect that at the beginning.

When I had cancer, sometimes Sophie would come into my room to sit on the bed and talk. She wouldn't say much of anything, honestly. But I knew not to move one single muscle, to just be there because this, this right here, was pure gold. The teenage sensitivity is so delicate, I realized, anything could disturb her. So I wouldn't. I'd tamp it all down and just be still as Pippa Mouse, listen, wait for her. Over the last year, she's come to me less. But when she does, Pete's snoring away, and she sits so far away I can't touch her on the end of the bed. But I'll do anything to keep her there, no matter how tired I am. I repeat like a mantra to myself the opening lines to a Randall Kenan story, "Hobbits and Hobgoblins": "The world whispers to those who listen."

Now, I think, all I have to do is wait. Slow down. Listen. Iris and I walk around the church. We go behind the church and then inside the church. We go into the café on the corner, we walk in large circles. Iris is now holding my hand, and I am squeezing her hand tightly, and I can feel her little fingers mushed together, but I can't stop. "Iris," I say. "Do you see her?"

"Mommy, you're hurting my hand," she says.

We are dizzy from going in circles, unsure whom to ask, where to go, we don't know this town at all, or what there is for scaffolding in an emergency. I don't know yet whether this is an emergency. When does a teenager wandering off constitute an emergency? Does anyone ever give parents a bulleted flyer with a list for "What to do when you're in an emergency, teenage edition"?

I am peering down the dark medieval streets; they seem to slope slightly, away and up from the square, as if the square were sunken. The small wooden-beamed buildings appear now to me more like *Hansel and Gretel* huts, not at all charming, and I can only think that stories like that one turn out not so great, there's often a wolf or a witch. I heard in a podcast once that it takes about five hours to find a missing child. Five hours. When you go past five hours, the possibility of the worst having happened goes up exponentially.

I look at my phone for the time. A clock starts ticking in my mind, every second lost could be the one that mattered. "Isn't there anyone who can help us?" asks Iris in a small voice next to me.

"There must be," I say, and put my free hand to my face as a visor so I can scan the square. I can feel panic rising in my chest. But I need to sound calm, move deliberately for Iris. If she falls apart it will make it harder. Go slowly, I tell myself, like you're approaching a growling beast, one hand outstretched. Watch the jaws. You need to think carefully. Later, I will think, Well, of course Iris knew I was flipping out.

Across the hot square, there's a man wearing a short-sleeved light blue shirt with badges on it, dark trousers, and a squarish hat that seems to confer some level of importance. "Iris, look—there's a policeman, I think."

We make our way to the man, and I can hear Iris's little pink Crocs squeaking a bit with her sweaty feet rubbing inside them.

"Hello, sir," I say. "I have lost my daughter." He looks at Iris.

"No—not this daughter, my older one—*plus grande—comme ça?*" I try to show him how tall Sophie is with my hand that isn't holding Iris's hand. Then I pull out my phone and say, *"Elle est là,"* pointing to a photo taken just that morning. Looking at it now, it seems to be eons ago, back at our campsite in the Dordogne, when I took a photo of both girls before we started driving. How has this day not ended yet?

The man looks at me now with the kind of attention that makes you feel, all of a sudden, safer in a situation like this. Attention is being paid. I can say this now because I know this now. He listens to every word, watching my face carefully, and then looks at the picture and pulls his walkie-talkie from his belt and speaks some fast and indiscernible French words into it. Soon a female cop arrives, wearing the same outfit as the man, except her navy blue trousers are a long navy blue skirt. She shakes my hand and looks at my photos and asks us when we last saw Sophie. I tell her, "Well, she went to stand in the shade, we were watching the show . . ." and I float my hand toward the square, where throngs of people are still blithely watching skits and musical acts as if my daughter isn't missing. "There was the one with the man in the harlequin outfit and the woman with the blond hair," I say.

"Oui, oui." The policewoman is writing down notes. Another policeman with jet-black hair and a mustache arrives. The last two confer with the first. They are pointing around the square as if making a search plan. They take this seriously, these French cops, not an ounce of irony or indifference. Not a single second of laziness. All professionalism and pride to do this important job.

"Does your daughter have a smartphone?" The policewoman is talking to me. She looks down at her pad of official light-blue carbon-copy paper to indicate she will be writing this down.

"No. She's not quite fourteen."

"An iPod or iPad?"

"Not on her."

"Any device by which we could track her—Type One diabetes with Bluetooth CGM or Fitbit?"

"No." I cast my eyes down.

And then Iris is wiggling next to me. I didn't realize that I had dropped her small hand as I was wringing my own hands. I pick it back up and try to smooth it with my free hand. My voice is shaking now and tears are starting to spout out the corners of my eyes. All the while, the professional policewoman keeps saying "*Oui, oui, oui*" and making notes, lots and lots of notes, about the material and color of Sophie's skirt, whom she might know in the town (*no one*, I say). I keep trying to think of every single detail I could possibly give this woman, when Iris says, "Wait, Mama!"

"Not now, Iris. Let me finish this thought—"

"Wait, Mama!"

"Iris, I'm talking to this policewoman."

"Mama, I did see Sophie talking with someone!!"

"You what?" The policewoman's pen poises above her paper.

"Why didn't you say this before?" I ask.

"I forgot. I forgot when it happened. I forgot it mattered."

"It matters, Iris. Please spit it out. Say!" I'm suddenly irrationally angry at Iris, as if all of what is happening depends on this one detail my child has not been forthcoming with. How embarrassing! I take her by her bare, tan shoulders; I want to shake her. I don't shake her. I see the fear in her eyes, too. They are my mirrors. Oh, my little Pickle.

"I saw Sophie for a second only. She was in the shade under that linden tree . . ." Iris says the word "linden" in such a way that it sounds like tinkling silver jewels, "LIN-den." "And Sophie was talking to the riding teacher, Marc, and the guy with the harlequin outfit, who was wearing the blond wig. You know? Well, you were texting and I was waiting. And then I saw them walk sort of near the church, maybe behind it, I don't know, because there was another thing happening on the stage, the thing with the huge puppets, and I was watching those, and watching them finally give water to the elephant, and when we turned back around, I didn't see her again."

The riding instructor. The man in the harlequin outfit with the diamonds of color. My daughter. I was texting. I was texting! That was all the policewoman needed, the mention of those two young men.

She calls to her two colleagues, who get on their radios, and then two more policemen arrive, clean-shaven, muscular. The four men start to fan out across the square, hunting, serious. Is this actually happening? I think.

I hear a distant police siren, and a small police car comes onto one of the blocked-off streets. The driver pulls into the square and parks in the shade of the church. Two more men hop out, speak to one of the first four men, and then all of them are dispersed, combing through the square. Six men, one woman, all working. The clock is ticking.

People at the festival are turning to look now. The policewoman leads Iris and me to the front of a store that sells belts and bags made of leather and asks me if I want a cup of water or coffee, a soda for my little girl. I nod, unable to speak. When the policewoman leaves to go into the café next door to the leather goods store, I turn to Iris. I try for a softer tone, though I'm sure she can hear me clenching my teeth. "Is there anything else you haven't told me?"

"No." Her shoulders are trembling now like she is cold. "No, there is nothing else, I promise."

The woman comes back with a water for me and a small glass jar of peach juice for Iris. She gets down, eye level, with Iris and hands her the juice and smiles at her, comforts my daughter in a way I can't right now. She asks us both, searching my face and then Iris's, "Is there anywhere else she could have gone that you can think of?"

"The château, maybe? We are staying at the castle, and the riding instructor—the man named Marc, the one who my daughter mentioned—he works there."

"Let's go there," the policewoman says, and she leads Iris and me to a small police car parked down three cobblestoned streets, left, right, left, and in a hot parking lot where everything smells like baking rocks.

"Mama, should we tell Daddy?" comes Iris's little voice from the back seat. I turn and see my little spindly daughter, eyes peering forward, alone. Everything is in IMAX theater intensity. Like that film we took Sophie to when she was little at the Boston Science Museum, where a huge snake seemed to poke up from behind your seat. We were stuck enduring the terror of that film until it ended. But at least we knew that a film had to end, would end.

"Oh," I say. "Oh." And then: "Let's see if she's in our room first, at the castle, at the pool, riding with Marc—anything. This will scare the living daylights out of Daddy." I imagine Pete's face, hearing this. My heart might stop if I have to tell him this.

The policewoman drives quickly with her siren on, and we pull up in front of the château's grand steps. She doesn't need to park in the lot. She hops out, maybe the car is still running, I have no idea, and I follow her, forgetting Iris, then doubling back to grab her hand, and all that is going through my mind is this: Please. Please. Please. God. Please. I am willing to believe in anyone or anything right now, even angels.

A backup police car arrives behind us, and two more female cops jump out and make their way toward the pool. I hear one of them say on a radio transmitter, *"Cherchez le fleuve."* The river. I get that much.

Iris and I rush to our room while our personal cop stays downstairs. She is busy summoning the manager when we get into the elevator. The key card shakes in my hand as I try to open the door. I drop it on the stone floor and I'm shouting, "Sophie, are you in there, Sophie!" Iris picks up the card for me and slides it into the little slot very carefully and pushes open the door. We burst into the room. Iris and I call. We look—ridiculous—under the beds, in the bathroom, in the closets. Iris is crying now, I knew this was coming and now here it is, the category 5 storm. I keep saying, "Iris, you gotta help me. Don't fall apart—not yet, honey, not yet. Iris! Goddammit. No, just keep looking."

When we go back down in the elevator empty-handed, our cop meets us at the door. From one look she knows we have not found Sophie upstairs. She goes back into the manager's office and closes the door.

Iris and I stand on that red carpet, under that big chandelier, the fountain bubbling next to us. "Mama," croaks Iris, "please call Daddy. I want Daddy." She starts to wail. We are in our own little cone of terror. Iris sits down on the rug and pulls her knees to her face and is sobbing. There is so much aloneness and loneliness in a crisis. No one ever talks about that.

"Okay, Pickle, okay." I can barely speak. I dial Pete. I notice that guests and red-vested staff are milling through the hotel like everything is fine. In the dining room, *apéro* have started, and people are eating little canapés and olive tapenade and drinking Aperol spritzes and Beaujolais.

Pete picks up on the first ring. "Hey." The warmth, the familiarity, the love I don't deserve, are all sent across the phone line as his voice floods through me. The yarn that ties us tugs, tightens.

"Pete. Pete." Tears are cascading out of my eyes. I know he can hear Iris crying in the background, but I feel like someone might have stolen my voice.

Immediately, Pete is on high alert. "Yes. Alice! Speak. What's wrong? What's wrong, Alice? Is Iris okay?"

"Sophie," I whisper.

"Sophie what? What's happened to Sophie?" Panic is creeping into his voice.

"She's gone." I think I might faint. Just those two words. Incredible. Impossible. They slice through the phone. I wince.

"Gone? Gone *where*, Alice?"

"I don't know. I lost her." Again, that word "lost." Like my breast. Like my lymph nodes. When I say "lost" this time, I am sure the word might finally kill me. Too many losts piling up, and now it is the mother of all losts: my child. The pain is physical, a mortal wound: a sword, a knife, a knitting needle, a bullet.

"You mean Iris, right?"

"No. What? Sophie."

"How do you *lose* a fourteen-year-old girl?"

"I don't know."

"How do you *not* fucking know?"

He needs the facts: "She was with me. She went to stand in the shade. Under a tree. A huge linden tree. I looked away. I have no idea. She just *fucking* vanished. Pete, she vanished." I'm starting to feel every inch of hysterical as the stark reality of what I am explaining has set in.

"Alice, have you called the cops?"

I nod as if he can see me.

"Alice?"

"Yes, the cops—they are here. They are looking."

"Is there anything else you can tell me? Could she have gone off with someone?"

"There's this riding instructor. He's like seventeen or twenty or—I don't know. Iris says Sophie was talking to him in the square."

Pete is silent then. How could I have done this to him? His daughter. His firstborn. The child who turned him into a dad. I can hear him breathing like a horse. In a way, it comforts me. I know that breathing of my husband's, it's concentrated breaths. He is focused. The high school lacrosse player; the Connecticut state record holder, for the second half of the nineties, in the 55-meter dash. This is the guy I met almost two decades ago, the guy who will stop at nothing, *my* guy, who just puts his head down and handles it.

"I'm getting on a plane. It's ten a.m. here. I'll call you from the airport."

"Okay." My voice is small. "Okay." I am nodding vigorously. "Just get here."

"Alice, Alice—listen to me, okay? Do not stop looking. Don't waste a minute. Don't fall apart. Not now. You got that? I will be right there. Hand the phone to Iris."

I hand the phone to Iris and hear her say, "Daddy?" She is a puddle, lying in the fetal position on the red rug in the middle of the lobby. She is still only wearing that little dress, she must be cold. Pete's talking to her, she's nodding, she's trying to sit up, then wailing, then lying back down, then sitting up. She hands the phone back. "Daddy wants you."

"Alice, I need you to get every person you can think of on the line. The guy in Provence who's a diplomat's son, anyone. Everyone. I need the entire country of France looking for my daughter. And fast. No time can be lost. Do you understand?" He says those last words slowly, gently. He knows I might shatter into a thousand pieces before he can even get here to help me.

"I understand."

"I will be there soon. You're not alone, Alice. I will be right there. Stay strong—Alice, just stay strong."

"Okay," I say. "Tell me when you are on your way." My voice is strangled, I can't breathe. We hang up, and I take Iris to a couch and ask her to sit with me; there is so much sitting in a crisis, I think. "Iris, I have to call some people. I need to find Penelope's number."

"What about Mr. Tumnus?"

"What? Didier?"

"Yes."

"He's in the Alps— "

"Mama." She looks at me patiently, accepting, wiser than I wish she looked. "We need *everyone*," she is saying with her eyes.

I text Didier: Hi. I know we just texted a little while ago and everything was fine. But we have lost Sophie. I have lost Sophie. The cops are here . . .

I see the ". . ." bubble of texting and then the phone rings. Didier's voice is at the same time thrilling and also incongruous to my life. All he says is "I'll be right there."

I find Penelope's number in my phone under our camping

reservation. I call and it rings and rings. I imagine everyone outside, sitting under the lemon trees, eating and smoking. Marie answers.

"Marie. Thank heavens it's you. It's Alice."

There's a pause.

"The American, Alice, who was camping there."

"Oh, Alice, *comment ça va?*"

"Poorly. I've lost Sophie. My older daughter. I need Georges."

"Oh, *mon Dieu*. Georges—" I can hear her yell. "Georges! *Viens vite!*" The phone is shuffling and banging around. Then I hear Marie whisper, "*C'est* Alice, *l'américaine—avec les deux petites filles. La grande fille est perdue.*" I hear Georges say in the background, "*Ohh-la-la. C'est pas vrai?*" Then Marie's voice says, "*Je sais pas. Tiens.*"

I hear the phone fumbling, then: "*Oui?*" Georges's deep voice fills my ear.

"Georges, my daughter—Sophie, the older one—you remember her—she is gone. I need your help." I'm gulping for air again, like there just isn't enough oxygen in the entire universe to help me say these terrible words.

"*Où êtes-vous?* I mean, where are you?"

"I am at this castle—the Château des Confluences, outside Lyon. Do you know it?"

"Okay. No—I will find it. *J'arrive. Tout de suite.*"

After we hang up, Marie texts: Addie and Alain are coming, too.

I text back: Ok. Thank you. Then I put the phone down.

"What do we do now, Mama?" Iris looks at me expectantly. I am the parent, the one who needs to know what to do.

"We wait," I say. That much I know. I don't call my parents, though the little girl in me wants to. What could they do from so far away? When I had cancer, I said the same thing to myself, and then to them: "There's nothing you will be able to do here. I just have to go through this."

But this, *this*, is so much worse. The helplessness of knowing there is nothing they can do—my parents!—and nothing I can do makes me want to wail. Staff from the hotel bring Iris and me tea and water as we wait and wait and wait. I watch people leave the restaurant to stroll the gardens and others go out to dinner. I see others still come in for dinner. I see kids get tarts and *crêpes flambées*. I see people check in and check out. Time bumps along so slowly into the future while the past is slipping away too quickly, before I can grab it properly, hold it, make sure it is mine.

Pete calls and tells me he can't get a direct flight so he is flying to Lisbon and then to Lyon—we won't see him until after midnight. Didier is in the car, Georges is on his way. All my second daughter and I have to do is sit still, listen, hope, pray, cry, drink water, use the bathroom. And as small as these tasks might seem, they are excruciating, like climbing Everest, each one.

42.

IRIS

A new female cop wants to talk to Iris. She says in broken English, "Tell me everything your sister told you. Everything you know about this guy, this guy Marc." Iris is sitting next to her mother on the bench in the lobby and her face feels like it's been cast in cement. Her mother, beside her, looks gray and very old to Iris and Iris notices that her mother is chewing her fingers. Iris has also noticed that her mother's pinkie is bleeding next to her fingernail. If Iris were to use words right now to describe how she feels, she would say "scared," or "sad." But no one has asked her how she feels. She must just supply more information, information she feels afraid she might not have, or she might get wrong, and somehow she could make it harder for the police to find her sister and then it will be all her fault.

Iris's mother says, "Iris—please—answer everything you can think of. I am right here, Pickle. Give me your hand." She feels her mother reach over and hold her hand, gently, softly.

"Ummm." Tears start streaming down her face, they are hot

and burn her skin with their saltiness. "So there was the riding teacher, Marc?"

"Yes, where did you meet him?" asks the cop, who has a shiny badge Iris notes that reads "Saint-Pierre." Iris guesses that is her name, maybe her last name.

"My sister and I went on a riding lesson with him earlier today."

"Was there anyone else?"

"Yes, there was Nadia."

"Who is Nadia?"

"She is a Russian girl who is staying here with her family?"

"Okay." Officer Saint-Pierre writes that down.

"We didn't really talk to her."

The officer writes that down. "*Et* Marc?"

"He said he was from New York City. Like us."

"How was his English?"

"Perfect."

"Did he tell you more?"

"He told Sophie. I was just there. He didn't really tell me. But he told her he went to Dalton, which is a school back home. Sophie knows kids there, she told him. And his mother still lives in New York. But he said his father lives in France."

"So he is American?"

"I don't know. I don't know." Iris can't stop the tears, they are a waterfall. "That's all I know."

"Did he show any special interest in your sister?"

"I don't know. They talked. That's all I know. He was riding alongside my sister, and then there was Nadia in the middle, and I was in the back. When we went on the trails."

"Did anything out of the ordinary happen?"

"I don't know. I don't know!" Iris is having trouble breathing, there is snot in her mouth; Iris wishes her mother could get her a tissue. Her mother just holds her hand. Iris keeps thinking, but doesn't say out loud, "If only I had kept my eyes on Sophie and not turned back to the festival, this never would have happened."

The officer pulls a tissue packet out of a zippered hip pocket and hands it to Iris. Then says, "Thank you, you told me a lot. If you think of anything more, please tell me." Iris wipes her face with the tissues. Before the officer walks away, Iris hears her mother say, "My husband. He is on his way. He has called the US embassy." Iris can feel the power in her mother's voice: My husband. The US. The embassy. The might of it.

The officer nods, speaks into her walkie-talkie, then goes to speak with the manager of the hotel.

Iris turns to her mother. "Why is everyone asking me like they think this is my fault? Like I am the one who lost Sophie?"

"No one thinks that, sweetie. They are just trying to get as much information as they can. And we need to tell them every single detail, anything at all, no matter how small. I've seen this on TV shows, the police go over and over the clues, thinking we might have forgotten something, missed it. That's all. How about we go get you something to eat there in the restaurant? Maybe some bread and cheese, some warm tea like the kind Penelope made you?" Iris nods, unable to say any more words.

So Iris and her mother go into the restaurant and sit down. Her mother orders Iris a croque monsieur and tisane de tilleul and an English breakfast tea for herself. Iris eats the sandwich guiltily, as if she shouldn't need to eat. She drinks the warm tea. Her nose and eyes keep weeping. She uses the one paper napkin that came with her sandwich for her eyes and nose, and balls it up and shoves it under the lip of her plate. Iris can see her mother is thinking everything through over and over, trying to find a way to discover a clue in the details of the day.

After a little while, Officer Saint-Pierre comes over to the table and squats down by her mother and says in a low voice: "The boy Marc, he has an iPhone. We tracked it at the square—where you last saw Sophie. We have also established who the player in the troupe was. He's an actor from the Czech Republic. Unfortunately, the devices both young men own seem to be off or left behind; they were last picked up near the church and the linden tree. We are working on a warrant to look through phone calls and texts. We have contacted the US embassy in Paris. And Metropole in Lyon. Shouldn't be too long now for more informations." Iris notes the extra "s" and wonders if it belongs there.

After eating, Iris and her mother go back to the lobby to sit on the couch near the fountain where they sat before. A woman with a big cart comes by and hands Iris a big fluffy blanket to curl up in on the couch. Time ticks by, and the police come and go while she and her mother watch. The police keep talking with each other in low voices, consulting their radios, standing silently and looking at their phones. "Isn't there more we can do?" Iris whispers to her mother. "I don't know what that would be," her mother says. "We just have to let the police do their job. If we leave the hotel, we could miss her. We have to wait."

The sun sinks and the night begins. The lobby empties out, the dining room is vacuumed, and plates and tiny glasses for the next day are placed. Iris is so tired, she slumps against her mother, holding the cowrie shell from Marie in one hand and the little cicada from Penelope in the other. She is knocking them together every few moments to hear a little tinkly sound that reverberates through the echo chamber of the shell. Outside the windows of the château, it is now so dark that Iris worries about Sophie in the darkness. Will she be eaten by wild animals? What if the sun never comes back? Day might never happen again. Eternal darkness. Sophie will never find them again. That is her last thought before she can't hold on any longer. The last thing Iris sees before she falls asleep is people at the bar laughing and popping the cork on a bottle of champagne. When she opens her eyes again, she sees her father.

Her dad is standing in the middle of the room. He is tanned but his hair looks grayer than Iris remembers from two weeks ago. He is wearing pants and a white collared shirt that is open at the neck. He is leaning over a table where four police officers consult a map on a computer. Iris can see, from where she sits, that her father is in charge, making decisions, staying calm. He is speaking a mix of the odd French word and English. His voice is clipped like the clops of a horse. Across the room, near a large porcelain vase filled with brightly colored flowers, she sees her mother from behind. She sees her mother's wrinkled linen jumpsuit and the way her back looks, slumped, airless, wilted. Her mother is talking to Mr. Tumnus.

43.

PETE

It wasn't exactly a piece of cake to get a flight in the middle of July 2022: Everyone and her brother, post-Covid, was flying to Europe. Pete had asked his assistant, Veronica (who was loudly sipping an iced watermelon-ginger-blueberry juice through a long paper straw), to find every and any flight she could while he took an Uber uptown. He called a friend of a friend who got him a contact at the US embassy in Paris and another at the French embassy in New York. He got to his apartment and quickly threw his deodorant, a change of underwear, a toothbrush, two black V-neck T-shirts, and one more pair of slacks into a duffel bag. He was wearing his gray slacks, a white shirt. He changed into his HOKA sneakers. None of this was important. By noon he was at JFK, passing through security without a single untied shoe, pat-down, or scan, all on embassy clearance, and boarding a TAP Air Portugal flight, first class to Lisbon, then on to Lyon. It was the only flight available. No Air France. No Delta. No British Airways. Nothing. After checking in, he stood on line, too amped to sit down, holding his Adidas duffel, his mirrored

Dukes of Hazzard–throwback sunglasses still on. Pete thought he was perhaps having a heart attack while he stood there, then he thought he might faint, then he realized that he was actually just crying. He pushed the sunglasses tighter against the bridge of his nose. He texted his wife, or Alice . . . okay, fuck, he really didn't know right now, was she still his wife?

Hey. I am standing in line. Ready to board. Fucking-A, Alice. I am freaking out. More tears seeped from behind his glasses and out; he caught them with the back of his hand. WTF, he thought.

. . . The three dots as he waited. Every second felt like a boat ride across an ocean.

I know. I know. I am here, waiting. I think everyone is doing everything they can. She has vanished. Our girl, Pete.

Did his heart stop for a second on that "our"? It felt like it did this little hitch thing, a thing he'd been noticing in the last year or so, when he'd be lying down, and suddenly, it was like his heart caught a snag, a piece of fishing line or floss, then jerked free and kept on thumping away.

The flight was announced, first class first. Pete went right down the gangplank onto the plane, stowed his duffel, and told the flight attendant, "Once you start service, I need a scotch. Make that a double." She was a lithe woman with very red lips and dark eyes. "Yessir," she said, her accent thick with smoky Portuguese. On an ordinary day, Pete might have flashed his George Clooney smile—who else maintained that kind of charisma as he got older? Obama, surely; Eddie Vedder, Bruce Springsteen, Gavin Newsom—but even the idea of being charming, as his daughter dangled somewhere, nowhere, and everywhere around him, made his stomach turn. The Police were on the stereo: "Every move you make / And every vow you break . . ."

Every vow you break. Every vow you break. Daggers in his eyes and heart. "This is all my fault," he murmured to himself as he took his seat.

A man standing in the aisle said, "Sorry?"

The thing about flying in a tube up in the sky is that you are sort of *in it* with the person seated next to you. And so, when the man Pete would learn later was named Jerry sat down next to him, a bushy guy with a round belly, a big beard, Pete felt relieved, less alone. There was something solid in the man's heavy breathing, the sweat on his brow, his backpack clanking with a rainbow of carabiners. "Excuse me," he said as he leaned Pete's way to shove his overfilled backpack at a bulging angle under the seat.

Pete waved an assent. He couldn't speak—his throat was swollen shut with fear, then rage, then incipient grief, each emotion having its way with him, throwing him up on the beach of time with the most ruthless of waves. Time was his enemy. He couldn't stop it, force it, manhandle it. He kept calculating how long the flight would take if they even left on time, which, with the slow way everyone seemed to be moving, did not look remotely likely. Then how long the wait was in Lisbon, then the next flight. All hours and minutes during which his daughter might come to more harm or maybe be found. What shape would she be in if they found her? Would they even know to ask the right questions when they did? How does that part work? he wondered. Horrors went through his mind.

He was not there and he needed to be. He needed to be there for Sophie, for Iris, for his wife . . . for Alice. Alice! Alice was the center of this for him. All those months Alice had suffered alone in their room while he and the girls tried to go on, with no idea if she'd live or die. Turns out cancer is never so clear, or so fast. Time is the only thing you have; cancer is measured in time and more time. Alice knew this, but he and the girls, they were in crisis mode for six months, a year, while Alice did all the treatments and lost her breast. He found himself suddenly thinking about the courage it took for Alice to start again as a writer and go off to France. But at the word "France" his mind went immediately to Alice finding someone else in France. For a second he had an epiphany that that, too, was actually his fault. And Alice now losing their daughter? Not her fault, he wasn't stupid.

As the man next to him got comfortable, Pete had a totally new and revelatory thought: What must Alice feel like to be Alice right now? He hadn't really done that before, asked himself this question. Not like this. And when he did, he was shocked by its sucker punch. The whole Alice-ness of the situation floored him, the bumpy hardship of it all, how resilient she had been. He was choking on salty, unwanted tears again. They made rain splatters on his gray slacks. He rubbed at the marks with the palms of his hands.

The burly man next to him was leaning closer, and Pete could see, through the prisms of tears in his eyes, the man's blurry face. He could smell the man's sweat, and he realized the man was talking to him. "Here," the man said. "I have no idea why I packed three, but I have three." He handed Pete a handkerchief and said, "I can make do with two on my trip. Take one." He was holding out a light yellow square of cloth with purple polka dots all over it, a garishly cheery design like you might expect to find on a fitted sheet for a baby's crib. "My name's Jerry." He stuck his other hand out. His forearm had black hairs that ended in silver tips like a coyote's. "Can't knock being upgraded to first, right?" The man smiled. Pete nodded, took his hand, shook it. (Pete always flew first or business.) He took the handkerchief gingerly and used it to awkwardly wipe his face under his sunglasses. He cleared his throat and said thank you.

"Scared of flying?" the man asked.

WTF? Pete thought, noting that he was now thinking in acronyms. But he saw the man was waiting for him to speak, looking at him peculiarly. "No," Pete whispered. (Why the fuck was he whispering?) "I just. I'm trying to get to Europe. My daughter. She's lost or stolen or kidnapped." Was this true? Could it be? Was he speaking fiction? It must be fiction. How had this happened? Saying it out loud was worse than keeping it in. He looked out the window and over the wing of the plane and at the little TAP Air Portugal red and green insignia on the end by a light.

Jerry whistled. And said, "Oh, dear." He reached a hand up and hit the flight attendant's call button. Pete wondered what was coming next. Was the man afraid that daughter snatching was contagious? Already asking to change seats since he didn't want to spend six hours in the air with a man who was dying inside?

Pete had started to say "I'm sorry to tell you that" when the flight attendant arrived, a young man wearing tight pants and a nylon bow tie. Jerry spoke first: "Hello—my friend here"—he waved one of his fat hands Pete's way—"his daughter is lost. Maybe even kidnapped in this crazy world. We need to get over to Europe quickly. Is everyone on the plane? Is the captain ready? What can we do?"

Pete was aghast. And moved. How unusual was it for a stranger to extend themself this way? He felt his top lip tremble for a second. He bit it. The flight attendant looked over at Pete warily, afraid, and then said, "I will go ask the captain what can be done." And was gone.

"Thanks, man," Pete said to Jerry. "For what it's worth, I expect to be in hell for at least the next ten hours, so." He smiled wanly.

"I am so sorry, my friend," said Jerry. "I wish I could help."

"Thank you," said Pete, and looked away.

But the man was still talking. "Have you prayed?"

"Not really," said Pete, looking out the window and willing the wheels to start rolling. Jesus. Jerry Garcia. Was he a Bible beater?

"I wasn't really a religious guy, my whole life. Then a few years ago I walked that Camino, the one that goes across northern Spain, do you know it?"

Pete nodded, still turned away. He thought, Oh God is he going to hand me a Watchtower?

"And I started praying in those cathedrals. First it was selfish stuff, like 'I pray my feet stop hurting' or 'I pray I don't die in this heat,' I mean, let's face it, I'm not a small guy. I've got some cholesterol issues. Type Two—that one's my fault. But then my prayers got bigger, more expansive, more hopeful, and less cynical. I'm just a small-town guy from Vermont . . ."

Figures, thought Pete.

"But the thing is, the more I included other people—or even plants and trees and animals—in my prayers, the more hopeful I became. And that changed things for me. I'm on my way now to hike along the coast of Portugal by myself. I want to see every cathedral on the way, and I will do the same, pray the whole way, likely about my feet, then maybe a few bigger things." He chuckled at himself. "I can pray for you, too. But . . . you know, so can you. Would you like me to lead you?"

"No, that's okay." Pete took in a deep breath and put his hand up, not quite making eye contact. "I'm okay—all good. I—I just need to get there. Thank you."

The man smiled. He looked like he felt sorry for Pete. And that irritated Pete enough to look away. Then he cast a glance back, partly hoping Jerry might try again. But Jerry had put his earphones on and was watching *Top Gun: Maverick*.

Pete was alone now, squinting out the window. The air-conditioning was insubstantial, the July heat radiating off the macadam. He felt the plane jolt as the blocks were removed from the wheels. He pulled out his phone, paid for and connected to the Wi-Fi, and started to text Alice. To say what? Well, anything. He would say anything. He would connect with his wife while she was still his. His Alice.

Hey, I am on the plane. They just started rolling for takeoff. How are you?

He hit send and then immediately hit edit and deleted "How are you?" What a dumb fucking question. He looked at his phone and then he saw the ". . ." of her texting him. Had she seen his edit? He wasn't sure.

I am sick with worry, she wrote.

I know. I am too, he wrote back. I will land in Lisbon in about 6 hours. Text me if anything changes. Pete started to write "I love you." Then stopped. He wrote, I love you guys.

Fly safely was all she wrote back. And then they were up and in the air, flying into the longest afternoon of Pete's life, one long, *long* golden hour, straight into the sunset, across the Atlantic, and into unlucky darkness.

44.

ALICE

When Pete walked into the château, it was four in the morning, not yet light. Didier was there, and I was grateful he'd come. But something about his presence, though pulling at me even in this crisis, felt a nuisance, the slightest bit. He didn't really know us—me, Iris, or Sophie. His ability to translate for the cops and back to me was helpful—necessary—he was playing an important role. Georges was not yet there, the road from Provence very long, and Pete had landed by then in Lisbon and taken the first flight to Lyon. He was coming by driver the rest of the way. Didier was my first responder.

But then, my husband: I was standing at the top of the stairs, looking at the bank of glass doors, when I saw the black car arrive, saw him get out, the white of his shirtsleeves. I watched him take a second to thank the man, of course he would do that. Then he opened the door to the château. There was a second when he didn't see me and I was able to take in his midnight shadow, the wrinkles in his white shirt, his plain flat-front gray chinos, his bright orange and blue HOKA sneakers, his cop glasses dangling from his shirt pocket; though tan, his face was puffy, tinged, grayish in that dark hour before the day begins again, making him look a bit like Mark Ruffalo.

When he looked up at me, his face was set and his intelligent eyes said everything silently, forcefully: "I am here. This is our daughter. We will find her." I stood at the top of the stairs and waited for him. He came up and kissed my forehead, put his duffel bag down, and held me for a long moment. I took his hand and led him to the hub the police had created in the middle of the lobby—a hotel table, some radios, two cops. I introduced them and then I introduced our translator, Didier. I didn't tell Pete with my voice or body that this was the man, this *is* the man. I just let it be. We needed everyone on the one problem. Later, I told myself, I would confess.

By then Marc's father, Pierre Ricard, had been found at his vineyard not far away in Beaujolais. Marc and his friend, the guy with the wig and the harlequin suit in that lewd and bizarre skit, had also been found by the police and questioned, we were told, at the police station in town. The two young men were being held for additional questioning and to "sober up." They had been out at the country estate of a Russian businessman, in oil. The manager of the hotel had told Didier that Russian oil money paid for Monsieur Ricard's vineyard. Both young men had said they had no idea where Sophie was. They had brought her to a party and she had vanished, that was their word. They had no more to say, they said, until Monsieur Ricard's lawyer arrived.

As Pete was getting up to speed, talking over the details, getting the facts translated by Didier, whose translator presence, I was relieved to see, he just accepted, I walked into the bathroom to be alone. And then I was remembering how early Sophie walked, barely eleven months, how good she was at walking!

My little marvel. She was considered, thoughtful, with every step she took. I was remembering nursing her on my left breast, which was her preferred side, and of course, became the breast I got cancer in (I can still feel the tug of her sweet mouth, the way the milk let down). I used to sing songs to her that I made up about birds and trees and whales, and one was about a girl named Ingmar and a cat named Sophie, which she found so silly, laughing with the deepest belly-shaking laugh in the world. I was thinking about how I would lie down on the floor beside her crib until she fell asleep each night and we'd watch each other through the slats, a high-stakes game of who would fall asleep first. When she couldn't keep her eyes open any longer, I'd crawl out of the room. I was thinking about how petal-soft her skin was, how clean she always smelled, how strong her back had always been, and how capable she'd grown to be. I couldn't remember enough of her young life; my mind was flitting from image to image like a slide carousel that was possessed, circling back over the same images, catching clumsily before jumping ahead to the next one. I thought about hiking behind her in the Pyrenees. I could see her smooth ankles. I took a hand towel from a stack and wadded it up and pressed it into my mouth as I howled.

And then I washed my face and walked out and stood next to Pete. He could never possibly blame this on me any more than I blamed this on me.

45.

IRIS

It was Iris who first saw Sophie return.

Just a little while before, she had seen her mother handing out coffee. Was this before or after she was talking with Mr. Tumnus? She couldn't quite remember. She must have dozed again.

At some point, she woke up with a breath caught in her throat and looked around and saw her mother staring at the fountain, as if it were possible to count the drops of water. Her father was talking to a policeman and had his hand pinched on top of his nose as if something hurt. Georges and Alain and Addie were speaking with the policewoman from earlier. Mr. Tumnus was drinking a coffee. The hotel staff was restocking a little table with juice, pastries, cheeses, grapes, baguettes, more coffee, and Oranginas.

Earlier, when her father had arrived, she had shouted, "Daddy!" And run and jumped, and he had held her. Then her mother was there and the three of them were holding on to one another under the chandelier, holding and holding and holding, and Iris was saying, "Daddy, Sophie, Daddy, find Sophie." He had pulled her out so she could see his face and he had said, in that way he had of being so sure, so capable, "Pickle, I am going to do everything to get your sister back. I absolutely promise." He could fix this, he was the kind of guy who fixed things, her dad.

"Here's what I need you to do, Pickle. I need you to go back to that couch, and I need you to rest, okay? It's still the middle of the night. I am going to talk to these terrific police officers, and look—we have Georges and Alain and Adelard." He didn't mention Didier. "And we are going to find Sophie, I am sure of it. We have some good leads."

Iris did as she was told. But there was so much activity around her, so much noise and buzzing, that she couldn't fall back asleep. And then she must have, because the next thing she knew, it was dawn and the light outside the long castle windows was pinkening gray. She was drooling onto her chin, onto the red velvet couch, making a small wet red pool when she opened her eyes and looked out the big doors. For a moment, she felt peaceful wonder at the way the light outside was filtering through the warm mist rising off the topiary, arriving so gently, so slowly, so sweetly. Everything looked like it was adorned with Christmas tinsel.

And then her big sister simply opened the door and walked up the red carpeted steps and into the lobby.

"Sophie," Iris whispered. "Sophie. Oh my God, Sophie."

46.

SOPHIE

Sophie had gone into the shade, like she'd said she would. It was hot and she felt tired and she had stood for a while not far from the linden tree, looking up at the light green heart-shaped leaves that fluttered like a million butterflies at the slightest hint of a breeze. She was bored and, for a second, had closed her eyes, listening. There was a bar not far away, and, when she opened her eyes, she saw people milling in and out, sitting on the small terrace with coffees or cold drinks, eating salads. She found her mind wandering to the riding lesson earlier. When she had been riding with Marc, who was, let's face it, drop-dead gorgeous and tall, smart, had gone to Dalton, spoke perfect English, had the pedigree of the French, was a competitive jumper and jumping coach despite being only nineteen and in college still (École Normale Supérieure), was stylish and just cool, he had invited her to a party that night. Not even fourteen, she had been surprised.

Yes, she had breasts, her period now, her long limbs, and desire. But inside, she still felt young, attached to her mother, overly involved with her parents. So when Marc had asked her about coming along, she'd said, "Yes." Knowing full well she had the concrete wall of her mother to get through first, which meant her options were these: lie and sneak out or tell her and not go. Simple. She'd have to do option A.

But then, while sitting in the shade of the linden tree, Marc had appeared, sunglasses down, black T-shirt, tan arms, dark jeans despite the heat, dusty from the horses, a beer in his hand. She could, of course, hear Taylor Swift's song in her head as he walked toward her: "Oh, my God, look at that face / You look like my next mistake." Sophie should have heard this soundtrack as a warning. But didn't that song celebrate the bad guy? She'd seen the video. The point was that bad guys are cool, you want them, they take you in fast cars, they kiss you, and you dance around feeling sexy. Right?

"*Salut.*" Marc stood over her; her face was level with his crotch. He was swaying slightly, like a dog tethered by a leash who wanted to be set free to run after a chipmunk.

"Hey." Sophie tried for disinterested.

"Want to go for a walk?"

Sophie looked around. She saw that her mother and Iris were watching the skit. Marc followed her gaze. "Yeah, it's bonkers. That guy in the suit, that's my friend—he went to boarding school with me in England before I went to Dalton. He's from Eastern Europe. Lives in Paris. But he comes down to the château for the summers."

"Yeah, okay. I should go tell my mom."

"No, don't worry. We can be right back. She won't even notice."

Sophie looked at him. He was older. He was so sure of himself. She said, "Okay."

They started walking. Marc kept them to the shady side of the streets. They talked about music and New York. They came to a tiny courtyard overgrown with weeds and filled with butterflies and Sophie laughed at the beauty of it, and when she laughed, she felt Marc's hand on her hair, and then he was turning her so sweetly, so softly, so tenderly toward him, and he was kissing her, and she'd actually never done this before, had only seen it in movies and Taylor Swift videos and read about it and listened while her friends whispered about kissing boys, some of which they made up, of course. There was that one girl, Lizzie Spencer, she said she had kissed a boy from Trinity and, perhaps, done more, who knows, she talked and talked.

Marc was kissing her like in the movies and Sophie was trying to figure out where to put her tongue and stopped at one point, pushing him away a little bit to get her breath, which made him go at her a little harder—she noticed that—and then he was pushing her up against a wall and was touching her breasts and she could feel his penis grinding into the side of her hip. All of a sudden, his hand was up her skirt and he was pulling her underwear to the side, her panty liner catching and pulling on her pubic hair, and then his finger was inside her, poking, and her leg was hoisted up by his hip, and she felt pinned against the wall and she started to cry out, to say no, but he said, "Shhhh, it's good, this is good, you are supposed to feel good, you feel good, you like this." Like he knew.

• • •

He held her hand as they walked back to the square, and Sophie was not sure what to feel. She decided to decide that she had wanted that. She had gone, she was wet, she had kissed back, she had liked it, hadn't she? As they walked, he didn't really talk to her; he pulled out his phone, dropped her hand, and was laughing and saying he was texting with Vladko, the friend, the harlequin.

At the back corner of the church, they met Vladko, still wearing the harlequin suit and the blond wig. They were just in the shadows there, and Sophie could see her sister and her mother, and she wanted to run to them now, but she was scared to move. She felt stuck, embarrassed about running. For a tiny second, she thought she saw Iris turn her head and look. She swore their eyes had locked. Sophie wanted to throw her hands in the air and yell, “Iris, please come save me, this is not okay, I don’t think, but I’m not sure, I have never wanted you to interrupt me more than now. Please come.”

But Iris turned back to the next act, and her mother was lost in her phone, texting, and Vladko and Marc were talking about a party, and then they said, “Let’s go,” and Marc said, “Sophie, come on,” and he put his hand around the top of her arm, firmly. Vladko was laughing as Marc gave her a little jolt forward. He said to Sophie, “You can be our afternoon treat.” Both men chuckled together.

They walked away, the three of them, from her mother and sister to a small black VW Golf, and Sophie got into the back seat like the child she was and the men got into the front seat. The men opened a bottle of red wine, and Vladko took off his wig and unzipped the front of his suit and Sophie could see his chest hair. Marc drove out of the city across fields of sunflowers and along a river (was it the same river next to the château? Sophie didn’t know), and they got to a long driveway with iron gates and when they got to the house there were people wearing bathing suits and halter tops and minidresses and just shorts and no tops—men and women—everywhere.

Marc opened the back door of the car for Sophie but didn’t

wait. The two men walked ahead of her, and she scurried behind, feeling suddenly like she knew what Iris must feel, the younger person in the back. Then the guys were saying hello and kissing women on the cheeks and they never once turned back to her. For a while, Sophie stood and watched. The house was opulent, with a taxidermied lion and even a zebra in the marble foyer. In the living room off to the side, there were soft couches everywhere, and mirrors on all the walls, interspersed with dark paintings of what Sophie imagined must be ancestors. Of course, Sophie had seen *fancy* in New York City. Friends of hers, some of them owned apartments that stretched entire blocks. But most of the Upper West Side kids, the ones she knew, anyway, were low-key, the brick brownstones filled with plants and books, and the oodles of money it took to live in New York City wasn't so obvious.

She felt ridiculous all of a sudden in her short skirt, her damp underwear, her crop top. All around her were young women in long slinky dresses, bikini tops with high-waisted French shorts, dangling pearl earrings that were as large as grapes. She saw people drinking and she saw Marc and Vladko go into a room and shut a door. Sophie wasn't sure, but she didn't think people were speaking French—were they? She heard English and some other languages.

Sophie pressed herself against a wall in the living room, near a door that led to a kitchen. She was wide-eyed and hungry, but she didn't see any food, just alcohol, and she could smell the skunk of weed. On a couch near a window, a group was smoking something that smelled like burning sap, and they were all taking turns with a long snakelike thing attached to a bubbling glass ball. For a second, Sophie was elated—wasn't that Nadia from the riding lesson? But then she saw Nadia roll her eyes back in her head and lie against the couch cushions, and Sophie wasn't sure Nadia would be good for much right then. Marc and Vladko came out of the room, red-eyed and grinning. She could hear people splashing and yelling outside by a pool, and damp, half-naked people were walking back inside to grab bottles of wine to take out to the pool area. Sophie could see that Marc was undressing in the kitchen, his chest and legs covered with dark curly hair, and Vladko unzipped his harlequin suit, and both men, totally nude, their penises and testicles hanging between their legs, were pouring themselves wine. Vladko looked over at Sophie and stuck his tongue out and wiggled it like a lizard. She stared, wide-eyed. The two men spoke to each other, looked at her once more, and Marc started to walk her way. Vladko said something else, and Marc turned back. Then, miraculously, the men turned to go out to the pool. The last thing Sophie saw of Marc and Vladko was the hair on their asses. They never looked at her again. Not once.

There was a door out the back of the kitchen, in the opposite direction of the pool, and Sophie looked at it for a long time. With no other options she could think of, no way of calling her mother, and no idea how you'd call the police in France, she walked out the door, into the golden light of late afternoon. Sophie felt a little sob welling up in her throat as she walked down the driveway. She got to the end, and walked around the iron gate through the bushes, and came to the road, a small, dusty country road. She turned right.

Sophie was thinking about the wind on their last night in Provence. She had woken up needing to pee and realized that what had been a calm breeze when they went to bed was now howling through the tent, shaking the stakes. Outside, the Mediterranean Sea sounded like it might devour the cliff where they lay in their tent in one gulp. Sophie couldn't believe her mother and sister were sleeping through the sound, and for a little while, she covered her ears, her eyes open. Then, unable to hold it any longer, she unzipped the tent to go out to pee.

As she stood in the field overlooking the sea, the wind hit Sophie with a roaring fierceness that boxed her ears and was unlike anything she'd ever known, even in Maine when the wind came off the Atlantic Ocean cold and sluicing, full of rain and ice. This wind was hot, and the sea down below was beastly in the cove, slapping at the rocks and raking them back into its turmoil. Over the water, a half-moon made a chaotic but bright path, and Sophie could see whitecaps on huge, dark waves. How that placid, soft, salty water could be transformed into such a crashing creature, Sophie couldn't fathom in the dark.

She quickly crouched down to pee, and then, looking over her shoulder one more time, she got back into the tent and zipped it back up. Her mother moved in her sleep and blearily asked if everything was all right.

"It's just the wind, Mama. And the ocean. I mean sea."

"We will be okay, it's far below us. Come here."

Sophie had scooted her sleeping bag closer to her mother's and let her mother put her arm around her. Sophie lay there listening to the wind until the sun came up, when she finally fell asleep until Iris started making noise.

After yogurts, they went to swim before leaving, and the water tossed Sophie around, threw her up onto the pebbled beach, and then pulled her back out. Iris squealed and dove and loved it. When they finally left, Sophie was relieved to get away from that howling sea, even as they drove west toward the wreckage of wildfires. She didn't think she'd have been able to take another night of the noise and force of it, sleeping in that little tent on the edge of the earth. It was the way the wind made you feel insignificant, weightless. Worthless, even.

When Sophie was younger, maybe four or five, her parents would take her out to Riverside Park on Saturday mornings before the farmers' market on Amsterdam Avenue. The three of them took the long route, up through the green bits of park, then back around to the farmers' market after picking up bagels at Absolute Bagel. Sophie always walked in the middle, and her parents each held a hand. The entire way, her parents would chant "One, two, three, whoop," and up she'd soar into the air, laughing. One morning when they were crossing the road, her father squeezed her hand three times, and said as he squeezed, "I. Love. You." "Do it again!" Sophie burst out. He did it again and again. Her mother did it, too. "I love you. I love you." Squeeze squeeze squeeze. It was their secret language just for her: squeeze squeeze squeeze, whoop—they no longer counted one, two, three—she was thrown in the air, her feet slapping down. "Again!" she yelled.

Now, as Sophie wandered along on the dirt road, the light waned and she missed their little tent, her sleeping bag currently crushed into a damp pill shape inside their rental car. Sophie wanted her dad. She wanted her little sister. She wanted New York. She wanted Maine. She wanted her mother. "What have I done?" she asked herself over and over, sure that this was entirely her fault.

Sophie knew she couldn't ask for a ride, even if a car were to pass her, because she had been told by her mother to never *ever* get into a stranger's car. Marc hadn't been a stranger, had he? So she just walked. Her flip-flop Birkenstocks, though comfortable poolside or kicking around, were now grating between her toes, rubbing off the tender skin; small pebbles and bits of dirt were getting under her heel. Every time she tried to kick them out, her shoes came off. But she continued to walk. In the heat, she had no idea if she'd ever be found.

Then she worried she'd die without water. She didn't remember when she'd last had any liquid to drink. Was it as far back as the café, before they went into the square? She had been too shocked and overwhelmed to even chew on an ice cube at the party. Her mouth felt sour and dry. The sun was starting to slant, and, in the back of her mind, she knew that the earth would eventually tumble into darkness. That would be a strange thing, she thought, to be alone in the dark in a strange place. She had no idea how much time she had before that happened, or how far away she was from anything at all. But this road did seem to be deserted, as far as she could tell, save for a troupe of motorcyclists who whizzed by. She hadn't seen one car.

She continued to walk along the side of the road, afraid to approach any of the houses she saw, many with long driveways through vineyards and fields of sunflowers, until she smelled something muddy, dank, in the air. The sun was going down quickly now. She knew from when they were in Maine that as the air cooled and the hot earth released the heat of the day, it gave off a lovely deep aroma. But she also smelled something else, something feral. She felt herself stop, the animal inside her listening, aware, perceiving with all her senses the way she had witnessed mother deer do at the edges of clearings before venturing out with their young to forage. Sophie heard, far off, the slightest gurgle, a whoosh of water, and turned her body to the sound, traversing a field full of nettles that scraped and stung, and sunflowers that towered over her head like outsize creepy characters in a fairy tale. Seeing the sunflowers, she had to laugh at something Iris had said just yesterday: "The sunflowers are bowing their heads because Christ isn't coming anymore." When Iris had proclaimed these words, Sophie had made fun of her, and her mother had told her to stop and complimented Iris on her "deep and suggestive thinking." Now Sophie thought she knew what the sunflowers felt like, if they felt anything like what her little sister said they felt.

Soon Sophie came to a thicket of shiny-leaved hornbeam trees. She remembered them from drawings she had seen in a series of books she had adored when she was younger, about mice in *Brambly Hedge*, and the leaves, she remembered this, were like folded paper, with deep creases. All over the ground was pink crabgrass, which gave way to enormous ferns. The ferns reached almost to her shoulders. As she walked, parting the plants, ducking under branches, the muddy smell became stronger; the gurgle, she was sure, was running water. She stopped and caught her breath. Just as the last stripes of yellow light sliced through the trees, she parted the ferns to see a river, hopefully *the* river, the one called the Saône, the one she had seen on the map on her mother's phone and that she knew flowed right next to the castle where her mother and Iris were surely waiting for her. In their bathroom in the château, next to the toilet, there was an old watercolor that was framed. It was of a blue, rushing river with fields and trees on either side. Because it was watercolor, the river actually looked watery, the way it bled into the paper. Underneath, in neat cursive in black pen, it said, "Saône River, 1921, Just Before the Confluence." Sophie had asked her mother about the confluence, and her mother had told her it meant the meeting of two rivers, where they became one; she said it was where the Saône and the Rhône met, and then said the word, "confluence," with a French accent, which sounded like music. Sophie had no idea, but she figured a river was safer to follow than the road. At least this way, there would be no or fewer strangers. This river, she decided, was her only hope.

Sophie knelt down and washed her face with water, dipped her hand in, and grabbed a fistful of sandy mud to smooth over the edges of her scrapes and rubbed it into the stinging welts all over her legs from the nettles. She looked right, then left, and chose left, hoping that her internal compass was correct. She followed the bank, but at times it was too steep or overgrown and she had to walk in the shallow water, her feet wet and slipping all over in her sandals. When she could, she grasped at branches. If the river were her mother, she was a small child, unwilling to stray even an inch from her side. Sophie felt a hard thing in her, an unwavering strength, a focus she had never known she possessed. She was holding firm to the idea that this river was the key to her survival, and she was not willing to let herself think she could be wrong. Sometimes when she slipped, or her shoe came off, or she scraped a knee on a jutting rock, she felt she might break apart into a torrent of tears. She would think about her mother, her sister, their fear, what had happened with Marc, the strange way he had put his hand on her arm while he guided her to the car, like she was a dog on a leash. But whenever she started to veer into all those thoughts, those images, she looked back at the water and breathed in, three quick "rabbit breaths," as her father had taught her when they were running races during Covid across the fields in Maine, three quick nasal breaths to keep you going, your mind clear. What had her dad used to say? Oh yes: "Clear eyes, full heart, can't lose!" From the show the two of them watched, *Friday Night Lights*. Over and over, she said those words to herself: "Clear eyes, full heart, can't lose." Can't lose. Can't lose. Can't lose. Won't lose.

Soon it was dusky and getting darker, and Sophie could hear rustling in the shadows on the sides of the river. Sometimes the banks of the river were steep and she had to be careful. As her eyes adjusted to the darkening light, she saw the vivid yellow of flowers along the banks; she saw the dark blue of the deepening sky overhead. Once, she sat to rest on a rock by the side of the river, her eyes closed, her temples thumping with fear, her heart focused on what she must do. When she lifted her head, she saw four deer, one with a rack of huge antlers, swimming across the river, their noses snorting out water, their eyes trained with unwavering dedication on the far side. Just like those cave paintings they had seen only yesterday. Lonely now, she said hello to them: "Hi, deer," she said. "Hi, deer." She sounded ridiculous. She felt it, too. But if only the deer could take her with them.

Sophie kept going, taking off her wet, slippery sandals and walking barefoot. Soon she found that carrying the sandals made it so she didn't have the use of one hand. She needed both hands to steady herself on branches and rocks and logs, so she tucked the shoes, standing up, into her skirt, the soles rubbing against her back.

It got darker, stiller. She kept wading, walking. She was startled, suddenly, by a crash-thump, a growling snort, and then a high-pitched scream that sounded like a witch's. Sophie screamed, "Who's there?," her hair whipping around her face. The breathing sounded right next to her, the snuffling, another otherworldly scream. Sophie started running, slipped, fell, slid down a bank into the water. Doggy-paddling, she swam, then put her feet down, realizing the water was shallow where she was. With her hands as her eyes, she waded as far into the water as she could, thinking she might be safer in the middle of the river if she could get there. With her hands stretched out in front of her, she hit a large rock not far from the side of the river. She climbed it, and sat, perching. Shivering, she rocked back and forth, her knees clenched to her face, her tears hot, and said, "Oh my God, oh my God, oh my God," over and over.

Far off, she could hear cars, the buzz of a highway. She must be close to a town, to a city, to something. With her face on her knees, she could feel, in a pocket of her skirt, a tiny bump against her stomach. After a moment, she reached in and fingered around to find the silver cicada from Penelope. Clutching this familiar object in her hand, she must have somehow slept for a few minutes or an hour (more?), who knew, but the night seemed quiet all around her when she opened her eyes, her mouth stuck to her knees, her hair a curtain. All she could hear was water slipping by. She sat as long as she could bear. "Mommy," she said. "Mommy. Mama." Tears were gushing down her face. She had never wanted her mother this much. When she saw the first inkling of sky, pink tentacles spreading across the gray blue of dawn, she took a deep breath, put the cicada back inside the mesh pocket against her lower abdomen, and traversed the waist-high water, holding her sandals high above her head. When she got back to the bank, she turned right and continued.

By the time she reached the first small town, the sky was the color of the underside of a blooming rose. The river went through the town, and Sophie followed it until she could climb to a road and put on her sandals. She watched hungrily as a baker, wearing a long white apron, opened his wooden shutters and put out tables and chairs while the smell of bread wafted to the sidewalk. In the apartment above the bakery, she saw a dark-haired woman hanging a yellow sheet, cloth diapers, teeny socks, and washcloths on a clothesline she had strung outside the window. Sophie had never felt so grateful to see other people in her life. And though every core of her being wanted to run to this man, this woman, anyone, and beg for help, her lack of French, her fear of not knowing what to explain, her aloneness in this problem, stopped her, and she only watched from the sidelines, her throat hoarse with tears and thirst.

She continued to walk along a little viaduct, past a small mall, a grocery store, through the parking lot of a farm-supply store. She noticed that the parking lot was not paved over but, instead, had a grate for cars to park on, and in between each square was planted grass. By now, her sandals were dry, and though she was dirty and hungry, the tiniest shards of hope were starting to puncture the fears of the night. She could feel the mounting and needling pangs of yearning zinging through her breast.

She walked on and on, then came to the outskirts of another town. She followed the river a little farther, doubting herself that this was *the* town, who could tell? All these French towns had stone houses and iron gates and crooked streets. But on a hunch, Sophie went right and walked up a steep street, only to fall back down, winding past shops that were opening, the pungent aroma of a *fromagerie*, the sweetness of a macaron shop, the tantalizing mustiness of a fruit seller's wares being placed on a table in the shade by an old man with white hair. And then, below her, she saw the square and, unmistakably, the linden tree.

She ran for the tree. She ran for it as if it were an old friend, a grandmother, a mother. And when she got there, she looked around, wondering if anyone was watching. But it was early enough that no one was around, so she hugged it. She put her hands around the trunk, laying her face against the roughness, smelling the green leaves, the damp bark, and hearing the starlings in the branches making exuberant morning noises of survival. She stood and held on to that tree as hard as she could until her breaths calmed down.

Sophie would swear to herself, for years and years, that that linden tree had shuddered with gratitude and joy when she put her arms around it, when she laid her cheek against its cool, rough, shaggy bark. That it had heaved a sigh of relief that seemed to say, "You're back, you're safe, I am here." She would never tell another soul, it would always be hers, private, too subtle to really explain in words, what that tree meant to her and always would mean.

One day, a mother herself, Sophie would go find that linden again, still standing. And she would tell her children about all the people in the world who had come and found shade and respite under that tree. How it had stood through wars and fires and all kinds of personal dramas no one would ever know. How it had shaded generations and been a symbol of life and family and safety for so many. But Sophie didn't know any of that now. Not yet.

All Sophie had to do in this moment was walk across the square, down a narrow road, turn right and go along the river with vineyards on the other side, and she would be at the castle. She could be there before the sun was fully up. She took off, jogging. All she had to do was get there.

EPILOGUE

ALICE

I have tried to imagine what it was like for Sophie to walk into the castle and see Iris, then me, then her father, then Didier, the police, Georges, Alain, Adelard. She has told me she was only exhausted, grateful. She cried, she held me, Pete held her, Iris wouldn't let go of her. We didn't know yet what she'd been through. All we cared about at first was that we had her back. Her clothes were filthy and torn, and the cork sole of one sandal had come unglued.

I sat her down, took the shoes off, and ran to the bathroom to get some damp towels to wash her feet, which were cut, bleeding, blistered, and filthy.

While I was gone, someone from the hotel had known to get her an ice water, then another. Someone else made linden-flower tea, the sweet honey smell wafting from her mug as she sipped it. Pete had asked for a washcloth and was washing her brow; Iris was stroking her hand and had given her her blanket. I took my time with her feet, caressing and cleaning them.

Alain was standing off to the side, just watching her, his eyes trained on my miraculous daughter. I saw Georges talking to the police, and he came and stood next to me and whispered that the police would like to talk to Sophie. He told me that he had asked that she be given two hours to eat and bathe. The hotel manager brought Sophie a perfect soft-boiled egg and strips of toasted baguette with butter and hauled over a small folding table so that she could sit right there in the lobby without moving on miserable feet. She ate and drank the water, her chest still heaving with emotion, while Pete and Iris and I all kept one apostolic hand on her, never letting go. Of course, one day we would let go, again and again and again. But not now, not today.

I looked up once and saw Didier leaving out the front doors. I watched the back of his neck, the blond V of his hair dipping to just above his collar, the way his Levi's fit him so gorgeously, how square his shoulders were, and I thought, There he goes. Maybe that's just not my life. And then I whispered, "Thank you." I saw Pete turn and look, saw Pete watch the man who had been my lover walk from the doors to the parking lot, and I knew when my husband turned back to me, by the look in his eyes, both of us still holding on to our daughter, that he knew, he had known all along.

When Sophie had eaten, we, all three of us, took her upstairs in the elevator and I drew her a bath and I pulled the curtain around her. I let Iris watch cartoons, and Pete sat in one of the chairs looking out that wall of windows.

Georges was downstairs managing the police. Alain was with him, ever Sophie's sentry. I saw that this was a devoted son, boy, man—one who could not be shook off quickly. Adelard had been sent to town to buy Sophie a new pair of sandals. Marie was on her way to join us; Penelope would stay behind with the other two boys.

After Sophie's bath, we had some time before the police needed her, so I tucked her into one of the two beds we'd never slept in and told her to sleep for an hour. I texted Georges and said we needed more time—she was too tired to make any sense. He texted back: No problem. Alain and I are playing chess. The policewoman doing the interview is reading *Vogue*—all is calm. *Ça va.*

With Iris zoned out on cartoons and Sophie asleep, Pete turned to me from where he was sitting and spoke quietly. "I am on antidepressants, Alice. And for a few years there, I think I lost my way. More than my way . . ."

I nodded and said softly, "I didn't know about the antidepressants. I wish you'd told me. But I get it."

"Do you?" The relief on his face was unmistakable, the feeling of being heard, seen.

"I do. I've made mistakes, too. I am sorry. I am, Pete. I haven't said that enough." It felt good to say it.

We were silent then. The sun was coming in hot through the windows, and Pete was still wearing the crumpled shirt and gray pants and ridiculous running shoes he had flown over in. He looked at me, his face open, the most open I had seen it since before we had kids, and I said, "It's all surprising. How this has turned out. Life. Isn't it?"

"Yes," he whispered. His voice was hoarse, childlike.

"Who would have thought any of it would go like this?"

"Alice, I want you to come home with me. Please come home with me."

I looked out the window and then I walked over to Pete. I sneaked a glance at Iris, but she wasn't doing anything except watching the screen, the tinny sounds of French cartoons filling her head and the room. She looked exhausted, eyes glazed.

I kissed my husband, long and deep, holding my mouth to

his until I was sure I'd inhaled the familiar feel of his scratchy cheeks and his musky Pete smell. Until I was sure we'd weather whatever would come next, together.

"Okay," I said. "Let's get the first flight we can find."

"I'll get it organized," Pete said. "As soon as the police tell us we can go, when we can go. For now, this isn't a bad place to wait, is it?" His face looked hopeful, young, maybe a tiny bit fierce.

We were both looking out those tall windows across the moat and to the kingdom stretching for miles, it seemed, below. I was thinking how odd it all is: You can love and not love your husband; you can lose and not lose your children; you can be glued together and desperately need to be alone; you can be exhausted yet still awake; you can be at peace inside and also on the edge of war. It's all so complicated and unexpected, it takes my breath away.

"Not bad" was all I said, nodding to our view. This was a moment to say less.

"Will you still be able to write your article?" Pete asked, remembering that I might feel I'd failed at that, too.

"I don't know. But I do know exactly what I want to write now."

He smiled then, generous. "I can't wait to read it," he said.

Pete leaned his head back, that smile still on his face. He looked sleepy. "Sleep a little bit," I said, and reached out and touched his hair, smoothing it away from his ears.

I picked up my phone to set an alarm and I saw there was a text from Didier:

> Alice. I didn't get to say goodbye. Sophie is back and I am so glad. And I am glad you called me. You will need to go home and figure

this out. You've got these two girls. A whole life. That man, your husband, is the father of those girls. He came here for you. If you don't want him, ok. But go home. France will be here. I will be here. You know where to find me. "Don't doubt that the stars are fire," as the great poet said . . .

I started to write back. I imagine he saw the three dots. But I looked up and saw that Pete's eyes were closed. His face struck me as so innocent and vulnerable, so familiarly grateful we were all together again.

There was nothing more to say, anyway. Instead, I set my alarm and lay down next to Sophie. Ever so gently, I put my hand on hers and held on.

ACKNOWLEDGMENTS

No work of art is ever made by just one person. There are always so many kindnesses that help the artist forge ahead, work against the odds into folly or excellence, or some lucky combination of both.

To name every person who inspired or gave me the little extra *oomph* I needed on any given day would be next to impossible. Some days it might have been someone checking me out while I bought coffee at my local grocery store; another day, it was a nurse who was extra gentle with a blood draw; another, my husband who got up early with me on a Saturday (when it would have been so much nicer to sleep in) so that I could work before our kids got up and brought me breakfast at my desk. Other times, it was a best friend arriving with a thermos of hot tea for after a cold plunge in a November ocean; or a glass of wine handed to me by my neighbor when I'd been working all day and was coming over to have five minutes of real people, real time; or a text message telling me to keep going, that what I was doing was important.

These thoughtful moments tied me to everyone around me as I wrote this book and made it a kind of communal act. I was lucky enough that this story literally just poured out of me, as if I were possessed. It just came and went where it needed to; I didn't plan it out. I almost don't even remember writing it. But I will remember all the kindness that surrounded me as I did it. And then everyone who helped once I had it down.

I've come to think about the small and large ways we can help to support each other as millions and millions of concentric circles, radiating forever outward, into infinity. I like to hope that these kindnesses will change the world, even now, as darkness permeates. Change may come in glacially slow ways. But that does not mean we won't create a ripple effect. The great American playwright Tony Kushner has said, "Hope is a moral obligation." I believe it is, and yet I also know how hard it is to hold on to. My feeling these days is that it can start with just the smallest of gestures, the most genuine smile, an open compliment for a stranger.

Herewith, then, is an insubstantial list (I say insubstantial because I know for a fact there were so many more people and even animals, plants, and trees that inspired me) of many of the people who gave and gave and gave to me, which helped open up small slivers of hope in my heart and brain so that I could keep going. All of these people are knitted into the fabric of this book; without them, no book. We did it together.

My husband, Dan, who brings me coffee in bed every single morning and never stops cheering me on; my two sons, Marsden and Levin, who are the most exciting and interesting people I've ever met—I wake up and can't wait to hear what you two are thinking. Levin, you say so many priceless and brilliant things, I hope you won't mind that Iris had to borrow a couple. Your great heart is knitted into Iris; thank you for holding my hand in the car when I drive you around. Likewise, Marsden, you generously gave me a window into the canon of "teenage acerbic," which helped me craft words and attitude for Sophie. And, Marsden, truly, you saved me more than once with this book: You helped me realize the book needed to be in present tense, which was a huge eleventh-hour change. But you sat next to me and helped. And you were my consultant for music and text messages from the start. Also, when I needed it most, you let me hold on to your strong shoulder, and that made me feel safer. I love you both to pieces.

Our next-door neighbors who are our adopted family: Nora, Adam, Solomon, and Leo—if love is a currency, then our two homes have a million bucks between us.

My agent, Lisa Grubka, who is not only loyal but also hardworking, funny, intelligent, careful, and so organized as she gives structure and support to me in the chaos of creation. Sarah Stein, my editor, who intuitively understands what we're trying to do with fiction: make people feel deeply and thereby feel less lonely in their own lives, which will give them hope, too (see, those concentric circles again). Along with Team Lisa and Team Sarah come the most amazing people, who are also helping, caring, thinking. At Harper Books: Jackie Quaranto, Tanya Fox, Jocelyn Larnick, Katie O'Callaghan, Stephanie Mendoza, Olivia McGiff, Doug Jones, and Jonathan Burnham. At UTA: (Prince) Harry Sherer, Orly Greenberg, Hannah Geller, and everyone there who takes the extra time to vet contracts, distribute funds, care about the small stuff.

I had many readers and helpers on this book. Here are all the people who read drafts, corrected Italian or French, circled words, hearted thoughts, called me on the phone to talk about a scene that really worked for them or a moment I could expand, cheered me on when I needed it most, and just helped me make these characters as real for myself as they were becoming for them: Merry Fogg, Rachel James, Selina Rossiter, Julie Fraize, Craig Pospisil, Cat Rickman, Emmanuel Saint-Martin, Jared Shipley, Cathy Richard, Mateo Pacelli, Debra Spark, Christina Baker Kline, Alice Elliot Dark, Daisy Florin, and Elin Hilderbrand. And of course my husband, Dan, to whom I read every book out loud. He knows just when to laugh, just when to tell me something works, and is the first to tell me how much he loves it.

My parents, Robert Shetterly and Susan Hand Shetterly, gave me the gift of showing me firsthand that an artistic life is not only possible but an important contribution to the world; they also modeled their passionate wonder for plants, animals, trees—and a desire to protect wild things. My uncle Jay has been unfailingly loyal and generous to me, starting with buying me my first computer when I went off to Brown, and then my first laptop when I went off to New York City. He never hesitates to believe that I will succeed. My aunt Maggie loves books and reads each one I write with wonderful enthusiasm, which is a gift.

Thank you to four male friends who were there when I needed them most: Adam Darter, Mark Kelly, Rob Riggs, and Craig Pospisil.

I am going to conclude with a list of what I (and the MO might) call my "kitchen table"—female friends who show up without hesitation, over and over again, and are right there helping me hold on to my one wild and precious life: Merry Fogg, Nora Calderwood, Rachel James, Leah Whalen, Jessica Mellon, Emma Kelly.

Finally, to nurses everywhere. You are angels.

ABOUT THE AUTHOR

CAITLIN SHETTERLY is the author of *Modified*, *Made for You and Me*, and *Pete and Alice in Maine* and the editor of the bestselling *Fault Lines: Stories of Divorce*. She won the Maine Literary Award for *Modified* in 2017.

Her work has been featured in *The New York Times*, *The New York Times Magazine*, *Orion*, *Elle*, *Self*, *The Boston Globe*, *Medium*, *Lit Hub*, and *Romper*, as well as on Oprah.com, *This American Life*, *Hidden Brain*, *Studio 360*, *Weekend Edition*, and various other public radio shows. She is an editor-at-large for *Frenchly*, a French arts and culture online news magazine. A Maine native, she graduated with honors from Brown University and now lives with her two sons and husband in her home state. Caitlin is passionately committed to helping preserve, in every way she can, the peace of wild things.

www.caitlinshetterly.com